TWIN CITIES NOIR

TWIN CITIES NOIR

EDITED BY
JULIE SCHAPER & STEVEN HORWITZ

AKASHIC BOOKS
NEW YORK

Also in the Akashic Noir Series:

Brooklyn Noir, edited by Tim McLoughlin

D.C. Noir, edited by George Pelecanos

Manhattan Noir, edited by Lawrence Block

Baltimore Noir, edited by Laura Lippman

Dublin Noir, edited by Ken Bruen

Chicago Noir, edited by Neal Pollack

San Francisco Noir, edited by Peter Maravelis

Brooklyn Noir 2: The Classics, edited by Tim McLoughlin

Forthcoming:

Los Angeles Noir, edited by Denise Hamilton

London Noir, edited by Cathi Unsworth

Wall Street Noir, edited by Peter Spiegelman

Miami Noir, edited by Les Standiford

Havana Noir, edited by Achy Obejas

Bronx Noir, edited by S.J. Rozan

New Orleans Noir, edited by Julie Smith

This collection is comprised of works of fiction. All names, characters, places, and incidents are the product of the authors' imaginations. Any resemblance to real events or persons, living or dead, is entirely coincidental.

Series concept by Tim McLoughlin and Johnny Temple
Twin Cities map by Sohrab Habibion

Published by Akashic Books
©2006 Akashic Books

ISBN-13: 978-1-888451-97-9
ISBN-10: 1-888451-97-1
Library of Congress Control Number: 2005934823

Third printing
Printed in Canada

Akashic Books
PO Box 1456
New York, NY 10009
Akashic7@aol.com
www.akashicbooks.com

For Sylvia—*olehasholiem*

Acknowledgments

Thanks go out to all our bookselling friends, especially Pat Frovarp and Gary Shulze, Jeff Hatfield, Lyle Starkloff, Hans Weyandt, and Tom Bielenberg. Thanks also to Johnny Temple for giving us the opportunity, and to Johanna Ingalls for being Johanna Ingalls. And thanks to the Twin Cities writing community for their generosity and trust. If it weren't for you, there would only be an introduction.

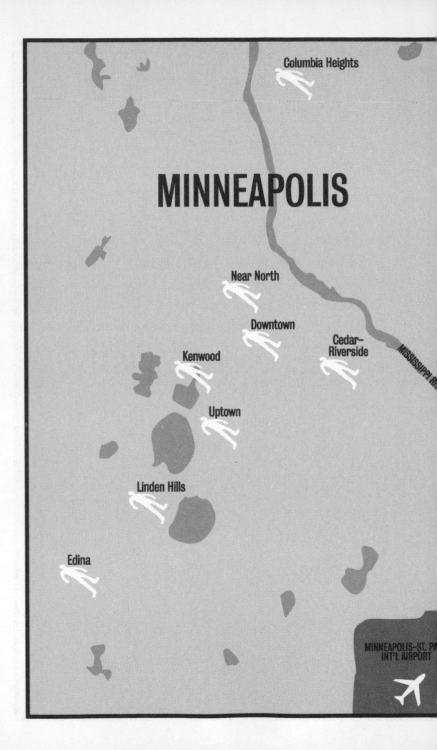

MINNEAPOLIS

Columbia Heights

Near North

Downtown

Cedar–Riverside

MISSISSIPPI RI

Kenwood

Uptown

Linden Hills

Edina

MINNEAPOLIS–ST. PA
INT'L AIRPORT

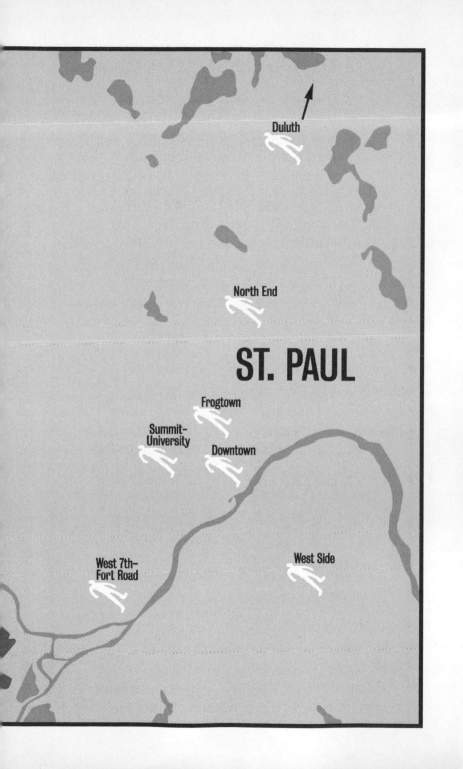

TABLE OF CONTENTS

INTRODUCTION
TALES OF TWO CITIES

Murder and mayhem are probably not the first things that come to mind when most people think of the Twin Cities of Minneapolis and St. Paul.

What comes to mind may be snow emergencies and sub-zero temperatures; Eugene McCarthy, Paul Wellstone, and Jesse "the body" Ventura; Dylan, Prince, and The Replacements; the Guthrie, Theatre de la June Lune, and Heart of the Beast; The Walker, St. Paul Cathedral, and The Mall of America; Mary Tyler Moore, Tiny Tim, and F. Scott Fitzgerald; Lake Harriet, Lake Como, maybe even Lake Wobegone, which, depending upon who you talk to, may or may not be real.

But not crime.

Everyone here has an opinion about what makes the cities different from each other and what ties them together. A type of social shorthand has developed over the years. Minneapolis is hip and St. Paul is working class. St. Paul is the political capital, Minneapolis is the cultural capital. St. Paul was built by timber money and Minneapolis from grain. There is some truth in these generalizations but the people who live here know it's not as simple as that and it never has been.

You don't have to look hard to find the darker underside. St. Paul was originally called Pig's Eye's Landing and was named after Pig's Eye Parrant—trapper, moonshiner, and proprietor of the most popular drinking establishment on the Mississippi. Traders, river rats, missionaries, soldiers, land speculators, fur trappers, and Indian agents congregated in his establishment and made their deals. When Minnesota became a territory in 1849, the town leaders, realizing that a place called Pig's Eye might not inspire civic confidence, changed the name to St. Paul, after the largest church in the city. The following verse appeared in the paper shortly after:

Pig's Eye, converted thou shalt be like Saul.
Thy name henceforth shall be St. Paul.

St. Paul was a haven for cons on the lam in the 1920s and '30s. Bad guys across the country knew about the O'Connor system. A criminal could come to St. Paul, check in with police chief John O'Connor, and walk the streets openly, as long as he or she promised to stay clean. Ma Barker, Creepy Alvin Karpis, Baby Face Nelson, and Machine Gun Kelley spent time in the cities. The system fell apart in the early '30s, about the time that Dillinger shot his way out of his Summit Avenue apartment.

Across the river, Minneapolis has its own sordid story. By the turn of the twentieth century it was considered one of the most crooked cities in the nation. Mayor Albert Alonzo Ames, with the assistance of the chief of police, his brother Fred, ran a city so corrupt that according to Lincoln Steffans its "deliberateness, invention, and avarice has never been equaled."

As recently as the mid-'90s, Minneapolis was called "Murderopolis" due to a rash of killings that occurred over a long hot summer.

Every city has its share of crime, but what makes the Twin

Cities unique may be that we have more than our share of good writers to chronicle it. They are homegrown and they know the territory—how the cities look from the inside, out. Some have built reputations on crime fiction, others are playing with the genre for the first time, but all of them have a strong sense of this place and its people.

Bruce Rubenstein, Gary Bush, and Larry Millett illuminate the past—the Irish cops, politics, radicals, and mob guys.

David Housewright, K.J. Erickson, and Mary Sharratt observe cultures colliding and the combustion that friction can cause. Pete Hautman and Judith Guest show us how amusingly dangerous life in the cities can be. Quinton Skinner, William Kent Krueger, and Ellen Hart illustrate what we're all capable of when lives are on the line.

In these fifteen original stories we see representations of the past, the present, and perhaps even a glimpse of the future. Maybe as importantly, we see who we are—Midwesterners, Minnesotans, and residents of the Twin Cities. We hope you enjoy reading these stories as much as we enjoyed putting this collection together.

Julie Schaper & Steve Horwitz
March 2006
St. Paul, Minnesota

MAI-NU'S WINDOW

BY DAVID HOUSEWRIGHT

Frogtown (St. Paul)

Benito Hernandez did not know when Mai-Nu began leaving her window shade up. Probably when the late August heat had first arrived—dog days in Minnesota. It was past 10:30 p.m. yet the temperature was eighty-six degrees Fahrenheit in Benito's bedroom and his windows, too, were wide open and his shades up. Just as they were in most of the houses in his neighborhood. That was one way to tell the rich from the poor in the Land of 10,000 Lakes. The ones who could afford central air, all their windows were closed.

The window faced Benito's room. Through it he could see most of Mai-Nu's living room as well as a sliver of her bedroom. Mai-Nu was in her living room now, sitting on a rust-colored sofa, her bare feet resting on an imitation wood coffee table. She was stripped down to a white, sleeveless scoop-neck T and panties. What little fresh air that seeped through the window screen was pushed around by an electric fan that swung slowly in a half circle and droned monotonously. It didn't offer much relief. Benito could see strands of raven-black hair plastered to Mai-Nu's forehead and a trickle of sweat running down between her breasts. Next to her on the sofa were a bowl of melting ice, a half-gallon carton of orange juice, and a liter of Phillips vodka. She was reading a book while she drank. Occasionally, she would mark passages in the book with a yellow highlighter.

Less than five yards separated their houses and sometimes Benito could hear Mai-Nu's voice; could hear the music she played and the TV programs she watched. Sometimes he felt he could almost reach out and touch her. It was something he wanted very much to do. Touch her. But she was twenty-three, a student at William Mitchell Law School—it was a law book that she was reading. Benito was sixteen and about to begin his junior year in high school. She was Hmong. He was Puerto Rican.

Still, Benito was convinced Mai-Nu was the most beautiful woman he had ever known. A long feminine neck, softly molded moon face, alluring oval eyes, pale flesh that glistened with perspiration—she was forever wrestling with her long, thick hair and often she would tie it back in a ponytail as she had that night. Watching her made him feel tumescent, made his body tingle with sexual electricity, even though the few times he had actually seen her naked were so fleeting as to be more illusion than fact. Often he would imagine the two of them together. Just as often he would berate himself for this. It was wrong, it was stupid, it was *asqueroso!* Yet when night fell, he would hide himself in the corner of his bedroom and watch, the door locked, the lights off, telling his parents that he was doing homework or listening to music.

Mai-Nu mixed a drink, her second by Benito's count, and padded in the direction of her tiny kitchen. She was out of sight for a few moments, causing Benito alarm, as it always did when she slipped from view. When Mai-Nu returned, she was carrying a plate of leftover pork stew with corn bread topping. The meal had been a gift from Juanita Hernandez. Benito's mother was always doing that, making far too much food then parceling it out to her neighbors. She had brought over a platter of *carne y pollo* when Mai-Nu first arrived as a house-warming gift. Benito had accompanied her and was soon put to work helping Mai-Nu move in.

It wasn't much of a place, he had noted sadly. The living room was awash in forest-green except for a broad water stain on the wall behind the couch that was gray. Burnt-orange drapes framed the windows and the carpet was once blue but now resembled the water stain. The kitchen wasn't much better. The walls were painted a sickly pink and the linoleum had the deep yellow hue of urine. Just off the living room was a tiny bathroom—sink, toilet, tub, no shower—and beyond that a tiny bedroom.

There was no yard. The front door opened onto three concrete steps that ended at the sidewalk. The boulevard between the sidewalk and curb was hard-packed dirt and exactly as wide as eight of Benito's size ten-and-a-half sneakers. Mai-Nu had no garage either, only a strip of broken asphalt next to the house that was too small for her ancient Ford LTD.

"It is only temporary," Mai-Nu had told Juanita. "My parents came from Laos. My father helped fight for the CIA during the war. They did well after they arrived in America—they owned two restaurants. But they believed in the traditions of their people, so when my parents were killed in a car accident, it was my father's older brother who inherited their wealth. He was supposed to raise my brother and me. Now that we are both of age, the property should come to us."

But six months had passed. The property had not come to them and Mai-Nu was still there.

Benito wondered about that while he watched her eat. Mai-Nu did not have a job as far as he knew, unless you would call attending law school a job. Possibly her uncle helped her pay the rent on her house. Or maybe it was her brother—Cheng Song was not much older than Benito, but he had quit school long ago and was now the titular head of the Hmongolian Boy's Club, a street gang with a reputation for terror. They had met only once. Outside of Mai-Nu's. She had been shouting at him, telling a smirking Cheng that he was wasting his life, when Benito had arrived home carrying his hockey equipment.

Benito was only a sophomore, yet his booming slapshot had already caught the notice of pro and college scouts alike. Several D-1 schools had indicated that they might offer him a scholarship if he improved his defense and kept his grades up, which Juanita vowed he would do—"*¡Si no sacas buenas notas te mataré!*" Cheng hadn't seemed impressed by the hockey player, but later he told Benito, "You watch out for my sister. Anything happen, you tell me."

Mai-Nu took the remains of her dinner back to the kitchen. When she returned she mixed a third drink and retrieved her law book. She kept glancing at her watch as if she were expecting a visitor. The phone rang, startling both her and Benito. Mai-Nu went to answer it, slipping out of sight.

There was a mumbling of hellos and then something else. "Yes, Pa Chou," Mai-Nu said, her voice rising in volume. And then, "No, Uncle." She was shouting now. "I will not!"

Benito wished he could see her. He moved around his bedroom, hoping to get a better sight angle into Mai-Nu's house, but failed.

"I know, I know . . . But I am not Hmong, Pa Chou. I am American . . . But I am, Uncle. I am an American woman . . . I will not do what you ask. I will not marry this man . . . In Laos you are clan leader. In America you are not."

She slammed the receiver so hard against the cradle that Benito was sure she had destroyed her phone. A moment later Mai-Nu reappeared, her face flushed with anger. She guzzled her vodka and orange juice, made another drink, and guzzled that.

Benito wished she would not drink so much.

The next morning, Benito found Mai-Nu at the foot of her front steps, stretching her long legs. She was wearing blue jogging shorts and a tight white half-T that emphasized her chest—at least that is what he noticed first. He was startled when she spoke to him.

"Benito," she said. "*Nyob zoo sawv ntyov.*"

"Huh?"

"It means 'good morning.'"

"Oh. *¡Buenos días!*"

"I'm probably going to melt in this heat, but I really need to exercise."

"It is hot."

"Well, I will see you . . ."

"Mai-Nu?"

"Yes?"

Benito was curious about the phone call the evening before, but knew he couldn't ask about it. Instead, he said, "Your name. What does it mean?"

"My name? It means 'gentle sun.'"

"That's beautiful."

Mai-Nu smiled at the compliment. Suddenly, she seemed interested in him.

"And Cheng Song?" Benito asked.

"Cheng, his first name means 'important' and my brother certainly wishes he were. Song is our clan name. The

Hmong did not have last names until the West insisted on it in the 1950s and many of us took our clan names. I am Mai-Nu Song."

"What about Pa Chou?"

"Where did you hear my uncle's name?"

Benito shrugged. "You must have told me."

"Hmm," Mai-Nu said. "Chou means 'rice steamer.'"

"Oh yeah?"

She nodded. "'Pa' is a salutation of respect, like calling someone 'mister' or 'sir.'"

"Why does he have a salutation of respect?"

"Pa Chou is the leader of the Song clan in St. Paul. What that means—leaders are called upon to give advice and settle arguments within the clan."

"Like a *patrón*. A godfather."

"Yes. Also"—Mai-Nu's eyes grew dark and her voice became still—"also they arrange marriages and decide how much a groom's family must pay his bride's family to have her. Usually it is between $6,000 and $10,000."

"Arranged marriages? Do you still do that?"

"The older community, my parents' generation, they really value the old Hmong culture. That is why they settled here in St. Paul. It has the largest urban Hmong population in the world. Close to 25,000 of us. They come because they can still be Hmong here. Do you understand?"

"I think so."

Benito attended a high school where thirty percent of the student body was considered a minority—African-Americans, Native-Americans, Asians, Somali, Indians, Latinos—all of them striving to maintain their identity in a community that was dominated by the Northern Europeans that first settled here.

"It is changing," said Mai-Nu. "The second generation, my generation, we are becoming American. But it is hard. Hard for the old ones to give up their traditions. Hard for the young ones, too, caught between cultures. My brother—he likes to have his freedom. I asked him, my uncle asked him, where do you go? What do you do? He says he is American so he can do whatever he likes. You cannot tell him anything. Now he is a gangster. He brings disgrace to the clan. Maybe if my parents were still alive . . ."

Mai-Nu shook her head, her ponytail shifting from one shoulder to the other.

Benito said, "What about you?"

"Me? I am bringing disgrace to the clan, too."

"I don't believe that."

"In my culture, a woman can only lead from behind. To be out front, to have a high profile, to be a lawyer—the old people, the clan leaders do not tolerate it. My uncle is very upset. He is afraid of losing power as the young people become more Americanized. Keeping me in my place, it is important to him. It proves that he is still in charge. That is why he wants me to marry."

"He arranged your marriage?"

"He is attempting to. He says . . . Pa Chou and my brother hate each other, but Pa Chou says he will leave all his wealth—my parents' wealth—to Cheng unless I agree to marry." She grinned then, an odd thing, Benito thought. "My bride price—the last bid was $22,000. If they wait until after I get my law degree, the bidding will top $25,000."

"You are worth much more than that," Benito blurted.

Mai-Nu smiled at him. "You are very sweet," she said. And then, "I have to run if I am going to have time to get cleaned up before class."

A moment later she was moving at a steady pace down the street. Benito watched her.

"Gentle Sun," he said.

It was nearly 10 p.m. when Mai-Nu went from her bedroom to her tiny bathroom—Benito saw her only for a moment. She was naked, but the rose-colored nightshirt she carried in front of her hid most of her body.

"¡Chingado!" Benito cursed.

Mai-Nu did not have a shower, Benito knew. Only a big, old-fashioned bathtub with iron feet. He imagined her soaking in the tub, white soap bubbles hugging her shoulders. But the image lasted only until he wiped sweat from his own forehead. It was so warm; he could not believe anyone would immerse themselves in hot water. So he flipped a channel in his head, and suddenly there was a picture of Mai-Nu standing in two inches of lukewarm water, giving herself a sponge bath. He examined the image closely behind closed eyes. Until he heard the sound of a vehicle coming quickly to a stop on the street.

His eyes opened in time to see three Asian men invade Mai-Nu's home. Flinging open the door and charging in, looking around like they were seeing the house for the first time. They were older than Benito but smaller, the biggest about five-foot-five, 140 pounds.

One of the men called Mai-Nu's name.

"What do you want?" Mai-Nu shouted in reply.

She emerged from her bathroom. Her hair was dripping. The short-sleeve nightshirt she had pulled on was wet and clung to her body.

"I have come for you," the man replied.

"Get out."

"We will be married."

"I said no. Now get out."

"Mai-Nu—"

"Get out, get out!"

The man reached for her and she punched him hard enough to snap his head back.

"You," the man said, and grabbed for her. Mai-Nu darted away, but the other two men were there. They trapped her between them and closed in on her, wrestled her writhing body into submission. Mai-Nu shouted a steady stream of what Benito guessed were Hmong curses while the first man begged her to remain still.

"It is for both our happiness," he said as they carried Mai-Nu toward the door.

Benito was running now, out of his bedroom, out of his house and toward Mai-Nu's front steps. He hit the first man out the door, leaping high with all his weight and momentum, catching the man with an elbow just under the chin, smashing him against the door frame, as clean a check as he had every thrown—his coach would have been proud.

The man bounced off the frame and crumbled to the sidewalk. The second man dropped Mai-Nu's legs and swung at Benito, but he danced away easily. He was more than a half-dozen years younger than the three men, but five inches taller and thirty pounds heavier. And years of summer league had taught him how to throw a punch. But there were three of them.

"I called the cops!" Benito shouted. "The cops are on their way."

Mai-Nu squirmed out of the third man's grasp and struck him hard in the face.

The man seemed mystified.

"But I love you," he said.

Mai-Nu hit him again.

The other two men turned toward Benito.

"The cops are coming," he repeated.

One of them said something that Benito could not understand. The other said, "We must leave," in clear English.

"Not without Mai-Nu," the third man said.

Mai-Nu shoved him hard and he nearly fell off the steps. His companions grabbed his shoulders and spoke rapidly to him as they dragged him to the van parked directly in front of Mai-Nu's house.

"Mai-Nu, Mai-Nu," he chanted as they stuffed him inside. A moment later they were driving off.

Mai-Nu watched them go, her hands clenched so tightly that her fingernails dug ugly half-moons into her palms.

Benito rested a hand on her shoulder.

"Are you okay?"

Mai-Nu spun violently toward him.

"Yes, I am okay."

Benito was startled by her anger and took a step backward. Mai-Nu saw the hurt expression in his face and reached for him.

"Benito, Benito," she chanted. "You were so brave."

She wrapped her arms around him and pulled him close. He could feel her exquisite skin beneath the wet nightshirt, could feel her breasts flatten against his chest.

"You are my very good friend," Mai-Nu said as she kissed his ear and his cheek. "My very good friend."

She released him and smiled so brightly, Benito put his hand on his heart, afraid that it had stopped beating.

"Are you all right?" Mai-Nu asked him.

Benito nodded his head.

"You are sure?"

Benito nodded again. After a moment, he found enough breath to ask, "Who were those men?"

"They are from the Kue clan."

"You know them?"

"Yes."

"What were they doing here? Why did they try to kidnap you?"

"It is called 'marriage by capture.'"

"What?"

"It is a Hmong custom. If a woman spends three days in a man's home, even if there is no physical contact between them, she must marry him as long as he can pay the bride price set by her family."

"By your uncle."

"It is becoming rare in America, but my uncle is desperate."

"That's crazy. I mean, they gotta know that you would turn them in, right? They have to know you'd have them arrested."

Mai-Nu did not answer.

"Right?"

"I could not do that to my people. For practicing a custom that has existed for hundreds of years, no, I could not do that."

"But you wouldn't marry him?"

"You are very kind, Benito. And very brave. I am in your debt."

"Mai-Nu, you wouldn't marry him."

"I must ask you one more favor."

"Anything."

"You must not tell my brother about tonight. You must

not tell him about my uncle. I know that he asked you to watch out for me, but you must not tell him anything. The way Cheng is, what he thinks of the old ways, you must not tell him. It would be very bad."

"Mai-Nu?"

"You must promise."

"I promise."

She embraced him. Her lips found the side of his mouth. She said goodnight and returned to her house, locking the door behind her. Benito stood on the sidewalk for a long time, his fingers gently caressing the spot where Mai-Nu had kissed him.

It was a soft, cool night full of wishing stars, unusual for August in Minnesota—a summer evening filled with the promise of autumn—and Benito was terrified that the weather might encourage Mai-Nu to close her windows and lower her shade. As it was, she was dressed in blue Capri pants and a boxy white sweatshirt that revealed nothing of the body beneath. She was sitting on her front stoop, her back against the door, sipping vodka and orange juice.

Benito called to her from the sidewalk.

"¿Qué pasa, chica?" he said. "¿Como te va?"

"Very well, thank you," Mai-Nu replied, and patted the space next to her. Benito sat down.

"My Spanish is improving," she said.

"Sí. I heard from a college today," Benito said, just to be saying something. "Minnesota State wants me to come down to Mankato and look at their campus."

Mai-Nu hugged Benito's arm and a jolt of electricity surged through his body.

"You will go far, I know you will," she told him.

"I need to get my scores up. I took a practice ACT test and only got a nineteen. That's borderline."

"It is hard, I know."

"Did you take the ACT?"

"Yes."

"How'd you do?"

"Thirty-one."

Benito's eyes widened in respect. Thirty-one put Mai-Nu in the top five percent in the country.

"I have always done well with tests," she told him.

Benito didn't know what to say to that so he said nothing. They sat together in silence, Mai-Nu still holding Benito's arm. She released it only when a Honda Accord slowed to a stop directly in front of them. Its lights flicked off, the engine was silenced. The man who stepped out of the vehicle was the largest Asian Benito had ever seen, nearly six feet tall. His jaw was square, his eyes unblinking—a military man, Benito decided. He smiled at Mai-Nu with a stern kindliness.

"You do not have a cordial word for your uncle?" he said.

"Why are you here?" Mai-Nu asked.

"We have much to talk about."

Benito started to rise. Mai-Nu reached for him, but Benito pulled his arm away.

"It is a private matter," he said, and moved to his own stoop. It was only a dozen steps away; he didn't figure to miss much.

"Did you send those assholes last night?" Mai-Nu asked.

"Mai-Nu, your language—"

"Screw my language," she said, and took a long pull of her drink.

Pa Chou's eyes became narrow slits. His voice was suddenly cold and hard.

"The way you drink," he said. "The way you talk. What has become of you?"

"I am angry, Pa Chou. Do you blame me?"

Pa Chou glanced around the street. Seeing Benito pretending not to listen, he said, "Let us go inside."

"Fine," said Mai-Nu. She stood and went into her house. Pa Chou followed. Benito gave them a head start, then dashed into his own house. His mother asked him what he was doing and he said he was going to his room to listen to music. Once there he stared intently through Mai-Nu's window, but could see neither her nor her uncle. Yet he could hear them. They spoke their native language. Benito did not have to understand their words to know they were angry.

He sat and listened for what seemed like a long time. Then he heard a distinct sound of skin slapping skin violently, followed by Mai-Nu falling into her living room. Pa Chou was there in an instant. He heaved her up by her arms, shook her like a doll, and slapped her again with the back of his hand. Mai-Nu shouted at him and Pa Chou hit her again. Mai-Nu fell out of sight and Pa Chou followed. There were more shouts and more slapping sounds. Finally, Pa Chou strode purposely across the living room to the front door. He shouted something at Mai-Nu over his shoulder and left the house. Mai-Nu walked slowly into her living room and collapsed to her knees, leaning against the sofa. She covered her face with her arms and wept.

Benito closed his eyes and braced himself with both hands against the bureau. Something in his stomach flipped and flopped and tried to escape through his throat, but he choked it down. A blinding rage burned at the edge of his eyelids until teardrops formed. He smashed his fist against the side of the bureau, then shook the pain out of his hand.

It was a family matter, he told himself. It had nothing to do with him.

But he could tell Cheng Song about it.

He could do that.

The headline of the St. *Paul Pioneer Press* four days later read: *Killing underscores problems in growing Hmong community.*

The story suggested that the murder of Pa Chou Song and the subsequent arrest of Cheng Song by St. Paul police officers was an indication of how difficult it is for many in the Hmong community to assimilate to American culture. But that is not what distressed Benito. It was the photograph of Pa Chou that the paper printed—a decidedly small man in his late forties standing next to the doorway of a Hmong restaurant.

Benito was confused. He rushed to Mai-Nu's house and knocked on her door.

"Who is it?" she called.

"Benito Hernandez," he answered through the screen door.

"Come in. Sit down. I will be there in a minute."

Benito entered the house and found a seat on the rust-colored sofa. There was a law book on the coffee table. Benito glanced at the spine—*Minnesota Statutes 2005*. He opened it to the page held by a bookmark. A passage had been highlighted in yellow.

524.2-803 Effect of homicide on instate succession,wills, joint assets, life insurance, and beneficiary designations.

(a) A surviving spouse, heir, or devisee who feloniously and intentionally kills the decedent is not entitled to any benefits under the will . . . Property appointed by the will

of the decedent to or for the benefit of the killer passes as
if the killer had predeceased the decedent.

Benito closed the book and returned it to the table when Mai-Nu entered the room. He stood to greet her. She appeared more radiant than at any time since he had known her. Her smile seemed like a gift to the world.

Mai-Nu was tying a white silk scarf around her head. She said, "It is traditional to wear a white headband when one is in mourning."

"Mourning for your uncle," Benito said.

"And my brother."

Benito was standing in front of her now, clutching the newspaper.

"Thank you for thinking of me," Mai-Nu gestured at the paper, "but I have already read it."

Benito showed her the photograph.

"This is your uncle?" he said.

"Yes."

"Pa Chou Song?"

"Yes, of course."

"It is not the man who came here that day. The man who beat you."

"You saw him beat me?"

"I saw—"

"Did you, Benito?"

Benito glanced at the open window and back at Mai-Nu.

"I saw," he said.

"And you told my brother?"

"I know now that you wanted me to tell Cheng what I saw."

"Did I?"

Benito nodded.

"There is no evidence of that."

"Evidence?"

"Did I tell you to go to my brother?"

"No."

"Did I tell you not to speak to my brother?"

"Yes."

"That is the evidence that the court will hear, should you go to court."

"I don't understand."

Mai-Nu brushed past Benito and retrieved the law book from the coffee table. She hugged it to her breasts.

"In Laos, women are expected to submit," she said. "Submit to their husbands, submit to their fathers, submit to their uncles. Not here. Here we are equal. Here we are protected by the law. I love America."

"Who was the man who came here that night?"

"A friend, Benito. Like you."

She reached out and gently stroked Benito's cheek.

"You must go now," she said.

A few minutes later, Benito returned to his bedroom. Dark and menacing storm clouds were rolling in from the northwest, laying siege to the sun and casting the world half in shadow. Mai-Nu's lights were on and though it was early morning, he had a good view of her living room.

He did not see her at first, then Mai-Nu appeared. She moved to the window and looked directly at him. She smiled and blew him a kiss. And slowly lowered her shade.

SMOKE GOT IN MY EYES

BY BRUCE RUBENSTEIN

North End (St. Paul)

L loyd B. Jensen's funeral cortege wasn't scheduled to leave the State Capitol for an hour, but a throng of thousands already lined University Avenue for a glimpse as it passed. The November sun wasn't doing much to warm them so they'd crowded together instinctively, three deep, all the way to the police cordon at Rice Street. It gave them a huddled-masses look appropriate to the occasion. A cynic might say that in this year of our Lord 1934, anybody who advocated the redistribution of wealth could draw a crowd, even if he was dead. As for me, I voted for him once, and I'd have done it again if the iron crab hadn't taken him down. I wasn't there to freeze my toes for a peek at his corpse though. I opened the door of The Criterion. It was warm inside, a few bar flies were gathered around their Manhattans, and somewhere in the murk a client was waiting.

Margaret Thornton phoned me after someone steered her to Slap Madigan, who'd recommended my services. The meeting place was my suggestion, but as soon as I laid eyes on her I could see it was a mistake. She wasn't the kind of woman a man should rendezvous with at a nightclub in mid-afternoon. She said I'd recognize her by the black hat she was wearing, and there she was in a corner booth, veil pinned back over one ear. The rest of her outfit, cloth coat, a glimpse of skirt before I sat down, echoed the darkness of the place as well. That didn't strike me as a good sign a year after her husband's murder, but she looked fine in widow's weeds. Her face might have hardened a bit since it graced the front pages, but there was still a girlish softness about her. I introduced myself. She nodded nervously. She had raven-colored hair, pale, luminous skin, and a few freckles around her nose that were barely visible in the dim light. Her slender, ringless fingers fidgeted on the table. One of them was chewed to the quick. I ordered a beer, and she turned down a refill on the Presbyterian she'd been nursing. I felt like a heel for arriving stylishly late. The poor kid had probably never been in a joint like this before, at least not alone.

I was in my mid-thirties then, she was about ten years younger, so these weren't fatherly feelings I was having, but I didn't stop to analyze them at the time. It wouldn't have changed anything anyway. We made some small talk. She told me she was Thornton nee Gallagher, a St. Agnes graduate. You can bet that tugged at my heart strings. In fact, it put a face to the premier fantasy in my rich array of hooch-induced fancies: Catholic school girls in Little Bo-Peep shoes, white knee socks, and those short plaid skirts they wear for God only knows what perverse reason. When I was a lad my pals and I would sometimes get a peek of alabaster thigh as they walked away. Of course, if we caught some Protestant or God forbid a sheeny doing the same, the gauntlet went down.

I managed to elicit a fair amount of personal information in the guise of professional inquiry. For example, why a proper young lady like herself married a muckraking Wobbly and a Methodist to boot, who'd published his high-minded broadside out of a cheap storefront on Selby. It came down to this: After eighteen years in the grasp of the nuns, and two more clerking at the Golden Rule department store, she wanted some excitement.

"Walter was always railing about something, and there were all these intcresting people around, some with beards even," she said. "I guess I just got carried away."

She told me she was living with her mother, that they made ends meet with help from their fellow parishioners at St. Andrew's and some Reds who'd admired her hubby. I told her Slap was my uncle on my mother's side, that I was unmarried, an irregular confessor. Close to an hour passed before we got down to business.

Margaret wanted what I had an unsullied reputation for delivering, the truth about an unsolved murder. "I need to get on with my life," she said.

She had a notion of what the truth was, and she made it clear that she'd be gratified if I validated it. That's not unusual, most of my clients want their preconceptions confirmed, but her problem was anything but routine.

"Walter was murdered because Harry Ford wanted to stop him publishing," she explained, and her blue eyes lit with sudden passion. "I don't blame Lloyd Jensen. I blame the man who has everything but the respectability Lloyd Jensen could bring him. I don't even care if Mr. Ford is tried for murder. I just want it on the radio and in the newspapers what a dreadful person he is."

"That's all? Nothing to it. It should be easy to get the goods on a defenseless fellow like Harry Ford."

"You can do it, Mr. McDonough. Your uncle says you never fail."

Her confidence was touching, but it was a daunting prospect. I'd heard rumors that Harry Ford was behind Thornton's murder, everybody had, but those rumors had no legs because most people loved the guy, and, more important

BRUCE RUBENSTEIN // 39

from my perspective, those who didn't knew better than to cross him.

She brought up the matter of my fee. I said we'd discuss that after I nosed around. I'd known her less than an hour, but she already had me putting first things last. I escorted her out the back, and opened the car door for her. There weren't many women drivers then, and to me she looked brave and vulnerable behind the wheel, all the more so because I recognized it as the same bucket that shared the front page with her the day after her husband's murder. They'd iced the poor stiff when he stepped out of this very automobile.

She gave me a little smile that faded quickly, exited down the alley, and over to Sherburne. That spared her a demoralizing sight around front. Lloyd B. Jensen's cortege was going past, and people were surging into the street, but not to kiss the governor goodbye. Harry Ford was seated at the passenger window of the hearse, and whether they knew it or not they were crowding up because they believed in what he stood for—redemption. They practically trampled each other trying to touch his cashmere coat, as if some of his magic might rub off on them.

According to the story that every Twin Citian knew, Harry Ford was born to a waterfront whore in Seattle. He'd spent his childhood scrapping for change on the docks, and took off for the Wild West at age sixteen. He worked as a saloon bouncer and a gold miner, then soldiered for Pancho Villa. It was in that latter capacity that he made his first fortune, selling the hides of the cattle slaughtered to feed Villa's army, about two thousand skins a month, at ten dollars each. Those hides were all he'd asked for in return for his valuable services making deals for supplies in U.S. border towns, but he went AWOL pronto when Pancho realized what a good thing he had going.

He spent the next decade "raising hell" (his term) in the Southwest. That must have included some smuggling, but mostly it was one long party that ended when the Feds fitted him up for a nose-candy charge in Denver. He hired some fancy lawyers who took his money but didn't beat the rap. He was broke when he went to Leavenworth, where he met Herbert Warren of Warren Enterprises, a St. Paul calendar manufacturing company. Warren was in for tax evasion, and terrified of the other inmates. Ford made a deal with him. He would protect Warren in prison, and Warren would give him a job when he got out.

Ford held up his end. Warren tried to renege many times, but Ford had some hex on him. He climbed relentlessly toward the top, and when Warren died mysteriously, he became president. He'd turned Warren Enterprises into the largest advertising company in the country, and made himself a legend in the process. Like many a millionaire before him, Ford dabbled in king-making. He'd palled around with Lloyd B. Jensen when Jensen was the county attorney, then bankrolled him for governor. He was ready to do the same for Jensen's shot at the presidency on the Populist ticket. The smart money said that with the Depression on and Ford's bucks behind him, Jensen could beat FDR. Then the poor man got cancer, and died. It was a sad day for many people when that happened, but it came a year late for Margaret Thornton's husband.

Jensen was famous for his reply when his gubernatorial opponent accused him of being a Socialist. "You're damn right I am," he said. That practically sanctified him among many Depression-weary voters, but he was no saint. He'd grown up poor in a mostly Jew neighborhood in Minneapolis. Many friends of his had joined the mockie underworld, which didn't seem to end their friendship, even though he occasionally had to prosecute them. You might say he had a past by the time he was elected governor, and started making the kind of deals he had to in order to govern. That didn't bother most voters, but it didn't sit well with some of his fellow radicals, especially Walter Thornton, who published a yellow sheet devoted to calling Jensen a crook and a sellout. The guy was a pain in the ass who might've hurt Jensen's chances of becoming president, but about the time he was getting worrisome, a car full of droppers pulled up as he arrived home one evening, and ended his career in journalism.

A mockie button man named Shay Tilsen was tried for Thornton's murder. He was acquitted, but everyone figured he'd done it. There just wasn't enough evidence to convict him. The prosecution offered him a sweet deal to rat on whoever hired him, and it was on the table up to the moment the jury walked in, but he never opened his mouth.

I had no skin in that game so I'd never given Ford's involvement much thought. I could find out though. My clients think it's sorcery how I get to the bottom of things, but my reputation rests on two solid facts: one—the majority of murders go unsolved. Your higher-ups don't spread that around, and since most people don't know it, they're also unaware of fact two—the shamuses usually know damn well who the perpetrator is, they just can't prove it.

The rest of the equation is pretty simple. I'm second-generation Irish, I know most of the cops in town, and I can find out what I need to by dropping into Tin Cups and buying a few shots for the right gumshoe. If there's any skill involved, it's knowing who to ask what. My first stop wasn't Tin Cups, however. I dropped into Kuby's Place on Front Avenue the next morning. Kuby's served as a living room for many a retired St. Andrew's parish fellow, and sure enough, there were about ten of them there, a few alone at the bar, the rest gathered around the wood stove, warming their ale on the firebricks.

When in Kuby's, do as the Kubans do. I pulled up a stool, ordered coffee and brandy, and put my nose to the crossword puzzle. It wasn't long before I felt a hearty whack on the back. They don't call him Slap for nothing. He was freshly shaved and nattily attired, the picture of contented leisure. I don't know how he does it, I thought, for the umpteenth time. By rights he should be in a bread line.

"Top of the morning," he said.

I nodded. "I need a four-letter name from Shakespeare that epitomizes cunning."

"I don't read that limey bastard, Martin. How did it go with the widow Thornton? And isn't she a fine example of lace-curtain womanhood?"

"She is, and a welcome respite from the molls I generally consort with. But why did she come to you, Slap?"

"Ah, give me a moment . . . Yes, a fifteen-letter name that epitomizes cunning. Martin McDonough."

We both knew why she'd been steered to Slap. Eight years ago Slap was an investigator on the St. Paul force. A bootlegging operation he was looking into with little or no enthusiasm led him straight to the late Lloyd B. Jensen. That piqued his interest, and when Slap got interested he found things out. He's always clammed up on this, but he must have known plenty. That was why the chief summoned him one day and told him an early retirement was called for. No scandal, he assured him, just a health matter (Slap will out-live me), a Patrolmen's Benevolent Association benefit, and he was a civilian again at age fifty. A lesser man would have been devastated. Not Slap. He lived with his wife and youngest son in a frame house on Oxford, just two doors from the tracks but he claimed that the sound of the Great Northern put him to sleep at night. I think it's a nip of the Irish that does it, but be that as it may, retirement agreed with him. I don't know how he maintained their lifestyle, but it was no mystery why Margaret Thornton was sent his way. He was an authority on Lloyd B. Jensen's affairs.

"What do you think," I asked, "was Ford behind it?"

"Nah. That husband of hers was preaching to the con-verted. All that Commie crap. It would've *helped* get Jensen elected."

He looked as serious as any guy with a nose like a potato and eternally twinkling eyes can, but he was shoveling a load of malarkey. "C'mon, Slap, he was also repeating rumors that you're familiar with, that you maybe could verify."

"Nobody cares about that old bootlegger stuff."

"A guy who was in bed with gangsters can get elected president?"

"Anybody who can end this Depression can get elected, Martin. FDR has my vote." He shook his finger under my nose. "What about yours?"

A few of the old gentlemen pricked up their ears at that, but I didn't take the bait. "Never mind politics. I've got other things on my mind. Who hired that mockie to drop Walter Thornton? And another thing. What kind of Jew is named Shay?"

Slap smiled. "I can tell you how to find out. Drop into a place of worship named Adath Jeshurin Synagogue, in Minneapolis. Tuesday night. It's their social evening. The scholars get together and discuss some Hebrew hocus-pocus, the businessmen talk business, and a bunch of radicals argue with each other so loud it drives everyone else nuts. I hear Shay Tilsen comes around. I wonder who he consorts with. So should you, Martin."

Slap never disappoints me, but I still have to crack wise. "Should I ask him why he dropped Thornton?"

"Nah. I was you, I'd talk to one of the Reds. Lou Rothman."

According to Slap, this Rothman and his buddies had Margaret Thornton's interests at heart. They took up a collection every week and sent it her way, in honor of her dead husband. "Maybe you can find out a thing or two from them," he said.

I agreed and stood to leave.

"When was the last time you talked to your mother, Martin?" he asked. I told him a week ago Sunday. "Well, I have a message from her," he said.

I should've seen that coming. I was halfway out the door before you could say *home and hearth*, but he shouted after me: "GET MARRIED, MARTIN—IN THE CHURCH!"

It was raining Tuesday night, a cold November rain. The kind that turns to snow. I had to park a block away and soak my brogans. I was pursuing Margaret's case so doggedly you'd have thought there was some money in it, but I'd already decided it was on the cuff. It was smoky and overheated inside. I took off my hat out of decent respect for an alien faith, but soon noticed that everyone else had theirs on. When in Hymietown . . . I put mine back on, wet as it was.

There must have been fifty or more men gathered in groups, in a room way too small to hold them. I stood around until an old gent in a black skullcap offered me a glass of disgustingly sweet wine and asked what brought me there. It turned out he was some kind of facilitator. He guided me back to a knot of fellows dressed like laborers. We waited around for a pause in their heated conversation, but it got louder. Pretty soon one guy grabbed another by the collar and twisted. "Stalinist bastard!" he said, and he almost burnt the other guy's big nose with a smoldering fag protruding from the corner of his mouth. I thought the brawl was on, but a guy about my age stepped in. He had a square jaw and a short, dark beard. He didn't say much, but whatever he said worked. They separated and rejoined the discussion. A moment later I thought I saw one of them launch a sucker punch, but he was just talking with his hands, a common mode of discourse here, I realized, as I looked around.

A few more minutes passed, then the old gent called out, "Lou," and the guy who'd short-circuited the donnybrook turned our way. His flat gaze came from behind fragile, wire-rimmed specs, but he looked hard nonetheless. When I told him my name and said I'd like to speak to him, he took off the goggles, came right up close, and squinted at me.

After a few moments he said, "Lou Rothman," and we shook hands. He had a grip like a teamster.

The face mirrors the soul, and I'm often required to make distinctions between one soul and another, so I pride myself on characterizing faces. Nevertheless, I didn't find the right simile for Rothman's map until years later, after Slap's son Danny became a Lincoln Brigadier in a fit of youthful ideal-ism. Spain cured him of that, and when he came home he said it wasn't the fascists who'd scared him, it was some of the characters who were nominally on his side. Rothman, it occurred to me, had a face you'd see in a doorway in Barcelona just before the bomb exploded. He was personable enough that night though. He laughed when he heard my first question.

"His name is Isadore," he said. "'Shay' is short for 'shaygus.' It's Yiddish for a certain kind of Eastern European bully that picks on Jews."

"So he beat up mockies?"

Rothman gave me another long look, best described as bemused. A couple of the other Reds were in earshot, which meant real close—the din of conversation and smoke-induced coughing in that room was something—but it suddenly got quieter on our end and the whole bunch, must've been a dozen of them, were all looking at me. The collar-twister edged my way.

"No," Rothman said. "It's an irony. When Isadore was a kid he beat up goyim who picked on Jews. He took pleasure in kicking their mick asses."

"Hey, I didn't mean anything by it."

"Okay, neither did I," he said.

The rest of his group resumed arguing, to my great relief. Now it was my turn to lean in so I could hear what he said.

"What brings you here, McDonough?" he asked. "You didn't come all the way from St. Paul to find out how Isadore Tilsen got his nickname."

"I'm here on behalf of someone you know. Margaret Thornton."

"Sure. We collect money for her."

"So I hear. But why? I thought you fellows, you know, you lefties, liked Lloyd Jensen."

"Lloyd Jensen and Walter Thornton were both Farmer-Laborers. They stood squarely with the working man, and their differences didn't matter to us." He gestured toward his bunch. "Jensen's widow will be well taken care of, and Thornton's shouldn't go begging either."

He was no Uncle Slap when it came to malarkey, but he

was right up there with any Tin Cups hoocher, and that's say-ing something. It inspired me to boldness.

"Margaret thinks Harry Ford paid Tilsen to murder her husband. Myself, I hear Jensen had a lot of friends in this part of town. Maybe one of them hired him."

"Lloyd Jensen grew up in the neighborhood. Many men in this room knew him personally. They liked him, they liked his politics. You could ask if anybody hired someone to kill Thornton, but it couldn't have been Isadore. The jury found him not guilty. What's the matter, you don't you trust our legal system?"

We were nose to nose, but nobody seemed to be taking any notice. In Tin Cups and other venues with which I'm familiar, going nose to nose was the penultimate gesture before fists flew, but Rothman didn't seem belligerent. He was just making a point.

"Can't stop people thinking though," I said. "Tell me, and this is another thing I'm just curious about, why did those two fellows you broke up almost come to blows?"

"They were arguing. Trotskyism or Stalinism."

"What's that about?"

"Trotsky doesn't compromise on world revolution. Stalin talks about Socialism in one country. No question he's warped the Soviet workers state to fit his own ideological deformity, but some of us wonder if that's what's required to fight fascism. The question is—what do the times call for? What is historically necessary? That's what Meyer almost punched Sherman about."

"Doesn't seem worth fighting over."

"There are two schools of opinion on that, McDonough. Some call it a trivial matter, others believe that perceiving historical necessity and acting to further it is a high calling."

"You should hear what us micks fight about," I said. "Nowhere near as elevated . . . Is Tilsen here?"

Rothman pointed him out through the smoke. "Come with me, I'll introduce you if you like."

Tilsen and a couple yeggs were yakking with each other on the far side of the room. They were positioned between a cluster of fellows in broad-brimmed hats and long coats and a group of more worldly looking men. We picked our way through, Rothman nodding to some, edging by others so as not to interrupt.

Tilsen was a big guy, late forties, with sloping shoulders and a thick neck. Rothman tugged the sleeve of his suit coat, and said something in his ear. Tilsen pulled a wad out of his pocket and counted off some bills.

Rothman motioned me over. "This is Martin McDonough," he said. "Martin, meet Isadore Tilsen."

His yeggs kept their hands in their pockets and their eyes on mine. He had big, hairy knuckles, reddish hair going gray at the temples, gold teeth. He didn't offer his hand, just nodded. "You know Louie?" he said. "Louie wants to change the world."

"Well, uh, it needs changing," I replied lamely.

"You think?" He nodded. "Nice meeting you, Mr. McDonough."

I was dismissed.

"He's a man of few words," I said on the way back to the radical caucus.

"He's short with the goyim, doesn't trust them," Rothman replied. "He's a big puppy with his fellow Jews though. When he was a kid he used to beat up the local shaygus for a favor. He wasn't much of a scholar, so that was how he earned respect."

He seemed in a forthcoming mood so I popped the obvious question. "What was that business between you and him, if you don't mind my asking?"

"Not at all. We usually collect ten or twelve bucks for Margaret Thornton, but we like to give her thirty. Isadore makes up the difference."

"Why is that?"

"You'd have to ask him," he said.

"No thanks. But I do thank you for everything."

"My pleasure. Now, if you don't mind, I'll rejoin the discussion. Stay awhile. Have another glass of wine."

I did. The wine was awful, but not so awful I couldn't drink it, and it gave me a chance to sneak a few looks at Tilsen. He and his boys were deep in some kind of conversation. With each other.

It was still raining when I left. I almost ran over a dog in downtown Minneapolis. The streets were deserted except for a few men sleeping in doorways. I nearly got lost trying to find St. Paul, but eventually made my way back to my Rice Street haunts.

Slap thought it unlikely I'd find a bride at Tin Cups, and upon reflection I had to agree. Women had started coming in unescorted after Prohibition—many a shanty-Irish lass, even a few kraut dames from St. Albert's—but they weren't the kind you'd bring home to Mom. There was a likely looking group of frails sitting at a table when I walked in, Maggie Quinn among them. She glanced up from a pig's foot she was gnawing and gave me the eye, but I paid her no mind. Margaret Thornton was in my thoughts, and I was there on business.

Jimmy Brennan was at his usual spot, on the inside curve of the second horseshoe, hard by the well, where only the most determined barman could fail to spot his empty glass. Jimmy was a percentage copper, on the take from two Rondo Street pimps, and possibly some petermen as well. At least, they seemed to have great success blowing safes when Jimmy walked the beat. He had a nose full of popped veins and shrewd little eyes. The way to his heart was through his wallet, so I saved him for special occasions.

I put a twenty on the bar. "What's your pleasure?" said the bartender.

"A nip of the Irish," I replied. "Top shelf. And one for my friend here."

Jimmy nodded, as if to say it was a start, but only just.

The good stuff was dear at Tin Cups. The change came to less than nineteen dollars. I tapped my finger on the notes. "Give me some information and I'll leave these when I go, Jimmy." He nodded again. I cut to the chase. "Slap doesn't think Harry Ford paid to kill the Thornton kid. How about you?"

He chuckled. "Lotta people think Slap is retired, but I get the feeling he still has a job."

"Why's that?"

"He ain't goin' without."

"They held a benefit for him, remember?"

"Yeah, I was there. Musta collected about, oh, nine hundred bucks. You could live for a year on that."

"What are you driving at?"

"Slap carries water for Harry Ford."

I can't say something of that nature hadn't crossed my mind, but blood is thicker than water, so I didn't disguise my displeasure. "You saying Slap is bent?"

"Hey, the man has to live. You sell what you got, to whoever is buyin'. I'm puttin' two and two together, that's all."

"Four."

What?"

"Two and two is four. I learned that in the first grade." I tapped the bills. "Information, please. If all you have is theories I'll keep the cash, and if all you have is theories that insult my family we'll be stepping outside."

"Okay, okay, relax. But that sheeny torpedo would've squealed unless he was paid to shut up. Somebody put a bundle down, and who but Harry Ford has that kinda money?"

"Another theory." I knocked back my shot, and picked up the bills.

"Hold it," he said. "The name Wicky Hanson mean anything to you?"

It did indeed. Harry Ford was known for hiring ex-cons, one more feather in a cap festooned with plumage. Most of them were nobodies, but Hanson's reputation preceded him when he came to work on the Warren assembly line. He'd been a Thompson-gunner for Capone in Chicago.

"What about him?"

"He's another guy lives beyond his means. He's learnin' to crack safes, but he still works the old trade occasionally. He was in on the Thornton hit. He knows Ford, he knows Shay Tilsen. Maybe he put'em together."

"Any chance he'd talk to me?

"He owes me a favor. You could buy it." He glanced down at the bar. "Not for eighteen bucks though."

A fight broke out on the other end of the bar, but we didn't let it distract us, and soon struck a deal. I'd be ashamed to say how much it cost in view of the fee arrangements on this matter. Jimmy said he'd be in touch. I ignored Maggie Quinn again on the way out. I'd decided to pay a call on the widow Thornton soon, with an update and a dozen roses.

I phoned Slap to tell him how things were going. "Jimmy B. says he can put me together with a member of the Thornton hit squad," I told him. "I didn't find out much in Minneapolis. Met Lou Rothman, but he had nothing to say."

"You didn't see who Tilsen talks to?"

"His palookas. Nobody else. Only interesting thing, he gave Rothman some cash for the widow. Maybe he feels guilty."

"He just handed the money over without a word, did he?"

"A few words."

"So he talked to somebody."

"That was nothing. Hell, he said a few words to me when Rothman introduced us."

Slap sighed audibly. "Well, press Wicky Hanson hard, Martin. He might have something."

"How do you know it's Hanson I'm seeing?"

He laughed. "Jimmy B.'s helping Wicky with his schooling."

Not much gets by Slap.

I didn't work the next few days, just waited for Jimmy's call, and planned my meeting with Margaret. There was a picture in my mind of her soft blue eyes, her cute freckled nose, and an expression on her face that was all yes. As it turned out, that picture was pretty accurate.

I'd decided to surprise her Sunday afternoon. I thought she and her mother would be finishing dinner around 3 p.m. That left a few hours of daylight, and I prayed for a nice afternoon. I thought we'd drive over to Como Park, maybe stop by the lake. I bought a dozen roses and kept them in the icebox Saturday night. Jimmy B. called that evening and said I could meet Hanson the next day. I told him I was indisposed.

"Christ, Martin, I thought this was important," he said.

"I've got something else going. What about Monday?"

"The guy works for a living."

"Maybe Harry Ford'll give him the day off. You know I work nights, Jimmy—anywhere he wants, Monday evening."

Sunday dawned mild and sunny, a September morn in November. Jimmy called about the time both of us should've been at Mass, and said to meet Hanson at Chan's, next evening around 7:00. I had to write it down I was in such a tizzy. This is very unlike me, I thought. I started slicking up for the occasion about noon, and looked my Sunday best when I pulled in front of the Gallagher residence a few minutes before 3:00. I was about to step out of the bucket, when the front door of the house opened and Margaret walked out arm in arm with Lou Rothman.

I processed this as quickly as possible under the circumstances. All I could think of was ducking those roses before they spotted me, but that was unnecessary. They only had eyes for each other. Hers were exactly as I'd pictured them. They walked past me in the general direction of Como Avenue. Margaret looked back when they reached the corner, probably to see if her mother was watching, then kissed him on the cheek.

I cursed the Sunday closing laws, and headed for the back door of a blind pig where a colored man sold me a bottle of something like whiskey. I made good enough use of it that I had a terrible hangover when Monday came. I also had a feeling in the pit of my stomach that had nothing to do with imbibing. Worse yet, although our pitifully one-sided romance was kaput, my business with Margaret was far from finished. She still wanted to know who was behind her husband's murder. The best I could do was suck it up and come out of this with my reputation intact.

Sorry as I felt for myself Monday evening, I still had some pity to spare for Walter Thornton. He'd stepped out of his flivver anticipating his wife's lovely face and welcoming arms. Instead, the pockmarked mug of the man across the booth from me ushered him into the next world.

"I could use a drink," said Wicky Hanson.

"So buy one," I replied.

"Jeez, I thought you wanted info."

"I do, and I already paid for it," I said, but what he told me almost made me sorry I'd been so short.

Hanson cautioned that Tilsen didn't confide in the non-Jews he occasionally hired, so all he knew was what he overheard. But he had sharp ears and a good memory. He explained that the mood among the five torpedoes on the hit was about what you'd figure—tense and silent on the way, relieved and talkative afterward. Tilsen was the wheel-man.

"There was this one mockie in the front seat next to him," he said. "Wasn't no dropper, even though he looked like one—hard guy with a fag in his mouth—but there strictly to finger Thornton. So we're waiting, car pulls up, guy opens the door, finger-man says, 'That's him,' jumps out, and motions us to follow. We step out and I overhear the mark say to the finger-man, 'Meyer, what're you doing?' And he says, 'Sorry, Walter, I'm an agent of history.' Then we start blastin' and his wife runs out screamin'. That's about it."

"You're sure his name was Meyer, and that's exactly what he said?"

Hanson nodded.

"Anything else?"

"Yeah. When we're drivin' away, we're all laughing and crackin' wise, even Tilsen. He turns around and says, 'May not look that way, but we changed the world today, boys.'

Then he nods to this Meyer character. 'Make sure you tell him we said that,' he says."

I put my head in my hands and thought hard. "That it?"

"Well, Jimmy B. says you want facts, not theories."

"From Jimmy. If you've got a theory, go ahead."

"It's just that the finger-man probably wasn't the guy ordered the hit. Tilsen told him to tell someone about this changin'-the-world joke he made. That's who was behind it."

I nodded. "I think you're right." I motioned to the waitress. "Give this man a drink," I said, and handed her two bucks.

Next day, two or three times, I was on the verge of calling Margaret and telling her what I'd deduced. It could change your whole life, I told myself. But I couldn't. Not yet. I wanted to nail it down.

That night I went to the synagogue. They were all there—the radicals, the scholars, Tilsen, the finger-man, the old gent with the skull cap. I took a wine and got right to the point with Rothman.

"You'd have liked to see Lloyd B. Jensen become president, wouldn't you?"

He knew something was up. He didn't take off the specs, just gave me a flat stare and nodded yes.

"Was he what the times called for? Was he historically necessary?"

"That's a complicated question, McDonough. What makes you ask? Thinking of joining the Party?"

"No." I stepped in closer to make sure he heard. "I'm thinking of telling Margaret Thornton who was behind her husband's murder."

He rubbed his beard and took that in. "Let me show you something," he said.

He took me by the arm and guided me into the thick of things. The air was blue with eye-stinging smoke, and there were so many people talking at once—gesturing, shouting, laughing, cursing—that nothing they said was intelligible. The word that came to mind was babble, but Rothman had another term, which he imparted by shouting in my ear.

"These are the masses," he said. "Every kind of person with every experience you can imagine is here. Hard workers, lazy bastards, money grubbers, thinkers, doers, devout men, unbelievers, gentlemen, killers. Somebody says something, somebody else hears, passes it on inadvertently or on purpose, pure or changed to suit his own self-interest, and sooner or later, who knows why, somebody does something that matters. Somebody acts."

"And then it's history."

"That's right," he agreed. "History is its own imperative. Anything can happen until something does. Then nothing else was ever possible. What are you going to tell Margaret?"

"I don't know," I replied, and I turned and walked out. I had goose bumps all the way to the bucket, wondering if someone was going to shoot me in the back.

I mulled it over for a while the next day, and then called Margaret on the phone. I didn't want to behold her disillusionment, which she made no attempt to disguise. "I don't know who was behind the killing of your husband," I told her, "but it wasn't Ford."

"There'll be no charge," I added, to break the silence.

She didn't thank me. "I thought you were infallible, Mr. McDonough," she said, in reference to my lost reputation.

To this day I wonder why I acted as I did. It had little to do with Rothman's denial, if indeed it was a denial. Maybe the look on her face when they were together did it, the way she kissed him on the cheek. When I told Slap, he couldn't believe it. "That was your last best chance for a decent marriage," he said.

It wasn't Margaret's, though. She and Rothman married. They have children now, three last I heard. Maggie Quinn moved in with me for a bit, but that didn't work. We brought out the worst in each other. I actually hit her once, which so mortified me that I decided it was time to end it, and she agreed.

I can't say that Margaret's face haunts my dreams. Hoochers don't dream, but we do have fantasies. Catholic school girls are mine. I've shortened their skirts and dirtied up their knee socks a bit over the years. They're still walking away, but now one of them is looking back over her shoulder, at me.

NOIR NEIGE

BY K.J. ERICKSON

Near North (Minneapolis)

You could spend a lot of time trying to figure out how three guys as different as Tom Leigh, Earl Dethaug, and Jorge Mendez ended up working together at the Minneapolis Impound Lot. What it came down to was that each of them, in his own male-impaired way, loved the other. But it took a lot of time and bad luck for them to figure that out. And like a lot of love stories, it ends as a tale of revenge.

The only snow Tom Leigh had seen before moving to Minnesota was snow that melted as it hit the ground. So he wasn't prepared when he woke on an early November morning at his girlfriend's apartment. Hung over. No idea that seventeen inches of snow had fallen since his last conscious moment. Or that the city of Minneapolis had something called Snow Emergency Rules. Rules so complicated they took three pages of closely printed type to explain.

His girlfriend got up first, took one look out the window, and said, "Shit."

Tom rose on one elbow, eyes clenched shut to avoid light.

"Where'd you park last night?" Carla said.

Tom leaned forward slowly. A faster motion would have been disastrous for his gastrointestinal tract. Not to mention Carla's bedding.

"Where'd I park?"

"There's serious snow out there, and the tow trucks just hit my block. If you parked on the street . . ."

"Tow trucks?" Tom said, still not hearing anything that warranted opening his eyes.

"It's a snow emergency, numb nuts. You park on the wrong side of the street, wrong day, wrong time—during a snow emergency—and your car gets towed. And from where I stand, it looks like my side of the street just hit the snow emergency trifecta. They've already loaded a bunch of cars . . ."

A surge of bile hit the back of Tom's throat. He dropped back on the pillow. He was pretty sure he'd parked directly in front of Carla's apartment, but he was also pretty sure he didn't much care.

"So they tow my car. They've got to bring it back after they plow, right?"

Carla was still at the window when she said, "There it goes. That is definitely your car. A pile of snow fell off when they loaded it on the flatbed. And no. They don't bring it back. You have to go get it. Which is going to be a problem. Buses probably aren't running and there's no way you're going to get a taxi in this weather. With tow fees and fines, it's going to cost you, like, two hundred dollars to get your car back. And impound fees, if you don't get down to the impound lot to pick it up . . ."

Tom was out of the bed, naked and farting, running toward the door. He grabbed his jacket off the couch and made it down to the front door in seconds.

Then he hit the snow. It would take a shovel and fifteen minutes to get him from where he was to the street. All he could do was stand there, watching the tow truck turn the corner, heading toward downtown, Tom's car on the flatbed.

It was then he felt the cold. It was then he realized he

wasn't wearing his jacket. He was wearing Carla's jacket, which stopped about seven inches north of his cold-withered dick. And it was then that his beleaguered gut gave way, leaving Tom no choice but to drop his butt down in the snow and let loose. Standing up, he made the mistake of looking back at the darkened snow where he'd sat. His reaction to what he saw was reflexive, born out of years spent as a floundering French major. *Noir neige*. Black snow. Who said being a French major had no practical application?

The city impound lot is located under the I-394 overpass at the western edge of downtown Minneapolis, shadowed by tons of concrete. A couple dozen columns, each maybe six feet in diameter, support the nonstop vibration of cars crossing the overpass. It's a forbidding sight. But what was really depressing was the line of people snaking toward a concrete block building at one end of the lot. There must have been two hundred of them. Miserable-looking people. Cold. Unkempt. Mad. Every one of them looked mad.

Tom had not been able to feel his feet for more than an hour by the time he made it through the line to a bleak, unheated hallway leading to the service windows. Behind the windows, two guys processed tickets. And behind them were handmade signs that made clear this was the kind of place where the customer was never right.

Minnesota Nice Stops Here
We charge extra for excuses
We don't make the rules, we just take your money

It was Tom's first sight of Earl Dethaug, one of the two guys behind the windows. The first thing you noticed about Earl was that he was fat. The way you get fat if you only eat white, yellow, and brown food. What Tom could see of Earl's clothing was a dirty T-shirt and a down vest with wisps of white feathers sticking out of the seams. His arms were heavily tattooed. The tattoos suggested Earl had once been thin; they had faded as his skin spread over expanding girth.

The next thing Tom noticed about Earl was how unconcerned he was by the nonstop abuse he took from each and every person who presented themselves, rumpled tow tickets in hand.

The guy directly in front of Tom drove his fist into the window after finishing his business with Earl. It was a mistake. The window was bullet proof, and from the sound of the impact, Tom guessed the guy broke some bones.

From the window speaker, Earl said, "Next."

At which point the guy turned fast, bumping into Tom. He spat in Tom's direction and said, "Move your dumb ass!"

Tom didn't even have to think about it. "*Fiche-moi le camp!*" he called after him. And then, louder, "*Va te faire foutre!*"

Earl was staring at him as Tom stepped up to the window. "I personally impose a surcharge on anybody who don't speak English, buddy."

"I speak English," Tom said. "But I curse in French."

Earl continued to stare. "You speak anything else?"

"Spanish. Some German."

"Hot damn," Earl said. "You want a job? One of my guys is out sick. Georgie. The one that speaks spick. We're getting killed. How about it, Frenchy. I'll give you seventy-five bucks to work from now until 10 o'clock tonight."

Tom thought about it. How hard could it be? And besides, after he paid the tow ticket and fine, he wouldn't have any cash left for the rest of the month.

Tom said, "Is it heated in there?"

"We got infrared heaters above and floor heaters besides."

Tom said, "You cover my tow bill and fine, and I'll do it."

Earl grimaced. Then he said, "I'll cover if you stay until 7 tomorrow morning."

That had been four years ago. Since then, whenever there was a snow emergency, Tom's phone would ring and it would be Earl.

"Dirty drawers, Frenchy."

Dirty drawers was Earl's code for his personal snow emergency drill. Earl wore the same unwashed underwear he'd worn every snow emergency since he'd taken over the city impound lot. Tom made it a point not to ask how long that had been.

"It's like this, Frenchy," Earl said. "Snow emergencies—I don't shave, I don't shower. Hell, I don't brush my teeth. And then I've got my specially aged underwear going for me. Gives a guy an edge. Know what I'm saying?"

It had never entered Tom's mind that he'd be working at the impound lot for four years. When he thought about it, he considered the possibility he'd miss being the guy in control on the other side of the bullet-proof window when the pathetic hordes of towees showed up. He considered the possibility that he'd miss the drama of the twenty-four-hour snow emergency shifts.

There was always lots of drama.

Earl said, "I've had to duck twice working impound lots. The third time I have to duck, I'm out of here. Not gonna push my luck."

The first time Earl ducked had been back when he'd run a private impound lot. He'd handled cars parked illegally on private property. Earl operated out of a ten-by-twelve-foot ice-fishing shack he'd bought off his brother-in-law for fifty bucks. He'd had a hole cut in the shack and installed a piece of glass with a pass window in it.

Three months after Earl started business in the shack, he'd dropped a handful of quarters on the floor. An eye blink after he'd bent over to pick them up, a brick came through the glass window, right where Earl's head would have been if he'd been standing up.

The second time Earl ducked was after he'd left the shack to take a leak behind one of the impounded cars. He was maybe two car lengths away from the shack when he heard something behind him. Like a rock had hit the shack. It was another eye blink before the whole shack exploded.

The police bomb squad said somebody had lobbed a Vietnam-era grenade at the shack.

After that, Earl had a twelve-by-twelve cement-block structure put up. A bullet-proof window in front. A john at the back.

"Sweet," Earl said, "but volume at the city was better. And I got benefits. So I sold the private lot. Came out ahead. Besides, once I read the city's snow emergency rules—ka-ching!—I figured it was a license to print money."

Jorge Mendez—Georgie to Earl—said, "What I hear is people are gonna be able to sign up for an e-mail notification on snow emergencies. That could hurt our business some . . ."

Earl rolled his eyes.

"Georgie, Georgie, Georgie. You worked here how long? A year more than Frenchy, right? And you still haven't figured out that our customers couldn't get it together to move their cars if you and me went out and personally whacked each one of them over the head with a two-by-four."

As usual, Earl was right. Nine times out of ten, people who

got towed were people whose lives were already seriously out of control. These were people for whom bounced checks, parking tickets, and overdue rent were a way of life. They were running on a short fuse before they got towed, and getting towed was just one of a lot of things that lit their match.

Tom liked Jorge almost as much as he liked Earl, hard pressed as he was to explain what any one of them had in common with the other. Maybe the one thing that Tom and Jorge had in common was that neither could explain why they'd worked for Earl as long as they had.

"Does it bother you that he calls you *Georgie*," Tom said, "instead of pronouncing your name right?"

Jorge shrugged. "I corrected him a couple times when I first started working here. Then he put my name up on the schedule spelled, *Whore-Hey*. So I told him to skip it. Just call me Georgie. It doesn't really matter. What matters is, stuff like when my mom was here from El Paso. Earl gave me extra to take her out for dinner. And the second year I worked impound, I had mono, and he paid me the whole time I was sick. That came out of his pocket, but he made me take it. With Earl, what you see isn't necessarily what you get. Know what I mean?"

It was Tom's turn to shrug. "I guess."

Jorge said, "Does it bother you he calls you *Frenchy*?"

Tom said, "I never really thought about it. Just like I never really think about why I'm still here."

"I guess I like the flexibility," Jorge said, "and the money's not bad. It leaves me time for my music. That's what I care about. Kind of like you and your French." Jorge stopped, looking at Tom. "How long does it take to finish a French major, anyways? You've been at the U how long now?"

Tom thought a better question would be, how long had it been since he'd registered for a class at the U.

"It's not like there's a rule about how long it takes," Tom said. "I'm doing a lot of independent reading. I'll finish when I finish."

Jorge's eyes narrowed and he continued to look at Tom. "So you finish your French major or whatever. What do you do then?"

This was a question that Tom got a lot, and he liked it less every time somebody asked.

"It's not like with a French major there's a job that you do. I could do a lot of things. Like teach, or translate or—whatever." He changed the subject. "The thing is, I'll be qualified to do something. That's what you need to be thinking about, Jorge. You need to have options. You need to have a Plan B in case your music thing doesn't work out. You don't want to end up like Earl, working at the impound lot when you're sixty years old."

"I got a Plan B," Jorge said.

"Such as . . . ?"

Jorge looked away from Tom. "You ever been to First Avenue?"

"First Avenue?"

"The club down by the Target Center. You know. Where Prince filmed *Purple Rain*. The Replacements played there in the '80s. Every major rock and roll band from the '70s and '80s played there when they started out. It's, like, a historic venue."

"I was there once, I think. Music's never been that big a thing for me," Tom said.

"Maybe not for you, but for a lot of people, First Avenue is like Mecca. People who know anything about music, they'll, like, come thousands of miles to see First Avenue. Just to breathe the air. Just to say they've been there."

"I'm having a hard time figuring out how this music Mecca ties in with your Plan B."

A smug look settled on Jorge's face. "I've got two cans of the paint they used to paint the place. The original black paint."

Tom shifted around a bit. "I'm still not seeing two cans of black paint as being your Plan B."

"It was when I was helping out with the sound system at First Avenue. I found the paint in a back room at the club. One of the owners said I could have it. I'm going to sell it on eBay. It'll be worth a fortune."

"That's it?" Tom said. "Two cans of black paint from First Avenue? That's your Plan B?"

Jorge looked disgusted. "You really don't know anything, do you? Some guy just sold part of a cheeseburger Elvis bit into for thousands on eBay."

Tom shook his head. "All I can say is, good luck."

"Timing," Jorge said. "Timing is the thing. If they close First Avenue—if Prince dies—my price goes up."

Timing turned out to be important the third time Earl ducked.

Earl's third duck came during what everyone was calling the storm of the century. It started as an eerily balmy January morning: the sun dim early on, heavy clouds gathering as the day progressed. The snow started slowly, purposefully. Like it had plenty of time to do whatever it wanted to do.

What it wanted to do was bury Minneapolis. Not once, not twice, but three times over a five-day stretch.

Tom, Earl, and Jorge had been in place behind the bullet-proof windows for thirty-six hours, taking turns sleeping on an inflatable mattress Earl had in a corner on the floor, when the guy in the camel-hair coat showed up.

He came up to the window without standing in line. Ignoring the shouting from his fellow towees.

"Here comes trouble," Earl said. The guy in the camel-hair coat wasn't your typical towee. The only thing he had in common with your typical towee was that he was mad. Really mad.

"Money on it," Earl said. "He's the classic white Porsche parked in A-33."

Earl pushed the speaker button. "Back of the line, buddy."

The guy stabbed a leather-gloved finger against the glass, his mouth moving furiously. Behind him, a towee clapped both hands on the guy's camel-haired shoulders and started to move him away from the window. The guy spun, sucker-punching the other towee.

"That's it," Earl said. "I'm calling security."

In the minutes it took for security to show up, almost everyone in line was involved in the fracas. Earl turned the speaker on to tell security to take the guy in the camel-hair coat. Then he yelled, "Everyone else. Shape up, or nobody's getting their cars out of here today!"

The speaker was on long enough for them to hear the guy in the camel-hair coat's final words.

"This isn't over, jerkoffs. That car is worth more than the three of you will make in a lifetime. You don't know who you're messing with." Then he threw the tow ticket on the floor.

To the guy standing nearest the window, Earl said, "You. Pick up that ticket and pass it through."

Earl looked at the ticket and said, "Yeah. The classic

white Porsche. A-33. Just like I said." He tossed the ticket to the side and said, "Georgie. Frenchy. Watch yourselves when you leave. What I said first. This guy is trouble."

Nothing happened, except two days later a guy came to pick up the classic white Porsche. Not the guy in the camel-hair coat, but the paperwork was in order, so they released the car.

"A lackey," Earl said. "Some guy he's hired to clean up after him. Probably a full-time job."

Earl ducked on the fifth consecutive day of the snow emergency.

Things had wound down, mostly because every car that could possibly be towed had been towed by then. Lines at the window had dwindled and Earl, Tom, and Jorge were spending hours back on the air mattress, too punch drunk to organize themselves back to a normal schedule.

It had been just Earl and Jorge at the window when Tom, on the mattress, heard Earl say, "Oh shit. Look what they're hauling in. A junker. I've told them a hundred times, a car like that isn't worth the price of the ticket. It's just gonna sit here, and the city's gonna end up paying to get it towed out."

He turned. "Tom, take the window. I'm going out to tell the tow truck to get that thing the hell out of here."

From inside the service center they couldn't see what happened, but they heard it. First a small pop. Then a boom, followed by quiet, followed by a series of booms, sequential, one going off after the other. They could feel the explosions as much as they could hear them. The floor under their feet vibrated.

* * *

"I always said, the third time I duck I'm done with impound work."

Earl was still at Hennepin County Medical Center, Tom and Jorge standing beside his hospital bed.

"Everybody said I'm lucky. Once they get the metal or whatever out of me, I'm pretty much okay. Damn lucky that the first explosive didn't go full bore. Bomb squad said there were three bombs in the trunk. Then it hit the gas tanks on a couple other cars. Only by the grace of God it didn't take down the overpass."

He looked at Tom and Jorge. "Man, wouldn't that have been something? The whole shebang coming down?" I heard that first pop and I knew what was happening. Gave me time to duck." He paused. "I told them. Told the cops. It was the guy in the camel-hair coat. I can smell it. Knew he wasn't going to walk away from what happened."

"So they're going to get him?" Jorge said.

Earl frowned. "That's the only thing that really bothers me about quitting now. They say one chance in a million they'll be able to tie it to the guy in the camel-hair coat." Suddenly, tears welled in Earl's eyes. He reached out, putting bandaged hands on each of their arms.

"Not the only thing that bothers me about quitting. I'll miss the two of you guys. I won't forget that it was you guys who pulled me out."

Tears rolled down Earl's face. Embarrassed, he smiled. "I'm gonna will you my dirty drawers. The two of you will have to fight over who gets to wear 'em."

"It's okay, Earl," Tom said. "We've been talking. It won't be the same without you. We probably should have moved on a long time ago. We're through with impound work too."

* * *

They stood in front of the hospital for a while before they headed home.

Tom said, "Time to implement Plan B, Jorge."

Jorge was quiet for a long time, then said, "I already did. Go ahead. Laugh. It didn't work."

Tom looked sideways at Jorge. "You put the paint on eBay?"

"The day the place blew up."

"And?"

"Nothing. Not a nibble." Jorge's expression changed from depressed to angry. "I can't believe it. I mean, where are people's values, anyway? When a moldy cheeseburger is worth more than a piece of musical history . . ."

Surprising himself, Tom felt bad. At that moment, having Jorge's Plan B work out would have made him feel better.

"Like you said, timing is everything. Who knows, a year or two from now it could still go big. Prince dies, you put the paint back on eBay with all the history about Prince and First Avenue . . ."

Jorge shook his head. But his face changed again. He didn't look exactly happy, but he looked pleased with himself.

"Talking to Earl just now. It made me think. I don't want to spend the rest of my life hauling that paint around. It'll just make me feel like a loser. I've got another idea."

"Like what?" Tom said.

Tom pulled a wheeled piece of luggage behind him as he and Jorge walked down the parking ramp.

"You're sure about this?" he said.

"I've spent the last week checking everything out," Jorge replied. "Trust me. The setup is perfect for us. He's got the Porsche parked in a special section just beyond the checkout booth. Supposed to give him extra security. But the checkout guy faces in the opposite direction, sleeps ninety percent of the time. If the Porsche was in the other part of the ramp, there'd be security cameras. But there's nothing on the other side of the checkout booth. And it's mostly contract parking, so not a lot of traffic going in and out this time of day. Just act normal."

It was like Jorge said. The guy in the checkout booth didn't even look up when they walked by him. There was a Lincoln Navigator next to the Porsche that completely blocked the view between them and the booth.

"Another piece of luck," Jorge said, giving the Navigator a pat with his gloved hand. "You want to say something in French before we do this? Kind of like a baptism?"

"Let's just do it and get out of here," Tom said. He bent over and unzipped the suitcase, pulled out one can of paint, handing it to Jorge. Then he took out the second can and pried the lid off.

Together, it took maybe three minutes to cover the white Porsche in black paint. When there was maybe six inches of the thick, viscous old paint left in Tom's can, he said, "Jorge. Check the driver's side. See if the door's open."

"You want to do the interior?"

"No. I want to do the engine, if we can pop the hood."

They were a half-block down the street when Tom noticed their boots were tracking black paint.

"Damn," he said. "We've got to break our trail. Wipe down our boots over there, on that snowbank."

Tom looked over his shoulder at the snow after they'd cleaned their boots.

"Now I want to say something in French," he said.

"Shoot."

"*Très convenable*," Tom said.

"Tray what?"

"Very appropriate," Tom said. "The snow back there. Where we wiped our boots. It reminds me of something that happened the first day I started working for Earl."

BUMS

BY WILLIAM KENT KRUEGER

West Side (St. Paul)

K id showed up at the river in the shadow of the High Bridge with a grin on his face, a bottle of Cutty in his hand, and a twenty-dollar bill in his pocket. Kid was usually in a good mood, but I'd never seen him quite so happy. Or so flush. And I couldn't remember the last time I'd seen a bottle of good scotch.

It was going on dark. I had a pot of watery stew on the fire—rice mostly, with some unidentifiable vegetables I'd pulled from the dumpster behind an Asian grocery store.

I held up the Cutty to the firelight and watched the reflection of the flames lick the glass. "Rob a bank?"

"Better." Kid bent over the pot and smelled the stew. "Got a job."

"Work? You?"

"There's this guy took me up on my offer."

Most days Kid stood at the top of the off-ramp on Marion Street and I-94 where a stoplight paused traffic for a while. He held up a handmade sign that read, *Will Work For Food.* He got handouts, but he'd never had anyone actually take him up on his offer.

"What kind of work?"

"Chopping bushes out of his yard, putting new bushes in. This yard, Professor, I tell you, it's big as a goddamn park. And the house, Jesus."

He called me Professor because I have a small wire-bound notepad in which I scribble from time to time. Why that translated into Professor, I never knew.

I wanted badly to break the seal on the bottle, but it wasn't my move.

Kid sat down crossed-legged in the sand on the river-bank. He grinned up at me. "Something else, Professor. He's got a wife. A nice piece of work. The whole time I'm there, she's watching me from the window."

"Probably afraid you were going to steal something."

"No, I mean she's looking at me like I'm this stud horse and she's a . . . you know, a girl horse."

"Filly."

"That's it. Like she's a filly. A filly in heat."

I watched the gleam in Kid's eye, the fire that danced there. "You already have yourself a few shots of something?"

"It's the truth, swear to God. And get this. The guy wants me back tomorrow."

"Look, are we just going to admire this bottle?" I finally asked.

"Crack 'er open, Professor. Let's celebrate."

Kid and I weren't exactly friends, but we'd shared a campfire under the High Bridge for a while, and we trusted each other. Trust is important. Even if all you own can fit into an old gym bag, it's still all you own, and when you close your eyes at night, it's good to know the man on the other side of the fire isn't just waiting for you to fall asleep. Kid had his faults. For a bum, he thought a lot of himself. That came mostly from being young and believing that circumstance alone was to blame for his social station. I'd tried to wise him up, pointing out that lots of folks encounter adversity and don't end up squatting on the bank of a river, eating out of other people's garbage cans, wearing what other people throw away. He was good-looking, if a little empty in the attic, and had the kind of physique that would probably appeal to a bored rich woman. He was good companionship for me, always eager and smiling, kind of like a having a puppy around. I didn't know his real name. I just called him Kid.

The next evening when he came back from laboring in the rich man's yard, he explained to me about his plans for the guy's wife.

"She's got this long black hair, all shiny, hangs down to her hips, swishes real gentle over the top of her ass when she walks. Paints her nails red like little spots of blood at the end of her fingers and toes. Talks with this accent, I don't know what kind, but it's sexy. And she's hot for me, Professor. Christ, she's all over me."

Dinner that evening was fish, a big channel cat I'd managed to pull from the river with a chunk of moldy cheese as bait. I was frying it up in the pan I used for everything.

"If this woman is all you say she is, she could have any man she wants, Kid. What does she want with a bum?"

That offended him.

"I'm not like you, Professor. The booze don't have me by the throat. One break and I'm outta here."

"Dallying with a bored rich woman? How's that going to change your luck?"

Kid peered up from watching the fish fry. "I got inside today, looked the place over. They got all this expensive crap lying around."

"And you're what, just going to waltz in and help yourself?"

His looked turned coy. "She let me inside today when her old man took off to get a bunch of bushes from the nursery.

Asked if I wanted some cold lemonade. Starts talking kind of general, you know. Where I'm from, do I got family, that kind of thing. Then, get this, she tells me her husband's not a man for her. No lighting in the rod, you know? I tell her that's a damn shame, all her good looks going to waste. She says, 'You think I'm pretty?' I tell her she's the prettiest goddamn thing I've ever seen. Then you know what, Professor? She invites me back tonight. Her old man's going out of town and she's all alone. Doesn't want to be lonely. Know what I'm saying? When it's dark, I'm heading over."

"You're spending the night?"

"Not the whole night. She don't want me around in the morning for the neighbors to see sneaking off."

"You sure you're not on something?"

"Proof, Professor," he said with a sly grin. "I got proof."

From his pants pocket, he took a small ball of black fabric. He uncrumpled it and held it toward me with both hands, as if he were holding diamonds. "Her panties."

Thong panties, barely enough material to cover a canary.

"She gave you those?"

"Reached up under her skirt and slipped 'em off where she stood. Said they'd tide me over until tonight."

He went to his things and rolled the panties in his blanket.

"Hungry?" I asked.

"Naw. I'm going to the Y, slip inside and wash up. I want to smell good tonight. Don't wait up for me, Dad," he said with a grin, and he walked off whistling.

He didn't come back that night. I figured he'd got what he wanted from the rich man's wife and the rich man's house and I'd seen the last of him. What did I care? People come into your life and they go. You can't cry over them all.

So why did I feel so low the next day? All I wanted was

to get drunk. Finally, I headed to the plasma center on University, let them siphon off a little precious bodily fluid, and I walked out with cash. I headed to the Gopher Bar for an afternoon of scintillating conversation with whoever happened to be around. It was a place where Kid and I had sometimes hung out together, and I hoped he might be there.

Laci was tending bar. A hard, unpretty woman with a quick mind. She sized me up as I sat on a stool. "Starting the wake, Professor?"

"You lost me," I said.

She threw a bar towel over her shoulder and came my way. "I figured you were planning to tip a few to the memory of your buddy. Not that a piece of crap like him deserves it."

"Kid? Piece of crap? What are you talking about?"

"You don't know?"

"Know what?"

She turned, took a bottle of Old Grandad down from the shelf, and poured me a couple of fingers worth. "This one's on the house."

Then she told me about Kid. It was all over the news.

The night before, he'd been shot dead in the rich man's house, but not before he beat the guy's wife to death with a crowbar.

"Funny." She shook her head. "I never figured him to be the violent kind. But anybody beats a woman to death deserves what he gets. Sorry, Professor, that's how I see it."

I swallowed the whiskey she'd poured, but instead of sticking around to get drunk, I walked back to the river.

That night I didn't bother putting together a fire, just sat on the riverbank below the High Bridge, listening to the sound of occasional traffic far above, thinking about Kid. At one point I pulled out my notepad, intending to write. I don't know what. Maybe a eulogy, something to mark his passing. Instead, I picked up a stick and scratched in the sand. A few minutes later a barge chugged past and the wake washed away what I'd written. I ended up crying a little, which almost never happens when I'm sober.

Two years ago I had a wife, a good job as a reporter with the *Star Tribune*, a house, a car. Then Deborah left me. She said it was the drinking, but it was me. I was never reliable. The drinking only made it worse. Not long after that I lost my job because I was happier sitting at the bar than at my desk trying to meet deadline. Everything pretty much went downhill from there. Somebody tells you they drink because they're a failure, it ain't so. They're a failure because they drink. And they drink because it's so damn hard not to. But as long as they have a bottle that isn't empty, they never feel far from being happy.

That's me anyway.

Near dawn, I stood up from the long night of grieving for Kid. I was hungry. I walked the empty streets of downtown St. Paul to Mickey's Diner, got there just as the sun was coming up, ordered eggs, cakes, coffee. I picked up a morning paper lying on the stool next to me. Kid and what he'd done was still front-page news.

He had a name. Lester Greene. He had a record, spent time in St. Cloud for boosting cars. He had no permanent address. He was a bum. And he'd become a murderer.

The woman he'd killed was Christine Coyer, president and CEO of Coyer Cosmetics. Deborah used to ask for Coyer stuff every Christmas. All I remember about it was that it was expensive. According to the paper, she'd just returned from visiting family in New York City. Her husband had picked her up at the airport, brought her home, and while he parked the car in the garage, she'd gone into the house ahead of him. Apparently, she surprised Kid, who'd broken in with a crow-bar, which he proceeded to use to crack her skull. He attacked her husband too, but the guy made it upstairs where he kept a pistol for protection. Kid followed and the rich man put four bullets into him in the bedroom. He was dead when the cops arrived. The husband knew the assailant. A bum on whom he had taken pity. A mistake he now regretted.

The story was continued on page 5A with pictures. I could tell already the whole thing smelled, but when I turned to the photos I nearly fell off my stool. There was the dead woman. She was fiftyish, nicely coiffed, but not with long black hair that brushed the top of her ass. She was a little on the chubby side, matronly even. Not at all the kind of figure a pair of thong panties would enhance.

If the article was correct, she'd been in the Big Apple when Kid had been given that delicate little sexual appetizer. So, if Christine Coyer didn't give it to him, who did?

During my college days, my clothing came from the Salvation Army. I shopped there in protest against con-sumerism and conformity. I shop there now out of necessity. For ten bucks I picked up a passable gray suit, a nearly white shirt, and a tie that didn't make me puke. I washed up in the men's room of a Super America on 7th, changed into the suit, and hoofed it to the address on Summit Avenue given in the newspaper story.

Like a big park, Kid had described the place. His perspec-tive was limited. It was the fucking Tuileries Gardens, a huge expanse of tended flower beds and sculpted shrubbery with a château dead center. The cosmetics business had been very good to Ms. Coyer. And to her husband, no doubt. So good, in fact, one had to wonder why a man would do any of the dirty landscape work himself. Or hire someone like Kid to help.

I knocked on the door, a cold call, something I'd often done in my days as a journalist. I had my notepad and pen out, in case I needed to pretend to be a reporter.

A woman answered. "Yes?"

I told her I was looking for Christine Coyer's husband.

"He's not here," she informed me. "Do you have an appointment?"

No, just hoping to get lucky, I told her.

"Would you like to leave a message?"

I didn't. I thanked her and left.

I headed back to the river thinking the woman's accent was French, but not heavily so. Quebec, maybe. Her black hair when let down would easily reach her ass. And that body in thong panties would be enough to drive any man to murder.

What to do?

I could go to the police. Would they believe me? If I produced the panties, they might be inclined to look more skeptically on the rich man's story.

I could go to an old colleague. I still knew plenty of press people who'd take the story and dig.

But the influence of money should never be underestimated. Everybody's integrity is for sale if the price is right. So I knew that turning the information and the panties over to anybody else was risky.

I realized I was probably the only shot Kid had at justice.

I sat by the river, smelling the mud churned up from the bottom, but also smelling the perfume of the black-haired woman as it had come to me on the cool air from inside the big house. I couldn't stop myself from imagining what she wore under her dress. I could understand completely why Kid had been so eager and disregarded the obvious dangers.

For a long time, I'd been telling myself I was happy with nothing. Give me a bedroll and a place to lay it, a decent meal now and then, and a few bucks for a bottle of booze, and what more did I need?

But the circumstances of Kid's death suddenly opened the door on a dark, attractive possibility.

I thought about the lovely house and its gardens.

I thought about that fine, beautiful woman inside.

I thought about the deceased Christine Coyer and all the money she'd left behind.

I thought about all that I didn't have, all that I'd fooled myself into believing I didn't care about—a set of new clothes, a soft mattress, something as simple as a haircut, for God's sake, nothing big really, but still out of my reach.

I was a starved man looking at the possibility of a feast. In the end the choice was easy. After all, what good did justice do the dead?

I got the telephone number from a friend still employed in the newspaper business. I kept calling until the rich man answered.

I identified myself—not with my real name—and told him I was a friend of Lester Greene.

He scraped together a showing of indignity. "I can't imagine what we have to discuss."

"A gift," I told him. "One your wife gave to him. Only she wasn't really your wife. She just pretended in order to lure Lester to your house to be murdered."

"I'm hanging up," he said. But he didn't.

"Ask the woman with the long black hair," I urged him. "Ask her about the gift she gave to Lester. Here's a hint. It's black and silky and small enough to be an eye patch for a pygmy. Ask your beautiful friend about it. I'll call back in a while."

I hung up without giving him a chance to respond.

When I called back, we didn't bother with civilities.

"What do you want?"

Justice for Kid is what I should have said. What came out of my mouth was, "One hundred grand."

"And for one hundred thousand dollars, what do I get?"

He sounded like a man used to wheeling and dealing. According to the paper, he was a financial advisor. I advised him: "My silence." I let that hang. "And the panties."

"You could have got panties anywhere," he countered.

"She's beautiful, your mistress. Who is she, by the way? Your secretary?"

"Christine's personal assistant. Not that it's important."

"But it is important that she's not very bright. She took the panties off her body and gave them to Lester. A DNA analysis of the residual pubic hair would certainly verify that they're hers. I'm sure the police would be more than willing to look at all the possibilities more closely. Do you want to take that chance?"

"Meet me at my house," he suggested. "We'll talk."

"I don't think so. Your last meeting there with Lester didn't end well for him. We'll meet on the High Bridge," I said. "I get the money, you get her panties."

"The panties I can verify. What about your silence?"

"I talk and I'm guilty of extortion. Jail doesn't appeal to me any more than it does to you. The truth is, though, you have no choice but to trust me."

"When?"

"Let's make the exchange this evening just after sunset. Say, nine o'clock."

I wasn't sure he'd be able to get the money so quickly, but he didn't object.

"How will we know each other?" he asked.

We'll have no trouble, I thought. We'll be the only cockroaches on the bridge.

The High Bridge is built at a downward angle connecting the bluffs of Cherokee Heights with the river flats below Summit Avenue. Although it was after dark, the sodium vapor lamps on the bridge made everything garishly bright. I waited on the high end. Coming from the other side of the river, the rich man would have to walk uphill to meet me. I found that appealing.

The lights of downtown St. Paul spread out below me. At the edge of all that glitter lay the Mississippi, curling like a long black snake into the night. The air coming over the bridge smelled of the river below, of silt and slow water and something else, it seemed to me. *Dreams* sounds hokey, but that's what I was thinking. The river smelled of dreams. Dreams of getting back on track. Of putting my life together. Of new clothes, a good job, and, yeah, of putting the booze behind me. I didn't know exactly how money was going to accomplish that last part, but it didn't seem impossible.

The evening was warm and humid. Cars came across the bridge at irregular intervals. There wasn't any foot traffic. I thought for a while that he'd decided I was bluffing and had blown me off. Which was a relief in a way. That meant I had to do the right thing, take the evidence to the cops, let them deal with it. Kid might yet get his justice.

Then I saw someone step onto the bridge at the far end and start toward me. I was a good quarter-mile away and at first I couldn't tell if it was him. When the figure was nearly halfway across, I realized it wasn't the rich man. It was the personal assistant. She stopped in the middle of the bridge and waited, looking up at the Heights, then down toward the flats, uncertain which way I would come.

What the hell was this all about? There was only one way to find out. I walked out to meet her.

I wasn't wearing the gray suit, but she recognized me anyway.

"You were at the house this morning," she said in that accent I decided was, indeed, French Canadian. Her hair hung to her ass and rippled like a velvet curtain. She wore an airy summer dress. The high hem lifted on the breeze, showing off her legs all the way to mid-thigh. Killer legs. Against this, Kid hadn't stood a chance.

"Where is he?" I asked.

"Who cares, as long as I have your money." Her lips were thick and red around teeth white as sugar. I smelled her delicate perfume, the same scent that had washed over me that morning. It seemed to overpower the scent of the river.

"Show me," I said.

"Where are my panties?"

I reached into my pocket and dangled them in front of her. "Where's my money?"

From the purse she carried over her shoulder, she pulled a thick manila envelope. "The panties," she said.

"The envelope first."

She thought about it a moment, then handed it over. I looked inside. Four bundles of hundreds bound with rubber bands.

"Want to count it?" she said.

All I wanted was for the transaction to be over with and to be rid of this business. "I'll trust you," I said.

She took the panties and threw them over the bridge railing. I watched them drop, catch the breeze, and cut toward the middle of the river, swift as a little black bat.

"Gone forever." She smiled.

"You didn't even check to make sure they were the ones. For all you know, I could have bought a pair just like them at Marshall Field's."

"They would never let a bum like you into Marshall Field's." She turned with a swish of her long, scented hair and walked away, her dress lifting on the breeze.

I watched until she'd grown small in the glare, then turned and headed back toward the Heights.

I was ten feet from a new life when he spoke to me out of the shadow of the squat pines at the end of the bridge.

"I'll take the money."

He'd probably come across in one of the cars during my meeting with the woman. I couldn't see his face, but he thrust a gun at me from the shadows and it glowed in the streetlights as if the metal were hot.

"I give it to you, I'm dead," I said.

His voice spat from the dark. "You were dead from the beginning."

I sailed the envelope at him like a frisbee. It caught him in the chest. The gun muzzle flashed. I felt a punch in my belly. I spun and stumbled into the street in front of an MTC bus, which swerved, its horn blaring. I fled toward the dark, away from the streetlights.

The bus passed, and he came after me on foot, a black figure against the explosion of light from the bridge. I ran, making my way along the streets that topped the Heights. I cut into an alley, across another street, then into another alley.

Suddenly, inexplicably, my legs gave out. They just went limp. I sprawled in the gravel behind an old garage. A street-lamp not far away shed enough light that I could easily be seen. I managed to crawl into the shadow between two garbage cans, where I lay listening. I heard the slap of shoes hard and fast pass the alley entrance and keep going. Then everything got quiet.

My shirt was soaked with blood. My legs were useless. I'd hoped to make it to the river, but that wasn't going to happen. The end was going to come in a bed of weeds in a name-less alley. Nothing I could do about that.

But about the man and the woman who'd killed Kid, there was still something I could do.

I pulled the pair of panties from my pocket, the pair she'd given Kid and whose twin I'd found that afternoon at Marshall Field's and bought with money made by selling my own blood. I drew out my pen and notepad and wrote a brief explanation, hoping whoever found me would notify the police.

I was near the river, though I would never sit on its banks again. I closed my eyes. For a while, all I smelled was the garbage in the bins. Then I smelled the river. When I opened my eyes, there was Kid, grinning on the other side. Like he understood. Like he forgave me. I started toward him. The water, cold and black, crept up my legs. The current tugged at my body. In a few moments, it carried me away.

BLIND SIDED

BY ELLEN HART

Uptown (Minneapolis)

I was born in the time of monsters. My earliest memories were of my mother crying because she was frightened for my father, who was off fighting Japan in the Pacific. The names Hitler, Mussolini, and Stalin swirled around my young mind like menacing black crows.

I've always had a rather mixed relationship with the concepts of good and evil. I know the atom bomb was a horrible genie to release on the world, and yet if the U.S. hadn't dropped the bomb on Hiroshima and Nagasaki, my father would surely have been killed. He flew a small plane that was slated to be part of the advance group sent to Japan to soften up their defenses just prior to our invasion. The invasion never happened. Instead, my father came home when I was six years old.

In our house, the bomb was considered miraculous. As a young child, I never thought of it with anything other than a kind of exhilarated wonder. I'd longed to have my dad come home to us, and the bomb made that possible. But after he'd been back awhile, I realized, much to my astonishment, that he was a stranger. I wasn't even sure I liked him. A year later he was dead. The bomb saved him so he could be knifed in a bar fight and bleed out on a barroom floor. That's when I was first introduced to the concept of serendipity—another thing I've been thinking a lot about lately. I'm not depressed—or crazy. At least, I tell myself I'm not, but I guess I'll let you be the judge.

As I grew up, the atom bomb was like a piece of coal flickering blue in my mind, never letting me forget what it had given and what it had taken away. I came to the conclusion in college that people's views of right and wrong tended to be both situational and generational. But that never really satisfied me, because although I wasn't religious, I wanted to believe in absolutes. Right and wrong. Good and evil. Maybe that's a flaw, but it's who I am.

My name is Leo Anderson, a suitably Minnesota sort of name for a boringly Minnesota sort of guy. I'm sixty-six, part Irish, but mostly Norwegian, a retired school teacher, the divorced father of two. And I'm going blind. Every morning, I wake up and look around my tiny bedroom to see what's been erased since the night before. It's a terrifying thing, this going blind business, and I hate it. I also hate being alone, living in this damn drafty apartment after being married for nearly thirty-eight years. Fact is, when I came home and told my wife about my diagnosis, it seemed to open up a sinister trap door in my marriage, releasing an angry accumulation of rabid emotions I never knew existed. Apparently, I wasn't a very good husband. That part didn't really come as a shock. I won't lie to you. It's another one of my flaws.

When I first met my wife, I was instantly attracted. She was tall and slender, with long brown hair and intense gray eyes—eyes that seemed to hold a secret only I could decipher. I was twenty-seven and a determined romantic. Karen was handing out leaflets at a peace rally outside Northrup Auditorium. We started talking. I don't know what got into me. I mean, I was usually pretty shy around women, but I asked her to have coffee with me when she was done. It all seemed so easy, so effortless, kind of like sledding down a snowy hill. By the time I got to the bottom and was able to stand on level ground, look squarely at what I'd done, it was two years later and we were married.

If Karen hadn't been pregnant with our first child, I probably would have left her. But when my son came along, everything changed. Not with the marriage, but with me. I finally had a purpose in my life. I believe I truly fell in love for the first time. My daughter followed a couple of years later. The marriage was never good, but my kids made it bearable. I feel bad now for the way I handled things. Maybe I should have ended the marriage, but I couldn't bring myself to do that to my children, and so ultimately I guess I made a mess of everything. For many years, my life revolved around teaching and family. But that's all behind me now. After such a noisy life, I had no idea this much silence existed in the world—so much space between a question and an answer. My days of working with kids had become ancient history. Or so I thought.

The morning it all started, the clock on the nightstand beeped at the usual 6 a.m. I reached over and flipped off the alarm. It was late October, and the light didn't hit my windows until closer to 7. The way the sun came in and moved around my apartment had become very important to me. I hated waking up in the dark. I figured I had the rest of my life for that.

After breakfast, I took my usual shower. Next to the mirror in the bathroom I'd taped up a page I'd torn from a dictionary. When I moved to this apartment on Columbus a few months ago, I'd been able to read the words while I brushed my teeth. *Official. Officiate. Officious. Offish.* But that morning, I had to squint at the page, bend very close, and even then I could just barely make out the words.

For the past few weeks, I'd spent part of each day moving around my apartment with my eyes closed. I was practicing, as I'd been taught. You can't go blind in Minnesota without being offered a lot of help—it's the way Minnesotans are. I'd been assigned a counselor to assist me with what they call "travel skill training," another counselor for "daily living skills," and I'd been given a list of therapists who could help me with the emotional aspects of going blind. We pay a lot of taxes, so we should get something other than the damn politicians for our money. Don't get me started on state politics.

I spent that morning in the kitchen, rearranging the cupboards for the third time. Everything had to be logical, and it took awhile to figure out what that was. I had a lot of memorizing to do before the lights went out for the last time. Nobody could predict when it would happen, but it wasn't far off. By early afternoon, I was sitting on the couch next to a bright reading light with a family album in my lap, my glasses resting on my nose and a magnifying glass in my hand. There was so much I wanted to burn into my memory—mainly, the faces of my children, the good times we had together.

Speaking of my kids, they don't like me much right now. Or more accurately, they both seem to be afraid of me—for different reasons.

My daughter is engaged to a man who has the body of an anorexic stork and a stretched, rubbery face that reminds me of the rooster in the cartoon movie, *Chicken Run*. Not a good combination. I figured one of the perks of blindness would be that I wouldn't have to spend the next twenty years looking at him across a dinner table. And on the off chance that they presented me with grandchildren at some point in the future, I would never know if the children favored the rubber-faced stork or my beautiful daughter.

Cary, that's my daughter's name, is afraid of me and her mother at the moment because she doesn't want to be reminded that love sometimes fails. I guess I understand. My son comes by occasionally, but I can always tell that he's watching me when he thinks I'm not looking. He's afraid of some inner biology that will cause him to end up like his old man—blind and alone. Instead of their father, I've morphed into a gloomy omen. I hope they get over it—for their sake as much as mine.

Anyway, by 3 that afternoon, I'd mustered up the courage to go for a walk. I slipped on my coat, grabbed my dark glasses, and headed outside with my cane in hand. It was only the second time I'd gone walking with my eyes closed. I'd already committed to memory the number of steps it took to walk along the hall to the front door and then down the outside stairs to the sidewalk. I tried not to cheat and open up my eyes as I walked along. I didn't intend to go very far, because if I didn't get home by dusk, I really couldn't see my hand in front of my face—unless I had my mega flashlight with me, which I didn't.

It hadn't snowed yet, so the sidewalks were clear. I figured I'd walk a couple of blocks, maybe as far as the convenience store across the park, and then call it a day. As I came to what I thought must be about midpoint in the block, I heard footsteps behind me. Before I knew what was happening, I was shoved to the ground. "What the—"

"Shut up!" snarled a young voice.

I twisted around, tried to make out the face, but it was just a blur.

"Your wallet. *Now.*" He slammed a boot into my ribs just to make sure I knew he was serious. "The wallet!"

I yanked it out of my back pocket. All I could think of

was that I didn't want him to hurt me. He could have whatever he wanted. Before I could give it to him, he grabbed it out of my hand.

"Hey," came a different voice, one that seemed to appear out of nowhere. This voice was equally young, but stronger. More confident. "The dude's blind. Give it back."

"Shit, man! Get the fuck away from me."

I looked behind me and saw the second kid. The late-afternoon sun glinted off something metal in his hand.

"That thing real?" asked my attacker, backing up a few steps.

"Give him the wallet back or you'll find out." The second kid's voice was taunting. Arrogant. But he was on my side so I cheered him on.

"Fuck." I felt the wallet hit my chest as the attacker sprinted off.

I was still dazed, but I sat up, touching the scrape on the palm of my hand. It had been chewed raw from hitting the concrete.

"Come on, man, I'll help you. Get you home."

My rescuer put a strong hand under my arm as I staggered to my feet. I was a good foot taller than he was, but to my frightened eyes, he looked immensely young and robust.

"Lean on me," said the kid, seeing that I was unsteady. "Where do you live?"

"The Standhope. At the end of the block."

He picked up my cane and pressed it into my hand, and then together we walked slowly back down the sidewalk to my apartment. We didn't talk until we reached the locked security door.

"Key?"

I fished for it in my pocket.

Entering the hallway, he asked my apartment number. I was grateful for the strong arm and never even considered that he might be as big a threat to me as the kid who'd knocked me down. Naïve is another one of my more admirable qualities.

After getting me settled in my Laz-E-Boy, he took off his coat. "Where's the bathroom?"

"Through the kitchen. It's next to the bedroom."

I wished he'd turned on a light. The apartment was growing dark. Something inside me warned not to let on that I still had some part of my vision left. He seemed to have a certain sympathy for blind people. If he knew I could see, it occurred to me, his sympathy might evaporate. I kept my dark glasses on so he couldn't see my eyes. I wanted to be able to study him without him knowing it. He returned a minute later with a washcloth, some antiseptic cream, and a bandage.

"Here," he said, switching on the overhead light. He washed off my palm with the soapy cloth. After applying the cream, he placed a bandage over the biggest scrape. "You don't want that to get infected."

"Thanks," I said, still a little dazed, and also a bit surprised at his gentleness and concern.

"You diabetic? That why you're blind?"

"No. An eye disease."

With the top light on, I could see a little better now. I watched him move around the living room. I guessed he was about fifteen. He had a stocky build and lank blond hair, and a dark patch on his forearm that I assumed was a tattoo. On his feet was a pair of bright red gym shoes. In the rear pocket of his jeans was an ominous bulge. That's when I remembered the weapon I thought I had seen in his hand. Without thinking, I said, "Are you carrying a knife—or a gun?"

"Toy gun. But it looks real."

In my forty-two years as a teacher, I'd developed a sixth sense about teenagers. I didn't believe him. "You could get hurt carrying that thing, even if it is a toy."

"I can handle myself. Besides, this is a rough neighborhood. A guy's got a right to protect himself."

I lowered my head, but kept watching.

"My dad was diabetic," he said as he checked out my CD collection. "I used to take care of him."

"Used to?"

"He died a couple years ago."

"I'm sorry."

"Thanks. I miss him—miss talking to him."

He ran a hand over an old Raggedy Ann doll sitting on a stack of magazines. The doll was something I'd brought with me when I moved out of the house. I'd given it to Cary on her fourth birthday, one of the happier days of my life.

"You got a daughter?"

"I do."

Glancing at the bookcase, he said, "Lots of books."

"I used to be a high school English teacher."

"My dad liked books too. You read Braille?"

I shook my head.

He glanced into the kitchen, then back at me. "Maybe I could read to you sometime."

I wasn't sure how to respond.

"I used to read to my dad all the time. I'm good at it. I kind of got what they call a dramatic streak."

"Well—" I didn't know a thing about this kid. He'd saved me from being robbed, but my instincts told me to be wary. But then, I guess my loneliness got the better of me. "Sure. I'd like that."

"When?"

"Well, first, do you live around here?"

"Not far. Maybe a mile."

"What's your name?"

"Ryan. What's yours?"

"Leo. You live with your mom?"

"Yup."

He didn't elaborate.

"How old are you?"

"I'll be fifteen in January."

"Brothers and sisters?"

"I got an older brother and a younger brother—and an older sister. Where'd you teach?"

"Washburn."

"What grade?"

"Tenth."

"I got a bunch of friends who go there. Me, I hate school."

The gripe was so familiar it made me relax a little. "So, how about tomorrow night? You can come for dinner if it's okay with your mother. I'll give you my phone number and she can call me."

"She won't care. She works evenings."

"Okay," I said, drawing the word out. I wasn't sure about any of this, and yet the prospect of not spending the evening all alone appealed to me. "How about six?"

"Six is great."

I wished I could see his face better, but as I said, I was afraid to take off the dark glasses and put on my regular ones. I was beginning to like him, so I wanted to come clean, tell him that I did still have partial sight. But something stopped me. I didn't know it then, but my life would come to hinge on that decision.

* * *

By the next morning, my left ribs hurt so much from being kicked that I called my doctor and made an appointment. I took four Ibuprofen while I ate breakfast, then got on a bus headed to Uptown. I had to sit in the waiting room for over two hours before I was allowed into the rear, where the examining rooms were located. My doctor wanted to send me for X-rays, but couldn't get me an appointment until the next day, so she gave me a prescription for some heavier painkillers and sent me on my way.

I filled the prescription at the Walgreens by my apartment, bought some bottled water, and took a couple before I left the store. It was going on 4, and the light was starting to fade. All my life I'd dreaded fall in Minnesota. The chill winds and early darkness seemed to seep into my soul and depress the hell out of me. There were some things I needed from the store for dinner. Instead of getting back on the bus and heading over to Rainbow, which I knew would take too long and put me out on the street well after sunset, I walked the three blocks to the convenience store not far from my apartment. Without my flashlight to shine down on the sidewalk, I wanted to make it home before dark.

Over the past couple of months, I'd made friends with the man who ran the store. His name was Chuck, although I figured it wasn't his real name because he was Vietnamese. I said hi to him as I entered. We usually exchanged small talk, so while I made a mental list of what I needed, I listened to him tell me about his newest grandchild. He almost glowed he was so proud of her. He said he planned to take her to Camp Snoopy at the Mall of America as soon as she was old enough.

"She so pretty. So smart," he said, grinning from ear to ear.

After a couple more comments, I drifted toward the meat counter. It wasn't large, but all I needed was a pound of hamburger. Walking through the aisles, I grabbed a bottle of spaghetti sauce, a box of noodles, and a half-gallon of milk. Thinking that Ryan would probably be expecting dessert, I passed by the frozen food section and found some chocolate ice cream. I wasn't much of a cook, but I figured most kids liked spaghetti and ice cream.

When I got back to the front counter, I had to wait while four other people paid for their groceries. Chuck was never in a hurry, so the minutes ticked by. Outside, the light was dwindling. I jingled the change in my pocket, cleared my voice a couple of times, but nothing I did seemed to register with Chuck that I was annoyed and wanted him to move faster. I could feel my palms begin to sweat. Finally, it was my turn. Chuck must have thought I was in a foul mood, because as soon as my stuff was rung up and I'd paid the bill, I rushed out the door.

A bitter drizzle had begun falling. I pulled the collar of my coat up around my neck and started across the street. The painkiller had finally kicked in, so I felt kind of floaty and loose, but no less anxious.

As I walked along, I could barely make out the sidewalk. Even with the drugs, I winced as I carried the sack of groceries. I was miserable and tense, and felt I'd made a big mistake in asking Ryan to dinner. I stumbled a couple of times over cracks in the concrete. The last time I nearly fell. And that's when I sensed it—the feeling that I was being followed. Maybe it was the Vicodin. Or maybe it was the dark closing in around me. I'd been warned to expect a range of emotions as my blindness became more complete, but paranoia wasn't on any list I remembered.

When I finally made it home, I locked the door and turned on every light in the apartment. I dumped the groceries in the kitchen, then slumped into a chair in the living room, breathing hard—breathing as if I'd been chased home by the boogieman. In the silence, the clock across the room sounded like a jackhammer.

I sat there for a while, until I was steady enough to get up. By then, the ice cream was melting in the sack. I pushed the carton into the back of the freezer and slammed the door. I hated feeling this fragile, this vulnerable. It wasn't a good night to be entertaining.

Back when I'd first retired, I contacted a group at my church that supplied "big brothers" to children without fathers. The woman who interviewed me was as rigid as an old-fashioned schoolmarm. It became clear pretty quick that she thought I was too old. They needed younger guys who could go sledding, skiing, skating, play softball. I had arthritis and a bad hip which prevented me from being as active as I used to be. When I left the office, I regretted being so honest with her about my physical limitations. I missed spending time with kids, and I figured I had a lot to offer a boy other than sports. Maybe that was another reason I wanted to get to know Ryan better. It was a chance to prove that know-it-all lady at my church wrong.

I'd just set a pot of water on the stovetop to boil when the doorbell rang. I buzzed Ryan in and stood by the front door, hands in the pockets of my khaki pants. As he walked past me into the living room, I could smell cigarettes on his clothing and alcohol on his breath. I decided then and there that this was one troubled kid—or, perhaps more accurately, this kid was trouble. But I'd always prided myself on being able to reach kids that others gave up on. Maybe I could help Ryan.

After all, I owed him.

"What's for dinner?" he asked, trying to sound casual, indifferent, cool.

"Spaghetti."

Behind my dark glasses, I closed my eyes. I'd never made an entire meal before without relying on what was left of my sight. I opened up the refrigerator to get the hamburger. "Help yourself to a Coke," I said, feeling around for the right lump.

"You haven't been blind very long," said Ryan.

"Is it that obvious? I'm not very good at this, am I?"

"Here," he said, moving up next to me. "Let me do it. You go sit at the table. I used to cook for my dad a lot, so I know what I'm doing."

I felt my way over to a chair. "There's some bottled sauce on the counter."

"Just relax, man. I got it covered."

While he made dinner, we talked. Ryan told me about his dad, that he'd been a construction foreman before he lost his vision. Ryan's family had lived in a house over on 43rd and Sixteenth, but they'd moved to a small apartment when his older brother and sister moved out. By that time, Ryan's mother was the sole breadwinner. She was an L.P.N. who worked the 4-to-midnight shift at a nursing home in St. Paul. And she had another part-time job that kept her away from the apartment on weekends. Ryan didn't see her much, but he shrugged and said it wasn't a big deal.

"What about the brother who's still living at home?" I asked.

"He's always on his computer. It's all he does. It's brain pollution, man. Boring."

"You don't like computers?"

"I don't like nerds." He went on to tell me about his best friend. I'm not sure what his real name was, but Ryan called him The Duck Man. I got the impression that The Duck Man was a little older than Ryan, and that he wasn't in school. They hung out together on weekends. The Duck Man was into motorcycles, music, and all things cool. He was in a band. Nothing ordinary. The music he made wasn't commercial. Commercial was crap.

While the noodles boiled, Ryan drifted into the living room and came back holding a book. "What's this about?"

"What is it?"

"It's called *The Fox and the Hedgehog.* Sounds like a little kid's story, but it's big—thick."

"It's a compilation of essays on that Greek saying."

"What Greek saying?"

"A fragment of a verse from an ancient Greek poet: *The fox knows many things but the hedgehog knows one big thing.*"

"What's that supposed to mean?"

"Well, I suppose you could say it's a way to categorize human beings. They're either foxes or hedgehogs. They either know one central important thing that guides their lives, or they know lots of smaller things." I paused. "Which do you think you are?"

No hesitation. "A fox."

"Why?"

"'Cause foxes are cool. Did you know that back in, like, the twelfth century, people were terrified of foxes because they thought that if you looked deep into a fox's eyes, it could, like, hypnotize you and then drag you back into the forest?" He stepped over to the stove, stirred the spaghetti sauce, then turned it down. "But actually, I think I'm a more of a hedgehog. I know one big thing."

"And what's that?"

His expression sobered. "That you gotta take care of yourself, because nobody else will."

It was such a bitter, cynical comment for such a young person to make, and yet with what he'd told me about his life, I wasn't surprised.

"What are you?" Ryan asked. "Fox or hedgehog?"

"I think I'm a fox."

"So what do you know that's so important?"

"Well," I said, feeling like I was being forced to take an exam I hadn't studied for, "for one thing, I think it makes you feel good when you help people."

His eyes rose to the ceiling. "Yeah. Okay. What else?"

"That it's important to love people. We're not complete unless we do."

"Shit, man. You sound like a fortune cookie." He seemed angry. I was about to respond when the phone rang.

Ryan handed me the receiver. "Hello?" I said, easing both of my elbows onto the kitchen table, turning away from him.

"Dad?"

It was my daughter. "What's up, honey?"

"Do you own a tux?"

"Me? No."

"Well, if you're going to walk me down the aisle in two months, you're going to need one."

"Oh. Sure."

"I made an appointment for you tomorrow night at Nelson's Tuxedo Rentals. I'll pick you up at 6 and we can head over to Southdale. Maybe have dinner somewhere first. That work for you?"

"Fine, sweetheart. I'll look forward to it." I turned in my chair. Glancing up, I fumbled with the phone, nearly dropping it. Ryan was standing in the middle of the kitchen, arms stretched out in front of him, holding the gun in both hands—the barrel pointed at my chest.

"Holy shit!"

"What did you say, Dad?"

I tried to cover, to stop my voice from betraying my shock. "I just mean . . . the wedding's getting so close."

"I gotta run, okay?"

"Sure, honey." The dark glasses hid the fear in my eyes, but I was afraid Ryan had picked up on it. Maybe I should have told my daughter to send the police. Except, by the time they got to the apartment, I could have been dead. I had to play this carefully.

"See you tomorrow night at 6," Cary said.

"See yah," I replied weakly, clicking the phone off. I was vibrating internally, but trying to hold it together. Sensing that my hands were shaking, I crossed my arms over my chest. "That was my daughter."

He didn't respond.

"So," I said, sucking in a deep breath, "where were we?"

"You were giving me your happy lecture."

"I was?"

"Tell me something real, man. Don't you have any, like, dark truths? Stuff about the evil side of life?" He held the gun steady.

My stomach vanished. "Does that seem more real to you than positive thoughts?"

"Hell yes."

I said the first thing that came into my head. "My parents thought evil was Auschwitz. Concentration camps. You know what they are?"

"I'm not stupid."

"I didn't say you were." I tried to regroup mentally and start again. "Truthfully, Ryan, I've spent a lot of my life thinking about evil."

"And?"

"Well, people today talk about it like everyone knows what it is. Like it's the weather. Everybody knows about the weather, right?" I paused, hoping for a response. When I didn't get one, I continued, "See, we play with the word. Evil is bad, but bad means good sometimes, right? Evil is rebellious, irreverent, sexy. It's what's forbidden. And what's forbidden is a mystery, and mysteries are cool. It's the uptight assholes, usually our parents or teachers, who tell us what's right and wrong, and what the hell do they know?"

He grunted at that one.

"For a long time, Ryan, maybe I thought a little like you. I saw evil as something that was darkly grand in a grotesque Third Reich sort of way. I liked to talk about evil in the rhetoric of Milton, of *Paradise Lost*. I romanticized it. Bad was dangerous, and that was cool. But you know what?"

"What?"

How did I explain this to him when most of the time I couldn't explain it to myself? I gave it a second, then said, "See, Vietnam taught my generation a different lesson from the one World War II taught my parents. It showed us not the evil of others—but the evil of us. And that's when I started thinking that evil wasn't grand and epic and biblical; it was shallow and messy, grimy and stupid. Why do people hurt each other, Ryan?" I gave him some time to respond. When he just stood there belligerently, I continued, "Because they can. Because they feel like it. Because they want something and they have the power to take it. That's it. Nothing grand or cool."

The gun lowered a few notches. He was finally listening. "Go on."

"I think we should stop talking about evil geniuses and instead talk about evil morons. And here's the bottom line. Being a victim—being somebody who's been hurt—is the world class excuse, the Mount Everest of self-justification. *He hurt me so I can hurt him—or someone else who just happens to get in my way.* People do evil because it's convenient, because of peer pressure and cowardice, because they're inattentive or under the sway of some idiot ideology. We're all victims of something, so we all have an excuse for what we do. Except, life shouldn't work like that. If it does, then all the hurt just continues on forever. People—men in particular—think that courage means stuff like driving a car too fast, or knocking someone down in a fight. But the kind of courage you really need in life is moral. That's the really hard kind of courage, Ryan. The courage not to be stupid, or shallow, or mean."

He stared at me. A long moment passed. And then he lowered the gun and stuffed it in his pocket.

"You're weird."

"I am?" I could smell the sauce burning. "Better check the food on the stove."

When he turned away from me, I collapsed back against my chair, waiting for the basketball in my chest to deflate. I struggled to think of a plausible excuse to get him to leave, but at the same time, I was afraid that if I ended the evening abruptly it would tip him off that I'd seen the gun in his hand. I figured that would put me in even greater danger.

The next few minutes were brutal. Something I'd said must have struck a chord because Ryan grew increasingly silent. He'd answer my questions, but with very brief responses. And then, slowly, his mood seemed to lighten. It was as if a light switch had been flipped on inside him, revealing a completely different kid. We ate our dinner and he talked animatedly about music, his main interest, and baseball, an interest we shared, and then he cleaned up. At one point, I remember he said, "You remind me of my dad."

"Is that good?" I asked.

"Yeah. It's very good. The best." He sat down on at the table across from me. "You know, I was just thinking, maybe you could use a kid around here sometimes."

The comment touched me, more deeply than I realized at the time. "Yeah," I said. "Maybe I could. And maybe you could use an old guy in your life—every now and then."

"Next time I come," he said, "I'll bring this book my dad liked. *To Kill a Mockingbird.* Ever heard of it?"

I smiled, told him I had.

"I think you'd like it. I'll read it to you, okay?"

I still wasn't sure I wanted a repeat of this evening, but before I could respond, he said, "Let me tell you something, Leo. Something I hate more than anything in the whole world. I hate liars. Like people who tell you they love you, but you know they don't. You know what I mean?"

I nodded.

"So don't ever lie to me, okay?"

I felt like a fraud. I was a fraud. He didn't know it, but I was already lying to him. "Okay," I said.

"You really promise?"

"I do. I promise."

When he left, he put a hand on my shoulder, and then, suddenly, he hugged me. "You're okay, man. I'll be in touch."

* * *

The next day, I couldn't seem to get him out of my thoughts. I'd been right to think he was a danger to me, but now that our evening together was over and the worst had passed, I started looking forward to seeing him again.

Dinner with Cary on Thursday night was something less than splendid. I told her about being mugged outside my apartment, and that the kid who'd knocked me down had bruised one of my ribs. Thankfully, it wasn't broken, just sore. But my daughter was so consumed by all of the wedding minutia that the story barely registered. After trying on a dozen tuxedos, and at least that many vests, she finally decided what looked best on me and we ordered it. When she dropped me back at the apartment, she gave me a peck on the cheek. I wanted more.

Over the next seven months, I got to know Ryan very well. We spent at least a couple of nights together every week—sometimes more. My vision stayed pretty much the same, but I was getting better at hiding it, so I don't think Ryan ever caught on. Sometimes we'd go out to dinner, but most often we stayed in. Ryan loved books, and I loved him for it. We read *To Kill a Mockingbird, Huckleberry Finn, Animal Farm, Lonesome Dove,* and *The Catcher in the Rye.*

I figured it was best we get to that last book together before he read it himself. It had been a problem for so many kids that I wanted to talk about it with him. As with most boys his age, Ryan agreed that the world was filled with phonies. And it was at that point that he really opened up for the first time, told me about his life, how he hated his mother. He went on and on about how she would say she loved him, then shove him out the door. I don't think he'd ever talked to anyone about any of this before, and the act of sharing his feelings, his pain, brought us even closer.

By March, I felt as if he'd become a second son. I had such high hopes for him. He'd been bringing his homework over for months. I'd help him with it if I could. Or, if he didn't need my input, he'd sit in the living room working on it while I listened to the TV. It wasn't like we were doing something together all the time. He seemed content just to be with me. And his grades improved. We started talking about college. When he'd leave for the night, he'd hug me. It made me realize how starved I was for affection—for the physical touch of another human being.

One afternoon in late May, I woke from an afternoon nap to find that my vision had suddenly worsened. The world was covered in an even thicker haze. By evening, I had developed a bad case of nervous energy. I hadn't seen Ryan all week and that was bothering me too. I listened to the news and all of David Letterman and I still wasn't tired. I got the idea in my head that I should buy a frozen pizza for the next time Ryan and I had dinner together. Chuck's Market stayed open until midnight, so I put on my coat, grabbed my big flashlight and cane, and headed out the door. I think part of the reason I went out was to prove that I could still do it—still be independent, still make it across the park, no matter what was happening to my sight.

Chuck was behind the front counter when I entered. "Busy night?" I asked.

"No," he said, stuffing his newspaper under the counter. "Slow. Bad business today. Bad economy. Make me worry."

I headed to the frozen food section. Adjusting my thick glasses, I squinted at the pictures on the box covers. I wasn't entirely sure what I was looking at, but I thought one was sausage, another pepperoni. There was an odd one that looked like it had mushrooms and something green on top. I figured the green stuff would put off a teenager. As I was dithering over which to take, I heard the door jingle open and then shut. A second later, I heard Chuck cry out: "You leave store! Go away, get out!"

I turned and saw two indistinct forms hovering by the front counter.

"The money!" said a young voice. "Now. Quick!"

My mouth opened. It was Ryan's voice.

"No money," insisted Chuck. "You go or I—"

Everything moved so fast after that, and my vision was so cloudy, that I can't tell you for sure what happened. I think Chuck must have reached under the counter, or at least looked like he was about to. The kid who'd come in with Ryan fired a gun and Chuck dropped down out of sight.

I heard Ryan swear. Then scream, "You freak! Why'd you do that?"

"Get the money!"

The kid with the gun burst back through the store, looking to see if anyone had witnessed the shooting. I backed into the shadows next to the freezer and ripped off my glasses. As I pushed them into my pocket, I realized I had my dark glasses with me. I quickly put them on. If the shooter thought I was blind, maybe he'd leave without killing me. My entire body was quaking as I watched him swing around the end of a row of canned goods, the gun held stiffly out in front of him.

"Not much here," called Ryan. "Maybe two hundred."

"Shit," said his buddy. And then he saw me.

"Come outta there!" he shouted.

I didn't move.

Ryan rushed to the back. When he saw me, he knocked his partner's hand down.

"Fuck, man! Why'd you do that?"

Ryan whispered, "He's blind, for chrissake. Leave him alone. Come on, let's get out of here."

The kid hesitated.

Ryan grabbed his arm. "Come on!"

The kid with the gun stared at me for another millisecond, then took off.

I guess I'm not much of a hero. I fell to my knees, shaking so hard I wet my pants. It took a long time to pull myself together. Minutes. Maybe longer. I finally struggled to my feet and raced to the front counter. Chuck was lying on his back with a big bloody hole in the center of his chest. I knelt down and felt for a pulse at his neck. If there was one, I couldn't find it. I grabbed the phone and punched in 911.

A woman's voice answered, "Emergency operator."

I told her where I was, that a man had been shot—the owner of the market. I think I may have been crying.

"Are you all right?"

"Yes." I couldn't seem to catch my breath.

"Are the assailants gone? You said there were two?"

I glanced outside, but all I could think of was Ryan, the trouble he was in. Why had he been so stupid? I was hemorrhaging internally for a kid I wasn't sure I even knew.

For my son.

"Sir, are you there?"

"Yeah."

"A squad car is on the way. Did you see the assailants?"

"What?"

"You called them kids."

"I did?" The air shimmered around me. My instinct screamed at me to protect him, but was that right or wrong?

"Can you describe them? Did you . . ." She paused.

Ten seconds. Twenty.

"Sir? Are you there? Sir?"

BETTER LUCK NEXT TIME
BY Brad Zellar

Columbia Heights (Minneapolis)

For years, every time I drive up Central Avenue into
Columbia Heights I'd start feeling like I had the barrel of a gun jabbed in the small of my back. If I hung
around the place long enough, I knew damn well I'd eventually have that gun between my teeth, and every night when I
went to bed I'd lie awake with the taste of iron and oil in my
mouth. I grew up out there in the Heights, and my old neighborhood was the bit I'd never been able to spit.

Whenever I made that trip over the last couple decades
I'd always had better things to do, and this particular occasion was no different.

I have to think hard here about chronology, because
some things from that day are still a little muddled in my
mind. This, though, would have been a Saturday. Francis
Greer, ringleader of the neighborhood cabal of my youth, and
my brother-in-law of several years, had been released from
prison a day earlier, and I had every reason to suspect that,
while an unwanted guest in my home, Greer had stolen two
tickets to a production of *Joseph and the Amazing Technicolor
Dreamcoat*. I had no particular enthusiasm for this musical
(which, I suppose I should mention, starred Donny
Osmond), but I had bought the tickets as a gift for my wife,
and she had been eager, even excited, to attend. This particular incident might seem relatively minor, and it was proba-

bly small potatoes as far as Greer was concerned. There was a long history, however, and the theft of the tickets was one more violation of an old trust and an even older loyalty.

I was seething that morning, and I'd had a spat with my wife Janice over the incident. Her natural inclination was to take her brother's side in our frequent disagreements regarding his behavior. Janice had gone to work pissed off, Greer was unaccounted for, and I had a day to kill. I'd driven out to the Heights to poke around on the off chance that I'd run into Greer, and to pay a visit to my mother. She wasn't home—my best guess was that she'd caught the free shuttle to the casino with some of her neighborhood cronies—and pulling up to the curb in front of her house had only served to bring back all sorts of bad memories. So that, at any rate, was how that day had started.

I've always known damn well that when you're lost, the first thing you should do is turn back around, but even the most conventional wisdom is useless to man who is constitutionally incapable of adopting it. I've always been a plunger. I just keep going, allowing myself to be carried along and blindly hoping that I'm going to eventually end up right back where I started. And oddly enough, that's exactly the way it always seems to work out for me, even though right back where I started is precisely the place I've spent my whole life trying to get away from.

A little useful background: From a very early age Francis Greer had presided over a sort of neighborhood academy of lawlessness, to which I was something of a helpless conscript. There were a bunch of us out there in the Heights, boys of around the same age who had grown up together. We were— thanks, I suppose, to the accident of geography and the influence of environment—an uncommonly tight group all the way through high school. Francis was a persuasive character, with a certain transparently criminal charisma. All through our childhood and adolescence he progressively upped the ante on our illegal exploits until there was no longer any pretending that we were just playing around.

Alone among this group of characters, I should have known better. I was from the good side of Central Avenue; the other four primary members of our little gang were from the other side. Two of them, Slim Chung and his younger brother Randy, lived in the trailer park in Hilltop with their mother Dolores, who was in a wheelchair. Greer lived with Janice and his parents in an apartment building adjacent to the trailer parks. Gilbert Borocha, the patsy of our group, came from a big family and shared a room with a couple siblings in a little house a few blocks south toward downtown, off the avenue, right at the edge of a railroad switching yard.

I recognized from a very early age that my life was substantially different from those of my friends. I grew up in a modest split-level home in a 1950s development. My father was an unambitious small-fry lawyer with his own storefront practice on Central. Every day he wore a suit and carried a briefcase to work, and he drank as much as he worked. Whenever I asked him what he did for a living, he'd say, "It's not important," and I never had any doubt that he believed this to the very core of whatever was left of his heart. He'd been a junior associate in a big firm downtown, but after years of being passed over for a partner position he'd apparently gotten the message and bolted for his nickel-and-dime private practice.

My mother is a decent woman, a privately pious housewife, and once upon a time she could actually muster a passable imitation of cheerfulness, at least in comparison with the mothers of my friends. She was tight with my older sister, who was my only sibling. Growing up, I always had whatever I needed, and got most of what I wanted. I guess the point I'm trying to make is that I had no excuses.

By the time I went off to the University of Minnesota, every one of my neighborhood pals had acquired juvenile criminal records of varying lengths. Somehow—and to this day I consider this the one miracle I may be given in this life—I managed to avoid the sort of serious trouble that would make such a mess of the lives of my friends. I had—as my mother would say—scrapes with the authorities, and my fair share of close calls, but I always exercised a certain prudence that was, I fully realize, essentially rooted in cowardice. The other members of my little gang were nothing if not imprudent, and after a certain age my primary role in their criminal enterprise became one of the consulting accomplice before and after the fact. I was the smart one, the confidante, the kid who always had to be in at a decent hour.

That didn't, of course, save me from the clutches of my chums, or, eventually, their predations. There was that old history between us, and for a very long time, perhaps naturally, I retained a soft spot for the people I knew as children. I also lived in a pretty serious state of denial for years; I was basically naïve, and didn't want to know the details of what Greer and the others were doing. To fully understand the extent of their crimes would have forced me to acknowledge the uneasy truth I had spent most of my life resisting. And the sad fact of the matter was that I had never been very successful at making friends once I left that old neighborhood behind.

At any rate, at one point, when I was married and living in a modest neighborhood in South Minneapolis, the Chung brothers and Gilbert Borocha showed up at my house with what I assumed were stolen tools and lumber, and began to cobble together a version of a serviceable flophouse in my garage. This project—carried out by some combination of my old friends, generally whichever ones weren't incarcerated or roaming aimlessly around the country committing crimes that would eventually land them back in prison—went on for almost two years, and over time these accommodations became quite elaborate. A presumably stolen portable out-house appeared in my backyard, stashed behind my garage, and remained there for more than a year. From this little clubhouse off the alley, my friends were free to come and go as they pleased. Perhaps needless to say, this arrangement was difficult to square with my wife and neighbors. I'll admit it also made me somewhat nervous, but none of my friends ever seemed to stay for any extended period of time, and they never—so far as I was aware, at any rate—caused trouble in the neighborhood.

Then one morning six years ago, I woke to the hysterical racket of crows, and from my kitchen window saw Randy Chung crucified to the picnic table in my backyard. He'd been stripped to his appalling bikini briefs and shot once through the head, apparently (this was determined later) in my garage and sometime before he was nailed to the table. I don't suppose I need to tell you that it's difficult for a respectable man's reputation to survive that sort of scandal. Anybody who has ever made the mistake of keeping ques-tionable company, and allows himself to become however tangentially embroiled in such an ugly incident—which was, of course, all over the local news—learns only too well that though a man can be officially exonerated, he can never again be perceived as truly innocent.

Two characters with whom I was entirely unfamiliar were eventually arrested and convicted for Randy Chung's murder, and the motive was allegedly some grievance over a drug deal gone bad. I felt terrible about the whole thing, of course. Randy was a simpleton, a quiet guy with a sweet disposition who had spent his entire life tagging around with his older brother Slim. What happened to him was horrifying, and literally beyond the range of my comprehension. And from a purely selfish standpoint, the real shame of it was that at the time I was in the midst of one of my phases as a respectable man, of which there have been several, each of them in their own way reasonably satisfying and successful.

I had never, unfortunately, been able to sustain any of them for long. In the aftermath of Randy Chung's death, my wife filed for divorce and our house was put on the market and sold.

The older I got the harder it was for me to understand why it was I had such a hard time playing the part of the solid citizen. Because—honest to God—it's always been easy enough for me to slip into that role. I've held three different teaching positions at junior colleges in and around the Twin Cities. For a time I successfully sold advertising for a Christian radio station. Characteristic for me, I'd taken the job out of desperation and found the work easy and, to some extent, satisfying.

Before my present marriage I'd been married twice, both times to wonderful, attractive, and modestly successful women, each of whom to this day maintains a life of the utmost respectability. I also had a teenaged son, made insolent, his mother assured me, by my erratic presence in his life. He was now playing in a band, Lounge Abraham, which, based on the tape I had received in the mail, was a very loud and angry proposition. The last time he came to visit I was stunned to see that he had acquired a tattoo on his arm—he is sixteen years old, which seems to me entirely too young for that sort of thing—that read, "*Death to the Great Satin.*" I was, of course, quick to point out what I felt was an inexcusable misspelling, only to learn that this was apparently an ironic tattoo, an allusion to a handmade T-shirt worn by some infamous psychopath who had shot up a California schoolyard with an assault rifle some years ago.

I couldn't pretend to understand my life, but I can tell you that I've always had legitimate money in the bank. I've never missed a car payment, and I've now owned three different homes, and would have turned a tidy profit on the first two if it weren't for complications related to my failed marriages. That said, crash landings and forced reinvention had long been my stock in trade. I can't tell you how easy it is to burn down your entire life and build a new one from the ground up. The hard part, of course, is to keep the damn thing standing. I'd always felt the key, though, was to do the demolition work yourself, or at least to never let go of the illusion that your self-destruction was purely your own work. It was a point of pride; I never wanted to give someone else the credit for ruining my life. I'd be the first guy to admit that I'd made plenty of bad decisions, but they were my decisions, even when my arm was being twisted so far behind my back that I was practically on my knees.

I'd been coming around on this philosophy, though. Maybe it was a copout, but by this time it seemed plenty clear that I'd allowed these old friends of mine to ruin my life—by not knowing better than to have taken up with them in the first place, certainly, and also by virtue of the fact that I'd never properly distanced myself from them and their behavior, even at the point—which was admittedly long since past—when it became clear that they were all irredeemable. Hell, by this time they'd ruined several of my lives, every one of them perfectly decent, with all the usual trappings, responsibilities, and satisfactions.

Francis Greer was the most complicated of my old friends. He was easily the most intelligent, the most cunning and untrustworthy. Greer had been in prison when Randy Chung was murdered in my garage. In the intervening years I had married Greer's sister, which was a complicated story in and of itself. I'd known Janice since we were kids, and had an on-again off-again relationship with her going back almost twenty years. The fact that she was helplessly related to Greer (and felt a genuine affection for him) had already created numerous problems in our relationship. Every time Greer got out of jail or needed something he was certain to show up on Janice's doorstep. Between his two prison terms and a handful of stints in county jails and workhouses, I had long since lost track of his criminal offenses, which always seemed to be compound infractions that ranged from driving under the influence and all manner of moving violations (improper registration, failure to provide insurance, suspended license, stolen plates) to automobile theft, receiving of stolen property, possession and distribution of narcotics, burglary, and parole violations.

Greer had, by this time, spent nearly a third of his life behind bars and he had apparently always approached prison as the ultimate leisure. I've said that he was intelligent, and I'll be damned if he didn't come out of prison the first time speaking Latin. Over the years he had read more books than I would ever have the time for, had supposedly translated poetry from Spanish, and had spent so much time in prison weight rooms that it seemed like no matter where I went I was sure to encounter a photograph on the refrigerator of a half-naked Greer flexing his muscles.

Thanks early on to our old friendship and later to my relationship with Janice, Greer had maintained a running correspondence with me in the years that he was away. Once, while I was teaching at a junior college in a suburb of St. Paul, he had tried to scam me into signing off on some non-existent coursework he needed to complete a degree. My refusal to do so had resulted in a serious strain in our friendship, and his letters to me became increasingly hostile and condescending.

Around this same time—I was in my late twenties—I wrote and published a crappy little novel, a formulaic thriller that looks increasingly dated and implausible. An agent who was an old college acquaintance of my father sold the book as a paperback original to a fairly prominent publisher, and I received an advance that was nothing if not modest. I was excited by the prospects and felt certain that I was on my way to a career as a writer. There were several delays in the book's publication—which I was assured was quite routine—and I had to wait more than two years for its arrival in bookstores, only to have all my confidence instantly transformed to out-right shame by the appearance of a blurb—attributed to, of all people, Karl Malden—splashed across the front cover: "*I really enjoyed this book!*"

As far as I know the book received exactly one review, a brief and entirely dismissive notice in the Minneapolis paper. Greer, from his cloister in prison, somehow managed to get his hands on that review, which he was kind enough to send to me along with a snide critique of his own.

* * *

The Friday afternoon that Greer was released from prison, Janice had driven out to Stillwater to pick him up. That evening we hosted—very much against my wishes—a party at our home in northeast Minneapolis. This was the second time I'd been forced to celebrate in a similar manner Greer's surely undeserved freedom, and I couldn't for the life of me understand what there was to celebrate. My wife, unfortunately, had inherited her mother's denial as surely as Francis had received his no-account criminal disposition from his father.

It was a mercifully small gathering. Slim Chung and Gilbert Borocha were there, as well as Greer's mother (lurching around the room with a cigarette clenched in her teeth and her oxygen rack gripped in her emaciated fist) and a handful of people who were mostly strangers to me. I had to hand it to Greer. He was a smooth and handsome character, a first-rate actor who could charm the pants off the most chaste woman in any room. He worked the party like he was running for office, and as the rest of the guests became progressively more inebriated, he never seemed to show the effects of the prodigious amounts of alcohol he was consuming.

It had been my understanding that Francis would not be staying at our house the night of the party, but as had so often been the case, my understanding was seriously flawed. After the last of the guests departed, he was still there at my kitchen table regaling Janice with some story, and a short time later my wife was hauling blankets and pillows out into the living room to make up Greer's bed on the couch.

Disgusted, I went up the stairs to my study. I had papers to correct and my mood was darkening by the hour. It was never good news when Greer showed up on my doorstep, and I thought I had noticed some clearly conspiratorial conversations between Francis, Borocha, and Slim Chung at several points in the evening. When Janice came up to bed I gave her the silent treatment. It was impossible to talk with her about Francis without setting off a prolonged argument.

I later ventured downstairs (I have a difficult time sleeping under the best of circumstances, and having Francis Greer under my roof made me even more restless than usual) and found him sprawled on the couch watching a pay-for-view porn movie on my television.

"That's going to show up on my records," I said to him.

"Yeah, Richie, I'm sure those records are of a great deal of interest to many people," Greer said. "Someone's probably scrutinizing them as we speak."

"You've been away, Francis," I said. "Things have changed. That sort of information is widely and irresponsibly disseminated these days. The real issue here is that I don't recall you asking my permission to dick around with my cable. You do understand that I'll be billed for that?"

"Relax, Rich. I'll go out first thing in the morning and sell some plasma so I can repay you your seven bucks. Would that make you happy?"

"What would make me very happy," I said, "was if you would go out first thing in the morning and find someplace else to stay. You must have friends here. Janice has mentioned that you were corresponding with a number of women while you were in prison."

"Those were old women, Richie. Christians."

"I'm sure old Christian women have homes and spare bedrooms," I said.

"Fuck you, Rich," Greer said. "You've really been getting on my nerves."

"I'd like nothing better than to get on your nerves, Francis," I told him. "You've already brought more than enough trouble into my life. So fuck you, too, and goodnight. And I'm absolutely serious: I want you out of here first thing in the morning."

The next morning Janice came up to tell me that Francis was gone. She was alarmed and wanted to know if I had any idea of where he might be. I told her, of course, that I had no clue, which was certainly the truth. I had no intention of recounting the conversation I'd had with Greer before I went up to bed. Janice was visibly upset and a short time later she left in a sulk for her part-time job at Target.

As I sat down to drink my morning coffee and read the newspaper it occurred to me that this was the day we were to see *Joseph and the Amazing Technicolor Dreamcoat* at the State Theater downtown. We had planned to have dinner somewhere beforehand. I went over to the bulletin board in the kitchen, where the tickets had been pinned next to the calendar. My intention was simply to confirm the date, but I discovered that the tickets were gone.

At this point Francis Greer couldn't have been further from my mind. There were any number of things in my home that I might have suspected Greer of stealing, but tickets to a Broadway show were not among them. I called Janice on her cell phone.

"Do you have the tickets to that Donny Osmond show?" I asked her.

"Oh shit, that's tonight, isn't it?" she said. "They're on the bulletin board in the kitchen."

"They're not there. And what's with this 'oh shit' business? I thought you wanted to see that fucking show."

"I did," Janice said. "But look, Richard, I just heard from Francis. He told me that you kicked him out of the house in the middle of the night. He's very hurt."

"Jesus, Janice, I did no such thing. Francis is a pathological liar."

"Francis might be a lot of things, Richard, but one thing he's not is a liar."

"That just goes to show you how good of a liar he is," I said. "If you honestly believe I kicked him out of the house in the middle of the night, you're out of your mind. I simply asked him what his plans were."

"Last night wasn't the time for that, Richard. Francis hadn't even been out of jail for twenty-four hours."

"Prison, Janice," I said. "Francis was in prison. There's a difference there I think you should be aware of."

"Oh fuck, Richard. I don't have time for this."

"Where the hell are those tickets?" I asked.

"I have absolutely no idea," Janice said. "I just told you. They were on the bulletin board."

"They're not there. Are you sure you didn't put them in your purse or something?"

"I'm positive. I never touched those tickets, and I don't feel like going to the damn thing now, anyway. I told Francis I would meet up with him later."

"Jesus, Janice," I said. "What the fuck is wrong with you?"

She hung up the phone.

I spent the morning fuming, and tried with little success to get through the pile of freshmen composition papers on my desk. By late morning I was sitting in the living room with the blinds drawn, drinking beer and watching women's beach volleyball. The phone rang at one point and when I answered I heard only silence on the other line, and then whoever was calling hung up on me. I checked the number on the caller-ID and saw that it was from a pay phone in Columbia Heights.

I showered, dressed, and drove out to the Heights. As I've said, I was just killing time. When my mother wasn't home I cruised through Hilltop to see if by chance Greer was staying at Slim Chung's, but got no answer when I knocked at the door of his trailer.

I was restless and ended up at this place on Central Avenue where I liked to play ping-pong. I've always found the back-and-forth, gnip-gnop nature of the game relaxing. It involved a concentrated engagement with a sort of reality that didn't involve actually feeling anything. The place attracted a crowd of blank obsessives, and I seldom communicated with any of my partners beyond the rudiments of keeping score.

That afternoon I played several games with a pigeon-toed old priest I often saw there. The guy played a very aggressive game with a lot of topspin. I've never been much of a player, and the priest kicked my ass every game. When I arrived he had been slapping ferocious returns at one of the weird little ping-pong robots this place had installed in a corner.

After I left, I headed downtown and spent a couple hours drinking and watching a baseball game in Runyon's. I honestly had no clear idea what I was up to, other than acting on a hunch I had no reason to trust. At a quarter to 7:00 I left the bar and walked down Hennepin Avenue, where I took up a surveillance position in a bus shelter across the street from the State Theater. Donny Osmond's name was stretched across the marquee. I waited probably ten or fifteen minutes before people started showing up in front of the theater.

Almost surely, I thought, if in fact Greer had taken the tickets it had been merely to spite me, but I also felt there was a possibility—Greer being a notorious philanderer, and now fancying himself something of a man of culture—that he would actually use the damn things to impress some woman. It was a long shot, I realized, but I figured he would have noticed the stiff price on the tickets and he was nothing if not an opportunist.

About a half hour before the scheduled performance, I saw Greer coming down the sidewalk toward the theater. He had a new haircut and the rolling swagger of an ex-con. He was wearing a pressed pair of slacks, a dress shirt open at the neck, and a suit jacket that I recognized as one of my own. I watched as Greer approached a group of people milling around under the marquee. He had his back toward me, but several members of the group bent their heads toward him and a conversation ensued. One of the men talking with Greer turned and waved a woman over. The man and woman conferred briefly and then the man fished some cash from his pocket, counted out some bills, and handed them over to Greer, who in turn gave the woman my tickets. He completed this transaction with a wide smile and an absolutely phony attempt at a courtly bow.

After handing over the tickets, Greer headed north back down the sidewalk. I gave him a half-block head start before following, from the other side of the avenue, at what I felt was a safe distance. He was walking at a brisk clip, and the sidewalks along Block E were crowded. When I saw Greer turn down 6th Street I had to make a dash through traffic to avoid losing him. I pulled up short in the middle of the block on the Hennepin Avenue side and watched him cross at the light to the other side of the street. There was a moment when I turned the corner that I was walking almost parallel with him, but I was stopped in my tracks when I saw him raise his arm and let out a shout. I looked east and spied Janice coming up the sidewalk from the opposite direction. I ducked into the exit of a parking ramp and watched as they embraced. Christ, I thought, anybody else would take them for lovers. Janice even took Greer's hand as they continued down the street and ducked into Murray's, the steak place where Janice and I had celebrated our engagement.

At this point things got very dark and confused. I've never been a violent man, and I don't even have much in the way of a temper. The rush of almost blinding rage that I felt building behind my eyes was startling to me. I broke out in an uncharacteristic sweat, and experienced what I felt sure was a panic attack.

I paced back and forth on the sidewalk opposite Murray's, infuriated by my inability to simply barge in and confront Janice and Greer with their deception. I've always despised public scenes. That, at any rate, was my dim and cowardly rationale at the time.

I tried to think my way through the situation, but I couldn't get my head around it. Greer, I felt certain, did not have transportation, unless he'd somehow borrowed a car from one of his criminal acquaintances, or—and this was certainly a possibility—stolen one. Janice would have driven her own car downtown, and must have parked in one of the ramps near Murray's. I crossed the street and spent half an hour wandering the levels of the garage nearest the steakhouse, but I didn't stumble across Janice's Honda.

My car was parked over on Washington Avenue, and I

thought of moving it someplace nearer, but there was no metered parking anywhere around Murray's. I figured I had perhaps an hour to hatch some plan of confrontation. A short time later, feeling increasingly desperate, I headed back down Hennepin to get my car. I have no idea how long I spent circling blocks on the maddening system of one-way streets that comprises downtown Minneapolis, but it felt like I trolled past Murray's at least twenty-five times.

Finally, just as I was turning down 6th Street one more time, I saw Janice and Greer emerge from the restaurant. I immediately pulled my car to the curb and illegally parked. I didn't have to wait long. They exchanged a few more words, Janice fished in her purse and handed Greer what was almost certainly cash, and then they embraced one more time and parted. Janice headed east along the sidewalk and Greer strolled west toward the heart of downtown. Sixth was a one-way going in the opposite direction, so I had to circle back around again onto Hennepin. At the intersection of 6th I saw Greer on the next block, and I drove up to 5th and wound my way back around to First Avenue. As I turned the corner I encountered Greer, perhaps fifty yards away, getting into a beat-to-shit blue Impala. I stopped and waited for him to exit his parking space, and then I followed him east through downtown and onto 35 south.

There was almost no traffic on the interstate at that hour—it must have been around 10:30—and Greer was driving at a surprisingly modest speed. I was trying to stay back at least several hundred yards, but I had to resist the growing urge to overtake him and drive him off the road. At the Crosstown Highway he turned off 35 and headed east again, toward the airport.

Holy shit, I thought. That fucker was going to climb on a

plane and skip town, probably with money he'd received from my wife. Greer continued right past the exits to the airport, though, and steered the Impala south onto highway 52. I was in familiar territory—I'd once taught at a junior college out that way—but I couldn't for the life of me figure out why Greer might have been headed in that direction. There was nothing much out there but drowsy suburban development, the grimy industrial sprawl beyond the airport, and a giant oil refinery, the gleaming spectacle of which was already visible in the distance.

Greer kept plunging further south, and I was blindly determined to stay on his tail, for what purpose I still had absolutely no idea.

He eventually pulled into the parking lot of a desolate-looking strip motel. The sign out front was faded and dark, and if it weren't for the presence of several pickup trucks backed up to rooms, the place would have appeared abandoned. I passed it and turned into the first street that I came to on the opposite side of the highway. I swung the car around and parked. The motel was perhaps two hundred yards away, and I could still see Greer's brake lights in the parking lot. The driver's side door was half open, illuminating the car's interior. Greer was clearly visible to me, and it appeared he was leaning over in the seat, studying something.

I popped my trunk, got out of the car, and fished a tire iron from the wheel well. Without thinking I dashed across the highway and crept along the edge of the service road toward the motel.

There was a cluster of scrub maples and weeds at the southern edge of the place, and I crouched in the darkness, breathing heavily, waiting for Greer to make a move. It seemed like I waited a long time. Greer remained slumped in the front seat. I could hear strains of rock music coming from the open door of the car.

Tiptoeing from the brush, I managed to get within perhaps twenty feet of the Impala, where I took shelter behind one of the trucks. I could smell marijuana, and peering across through the windows of the truck's cab I could see Greer, almost reclining, his head tilted back and his eyes closed, taking a long drag from a joint.

I crawled around the back of the truck and moved to a position directly behind the Impala. It took me perhaps two seconds to lunge forward and fling the car door wide open. Greer sat up straight, started to speak, and then turned his upper body away from me. The first time I swung the tire iron I hit him directly across the back of his head, almost at the base of his neck. When he hunched forward over the steering wheel, I hit him again, and he rolled over onto his back in the front seat. His eyes opened wide for a moment and then closed, and I heard a pitiful moan as I turned and ran.

Back at my car I settled in behind the wheel and tried to stop trembling. I rolled down the window and flung the tire iron out into the grass. I'd never really hit anyone in my life, and it was a strange, almost euphoric experience. The combination of rage and ecstasy is a feeling that I would have certainly described at that moment as wonderful. I tried to remember if I had said anything to Greer before I swung the tire iron, but I had no recollection, and regretted that I had not made some memorable statement. I also tried to recall at exactly what point, if ever, my actions had been premeditated. Did I even have what I could classify as a real memory of the moment I decided on a precise course of action, the instant I went to the trunk and removed the tire iron? I honestly don't believe I did. The whole thing just happened, but I felt an immense sense of satisfaction, and had absolutely no regard for potential consequences.

The bottom line was that Francis Greer had ruined my life, perhaps once and for all. And at that point, sitting there in the darkness alongside the highway, I truly didn't care. In that moment, for the first time in my life, the future literally did not exist in my mind.

I started driving back into the city. Somewhere en route I turned off highway 52 onto a dark little county road. There was no real thought involved in this decision. The road was entirely unfamiliar, but maybe I just felt like driving, and had some weird faith that I'd end up where I needed to be. I thought about all my days on the straight and narrow, all the times I'd awakened surprised to find myself where I was, and doing whatever it was I was doing; surprised by the clean-shaven face I'd see in the mirror every morning and the smiling man I'd frequently encounter staring me down from the family portraits around my house and on my desk at work. Some guys I suppose get a sort of disoriented feeling when they study a picture of themselves from an old high school yearbook. I've always had that same feeling whenever I see a photograph of my present self. I'm not saying I feel embarrassed or abashed; it's more a feeling of befuddlement, almost like I've literally never truly recognized myself in whomever I was pretending to be at any given moment.

I don't know, perhaps these thoughts came later. Maybe I wasn't really thinking or feeling anything that night other than the blank rush of adrenaline. I know I was driving very fast. They've told me that much. And then all of a sudden there were a pair of bright lights hurtling toward me down that dark road. I saw the approaching car swerve into my lane, and then the driver—some punk, I'd later learn, eighteen years old and roaring on Old Style—killed his lights.

I was in the hospital for almost two months, most of it spent in rehab learning to crawl back into my body. It was like my body was this empty suit in the corner and I couldn't do anything until I learned all over again how to put it on and move around in it. The whole time I was in that hospital there was a card from Francis Greer on the stand next to my bed. *"Tough break, Richie,"* it read. *"Better luck next time."*

The doctors tried to tell me that I had to learn to remember, and that I had no recollection of what happened the night of the accident. That's not true. I have a very precise memory of the accident; in fact, I know it was no accident at all.

The whole thing was deliberate, a game of chicken. The kid challenged me. I remember there was an instant when I could have jerked the wheel and conceded the lane, a moment when the collision could possibly have been avoided. I'd already yielded once; maybe two hundred yards before the crash I had instinctively swapped lanes with the oncoming car, but the other guy had followed my lead. And in those last few seconds I resolved I wasn't going to budge again. I'd done enough budging.

The kid who was driving the other car was killed instantly, and I'm told that neither of his surviving passengers had any memory of the accident. I know exactly what happened, though. The little bastard would too, if he'd lived: I won.

TAKING THE BULLETS OUT

BY MARY SHARRATT

Cedar-Riverside (Minneapolis)

For over two decades, Neil had worked as a nurse in the emergency room at Hennepin County Medical Center. Many people burned out after only a few years, but he stuck to it the way he stuck to everything else. Someone had to extract the rubble out of a motorcycle accident victim's raw thigh with a pair of tweezers. Someone had to be there to hold the hand of a teenager who'd just had a bottle of sleeping pills pumped out of her stomach. Neil never failed to comfort, even after seeing the fifth gunshot wound on a single day, the third woman with her teeth knocked out. He cleaned and disinfected their wounds. He bandaged them. He administered painkillers and spoke to them in a soft lulling voice. This routine had become such a part of him, he could practically do it with his eyes closed. He often wished he could indeed work blindfolded. In his twenty-five years in the emergency room, he had seen too much pain.

He tried to put it behind him the instant he stepped through his garden gate. In summer, he practiced his flute on the back porch, losing himself for an hour or more, playing Mozart, Debussy, or the Gaelic airs he had learned from his grandfather. But one particular evening, when he sat down to play, a string of obscenities exploded on the other side of the fence. The guy next door was yelling at his girlfriend again.

Neil hadn't had much luck with neighbors in recent

years, now that the neighborhood had become so rough and seedy. In 1969, when he and his former wife Gina had bought this little Victorian house, Cedar-Riverside had been vibrant and alive, the Twin Cities' answer to Haight-Ashbury. A poet used to live next door. Neil and Gina had kept their back door unlocked to welcome the stream of friends into their kitchen. He used to leave his bicycle out on the porch all night. In those days, Neil could live off his music and odd jobs. He played with a folk band, had gigs in the Triangle, the Riverside Coffee House, and once in Dania Hall. Like so much else, those venues had vanished. Dania Hall had burned to the ground.

Nobody stuck around for long anymore. People moved in and out of the rundown old houses; they came and went in a blur of rowdy parties and blaring television sets. Neil tried to be tolerant, but nothing disturbed him more than loud domestic arguments. His twenty-five years in the emergency room had shown too well where these fights could lead. Lowering his flute, he stared at the trembling leaves of the Virginia creeper he had trained to grow on his eight-foot chain-link fence. It was no good calling 911. That was what he had done during their last fight. The cops had come far too late, and the next day the neighbor, a ratlike young man with a thin face and thinner lips, had told Neil to mind his own goddamn business. The guy was not a person you could argue with. He had informed Neil that he owned a gun and knew how to use it.

On the other side of the fence, a door slammed. The boyfriend took off, leaving the girl behind. A few times Neil had passed her on the sidewalk. He remembered how she had gone bright red in the face when he made eye contact, how she had ducked her head. Now he listened to her jagged sobs.

If he were a woman, he could go over and check on her, offer sympathy and support, but he was a man, and her boyfriend was jealous, a gun owner. He raised his flute and began to play, although the peace his music usually provided seemed quite beyond him. Still, he practiced his scales before launching into Debussy. If only his music had the power to obliterate and transform. The sun disappeared over the top of his fence, glittered faintly through the Virginia creeper and chain-links, then faded.

Listening to the Mustang tear out of the driveway, Becky pulled herself up from the bathroom floor and groped for a washcloth, a towel, a bar of the jasmine-scented soap her mother had given her before she gave up on her daughter completely. She wet her hands and lathered her face, splashed herself with cold water, as if this would change anything. The first time he hit her, she had said, "I'm leaving." But here she was. Stuck. You're fucked up, she told herself. This could only happen to someone who was hopelessly fucked up.

"I didn't hit you," he said the first time. A slap with an open hand didn't leave a mark, didn't cause any real damage— it only stung a little. Hank's dad used to wallop him with a leather belt, used to beat the crap out of him. Hank told her she didn't know what real hitting was. Once when some guy at the Viking Bar tried to pick a fight, Hank followed him outside and busted his jaw. But slapping her, shaking her, pushing her to the floor or up against a wall—that was small stuff. A few weeks ago, she made the mistake of trying to confide in one of the other waitresses at work, an older woman named Joanne, who just rolled her eyes. "Do you have any idea what a real battered woman looks like?"

"You are a mess," she said aloud to the grubby walls and mildewy shower curtain. She turned her back to the mirror, didn't want to know what she looked like right now. Something awful and twisted inside her had drawn her to him, of all people. She was twenty. Last year at this time, she'd been in college—Mankato State—learning about the nineteenth-century English novel. When her financial aid had fallen through, her dad said, "Well, you weren't exactly college material, anyway." Becky sprang from a long line of failures. Her parents lost their farm when she was eight, and her father had been driving semis ever since. Her mom worked in a high school cafeteria. Originally Becky had wanted to study to be a teacher. "You, a teacher?" her dad roared. "Yeah, right. The kids would take one look at you, crumple you up in a ball, and toss you out the window."

Hank had been the one to comfort her. "What do you need college for? Why do you want to pay all that money for four years of B.S.? I never learned anything that really counted in school. You don't have to take that shit from your father, either. I never took shit from anyone." Hank had made her feel so reckless and wild. They used to go out on country roads late at night. He let her drive that old Mustang as fast as she wanted, egging her on until her foot ground the gas pedal into the floor and the wind roared through the open windows, whipping through her hair and bringing tears to her eyes. He said it was the closest she would ever come to flying.

When she started getting serious with Hank, his divorce had just come through. Although he was only five years older than she was, he already had two kids and a pissed-off ex-wife. But he told Becky that she was the real love of his life, the one he had been saving everything up for. Then his ex called Becky's mom and told her what a slut her daughter was. Becky's father said, "That's enough. Either break up with that loser or move out."

So she left with Hank for Minneapolis. On her better days, she told herself that they would work everything out. He could be so tender when he begged her not to leave. Sometimes he even wept. "I can't help it if I go crazy each time I think of you with another guy." The trigger for their last fight had been Becky getting a ride home from work with Ty, who was black and made her laugh. Hank looked out the front window and saw them laughing together in his car. When she came inside the house, he exploded. "I saw the way you were looking at him! You know, if there's one thing I can't forgive, it's betrayal." What would he do if she really tried to leave? She thought of the guy with the busted jaw.

Becky held her breath, wondering how long it would take for her face to turn blue. Eventually she would pass out from lack of air. At moments like this, she understood why people did drugs. She wanted to go numb, not feel anything. In the silence of not breathing, she heard her neighbor play his flute. That music drove Hank crazy, made him bitch and turn up the TV full blast. For Hank's sake, she had always acted like she hated it, too, but now that she was alone with the music, she had to admit she kind of liked it. It was pretty in a strange, sad way.

Going to the bedroom, she changed from her shorts and T-shirt into a black sweatsuit, dressing with the lights out and the dusk filtering through the window screen. She loved this time, which was neither day nor night but twilight, when everything seemed beautiful, even the condemned house across the street. She loved trying to blend into the twilight, imagining herself invisible and untouchable. Stepping out the back door and past the gutted wreck of Hank's old motorbike, she crept to the chain-link fence, metal cooling her cheek as she peered through the Virginia creeper. If Hank caught her doing this, he would twist it into something perverted, accuse her of having some obscene crush on the guy. But she just liked to look into his yard, which wasn't anything like her mom's and her aunts' with the marigolds and plastic deer. His garden was luxuriantly overgrown with all kinds of flowers bursting up between the vegetable beds. At dusk, the place was a mysterious darkened tangle with a few fireflies darting through it.

The neighbor had the porchlight switched on; she could see him as clearly as if he were under a spotlight. Even though he had to be at least fifty years old, he still had long hair. There was something about him, the way he could play for hours as if he were playing for his plants so they'd grow better. It seemed like the kind of thing a person from the '60s would believe in. Her neighbor was old enough to be her father, and yet he was as different from her father—and from Hank—as a man could be. How different would she have turned out if she'd had a father like him? His music infected her, the way it danced around her, drawing her to his fence.

Becky pressed her body against the metal mesh until the flute notes tapered off. She listened to the click as the neighbor went inside, locking the door behind himself. Lights went on and off in his kitchen and bathroom. How safe other people's houses looked from the outside. His face appeared in the bedroom window before he pulled down the shade. He never saw me, she reminded herself. I was watching him the whole time, but he never knew. That knowledge made her shiver and feel a little creepy, as if she were some kind of ghost.

* * *

Hank kept his gun in the top dresser drawer. Becky often saw him take it out and oil it. He was very proud of his gun. She had never been able to ask him why he bought it or what he intended to use it for. When he was gone, she opened the drawer and just looked at it. Would she ever have the nerve to aim it at someone, pull the trigger? Would such an act make her weak or strong, a heroine or a coward? Aim it at Hank? At her dad? Jesus, she was crazy to even be thinking like that. But sometimes when she wiped the counter at Denny's on East Lake Street, she imagined herself acting out a scene from *Thelma and Louise,* imagined the exploding bullet and seeing him—Hank, her father, their faces blurring together—crumple backwards, away from her, a puddle at her feet.

Neil picked bruised windfall apples from under the tree in his front yard. This earthy, brainless task calmed him. He tried to breathe deeply, rhythmically—his pulse was still ragged from the emergency room. Alicia, his favorite colleague, had a breakdown that day. They had wheeled in a ten-year-old boy with knife wounds from a fight that had taken place on the grounds of his elementary school. Alicia had an eight-year-old who went to the same school. She had started wailing, and the head doctor sent her home. The anguish on her face still haunted Neil.

He tried to focus on the garden. When he finished picking the fallen apples, he would throw them in the compost heap out back, then go to work picking tomatoes and zucchini, which were growing faster than he could eat, freeze, and can them. As he reached down, he felt a shooting pain near his lumbar vertebrae. Cautiously he pulled himself upright. A slipped disc was all he needed. He tried to reason with his body. It's just muscular tension. Have a hot bath and it will be fine.

Breathing in slowly, he heard footsteps coming down the sidewalk. Through the metal links of the front gate, he saw the young woman from next door lug a bulging sack of groceries. She staggered with each step. He raised his hand, about to call out something friendly, but her face was shadowed, downcast. He didn't want to startle her. Her grocery bag was printed with the logo of the local supermarket, which was understocked and exorbitantly priced. Why didn't she shop at North Country Co-op, he wondered, or one of the East African groceries? As she moved out of his range of vision, he thought of her emptying her wallet to buy mushy hothouse tomatoes, waxy apples, and rubbery broccoli in the zenith of the garden season.

In the distance firecrackers went off, or were they gunshots? Although this neighborhood wasn't nearly as bad as Phillips or Northside, he'd read in the paper that a Somali teenager had been shot over near the high-rise apartment blocks on Riverside Plaza—where Mary Tyler Moore used to live in the television show. He couldn't stop thinking of Alicia, how she had just lost it, unable to take in the sight of one more sliced-up kid.

Sound system blasting, the neighbor's Mustang boomed past, then screeched to a halt. Ten minutes later, as if by appointment, the yelling started again. In summer with the windows open day and night, there was no privacy. Seeking shelter in his kitchen, he tried out to drown out their voices by running zucchini through the food processor, but when he stopped the machine, he heard, "Becky, you stupid cunt . . ."

He started the machine again so he wouldn't hear the rest.

* * *

Becky opened the door to find a brown paper bag with deep red tomatoes and green and purple basil spilling over the top. Wasps buzzed around the bag. She glanced next door, but her neighbor didn't seem to be home—no sounds came from his house or yard. Hank was meeting his buddies after work, so he wouldn't be home until late. Hugging the bag to her chest, she carried it into the kitchen, set it down on the table, and flicked away the remaining wasps before pulling out the contents one by one, arranging them on the scarred Formica. A perfect head of romaine lettuce wrapped in paper towels. Cucumber and prickly zucchini. An old plastic yogurt container full of raspberries, a second one with gooseberries. Huge sweet bell peppers in green, red, and gold. At the very bottom, a small watermelon. After emptying the bag, she shook it upside down hoping to find a note from him, something like, *Hope you enjoy the veggies*, or, *Compliments of my garden*. But there was no message. She tried not to feel disappointed, but it would have been nice to find out was his name was.

The watermelon looked so good. Before she knew it, she had the big kitchen knife in her hand. She drove the blade through the rind and into the flesh until red juice ran over the kitchen table. After cutting herself a piece, she let the juice drip down her chin. It had been so long since she'd had really good fresh fruit. What was she going to tell Hank when he saw this stuff and asked her where it came from? She could already hear his voice, as cutting and sarcastic as her father's. "So did you hitchhike to the farmer's market? Or did the freak next door give them to you?"

On Sunday, Hank had caught her staring through the fence into the neighbor's garden—the neighbor hadn't even been home—but Hank had taken her by the shoulders.

"Trying to make me jealous?"

She laughed stupidly, like someone on TV. *Har, har, har.* Then he hit with his closed hand, his fist. Not a slap that time. It hadn't left an awful bruise or anything that makeup couldn't hide, but the skin around her cheekbone was still tender.

When do you turn into a battered woman? she asked herself, holding the container of raspberries and staring into that deep redness. How bad did it have to get, how much harder would he have to hit her, before it was real?

What would she do with the fruit and vegetables? Eat what she could now and throw the rest away? But they were so beautiful, so perfect. The neighbor had given them to her. He wanted her to have them and she was keeping them. She had to rock herself and laugh at the thought of something that was hers, that she wouldn't surrender.

Hours later, her voice dragged Neil out of a deep sleep.

"I'm warning you, Hank! If you ever do that again!"

"You're warning me, huh? Well, bitch, what are you gonna do about it? Just what are you gonna do?"

The hands of Neil's alarm clock hung suspended, green phosphorescence in the dark, spelling out the time—3:00 a.m.

"Damn it, Hank! I'm warning you . . ."

Slumped on the bed, Becky saw and tried not to see the ruined room, walls and ugly beige carpet smeared with the remains of the fruit and vegetables. What was worse was the pulp smashed in her hair and down the front of her clothes. Hank had locked himself in the bathroom and made no sign of coming out. Had he passed out in there? It was nearly 4:00 a.m. She had to get ready for work. Scooping the raspberry pulp out of her hair, she tried to hold it, then licked it off her fingers. In spite of everything, it still tasted nice, like the kind of raspberry purée she imagined they would serve in fancy restaurants.

One look at the clock—4:15—told her that she couldn't waste any more time. She would have to wash her hair in the kitchen sink and let it dry on the bus ride to work. Dragging herself to the dresser to get some fresh underwear, she instead found herself opening the top drawer where the gun was nestled among Hank's coiled belts. She picked it up, felt the smooth metal, its weight in her hands.

That evening there was no way to shut out the flute music. It was too hot to close the windows. The TV had been wrecked in the fight the night before. Hank stuck his head in his Discman and cracked open a beer. He acted as if the fight were a blank in his memory.

Becky didn't dare go near the fence but just sat down on the back steps, closed her eyes, and listened. Neil, she thought. When she had come home, she found a letter addressed to him that had landed in her mailbox by mistake—from some woman in Bainbridge Island, Washington State named Gina Martinelli. Before Hank arrived back, she had slipped it into the neighbor's mailbox.

His music was so beautiful that it pierced her. It sounded Irish, like one of those old laments. Everything was in a minor key, lovely but unbearably sad. She couldn't hold them in anymore, these stupid tears. She hated tears, hated her mother for the way she had gone off sniveling from her dad's outbursts, never sticking up for herself. Becky had thought she could be different, that she would never let herself cave in, but that was exactly what she was doing, crouching on the stoop and pulling her knees to her chest. Her body convulsed, arms, shoulders, neck heaving. This was it. She was losing it. Losing.

An explosion shattered Neil's sleep. Gunshots. Sharp, metallic, irrevocable. He jerked upright. The shots were being fired next door, barely thirty feet away from his bed. Counting six shots, he listened for her voice, for screams, pleas, cries, but there was only silence. Six shots, then that gaping void. Throwing on some clothes, he crept out into the backyard. The moon was just past full, now waning, sinking into darkness. Parting the Virginia creeper, he glimpsed her through the links in the fence. She clutched herself with crossed arms like a lost soul.

He wouldn't do it—he would not call the police or phone for an ambulance. He knew none of the neighbors would get involved. Rolling his head back, he stared at the scattered stars revolving in a dance too slow to see. Let her get away with it, he thought, shocking himself. Let her get away with murder. Going to the fence again, peering through the links at the moon-bleached woman, he called her name.

She walked numbly around the side of the house to his gate, which he unlocked for her. Shivering, she kept rubbing her skinny bare arms. The only thing he could think to do was put his arm around her and guide her through his door and into his kitchen, where she gazed blankly at the dried herbs hanging from the ceiling.

"Becky, do you want to tell me what happened?"

Turning to him, she took an unsteady step forward, then lost her balance. He caught her before she could fall. "He was too drunk to move," she said. "I shot him in the back. Like a real coward! I just shot him in the back, and after the first shot, I couldn't stop."

He cradled her as she wept, stroked her soft dark hair, cut

very short, exposing the fine bones of her face, her large and fearful eyes. He could feel her pulse, much faster than his own, like wings beating frantically—a small bird taking flight.

Becky awakened to insistent electronic beeps, the digital alarm. 4:04. Her hair was damp with perspiration. The sheets were clammy.

"Would you shut that fucking thing off?" Hank rolled over and covered his face with the pillow. He didn't start work until 9:00.

Her pulse raced as she remembered her dream. She had been a bird—a barn swallow—and she had been flying. That feeling of freedom and weightlessness had been so incredible, but then the dream had shifted, and she had turned into a hawk with talons for ripping flesh. Swooping down on a rabbit, she had torn into the soft fur until blood laced her feathers. But the killing and the blood hadn't seemed repulsive in her dream, just a thing of nature, a call she had to answer. Walking to the bus stop, she savored the dream, the sinewy power in her wings and talons. It was payday. She knew exactly what she had to do.

Neil was working overtime in the emergency room to cover for Alicia, whose breakdown had been even more serious than he had first thought—she had been hospitalized and would need to take a long leave of absence.

They always seemed to get their worst cases in August when the heat and the glare of the sun gave rise to the most sickening acts of violence. Like a factory line worker, he extracted bullets from flesh and disinfected wounds. Yesterday they brought in a homeless woman who had been raped and then stabbed twenty times. She had lost so much blood that she couldn't be saved. Alicia was the one who used to work with rape victims—she had done it very well—but the homeless woman was so far gone, not even Alicia could have given her solace. It was getting to be too much, even for him. All week he had been having dreams that made him lurch awake in sweat-soaked sheets: nightmares of the young woman next door gunning down her boyfriend.

Yesterday a letter from Gina, his ex, had arrived. They divorced in 1981. She had been sick of the neighborhood and his lack of ambition. "Everyone else has moved on, but you're not going anywhere," she'd told him. "You're stuck here like one of your plants." She had gone to Seattle to ride the waves of the software boom and then the dot-com boom. Presently she worked freelance out of her '20s bungalow on Bainbridge Island, her existence comfortably cushioned by investments and stock options. The one time he had visited her there, the thing that had struck him most was how white and affluent everyone was. He and Gina were still good friends. Since he was the only person on the planet who didn't have e-mail, they wrote letters every month.

For the past few years, she had been trying to convince him to move. He was welcome to stay with her until he found a job and a place to live. Just down the street from her house was a folk club where he could play his flute. He had to admit that her offer was tempting. Gina would help him find a job in some pristine clinic where his patients would be programmers and engineers, where he would never have to look at another torn-up, bleeding homeless person. If he didn't get out soon, he would end up like Alicia.

He arrived home from the hospital with a headache that made his garden shimmer like a hallucination. On the other side of the fence, something made of glass hit a hard surface and shattered. Then came muted grunting, the impact of a fist hitting something soft, and drawn-out weeping that didn't even sound human. Neil ran to the fence to see the guy next door straddle the gutted motorbike and punch the ripped seat. He was shaking as hard as Neil was.

Everyone's cracking up, he thought. There was no escape from it, no sanctuary from screaming and pain, even in his garden. Neil imagined that if someone saw his face, it would look like Alicia's when she had lost it that day. A wave of dizziness forced him to sit down. He rubbed his temples, rehearsed what he would say to Gina when he called her that night: "As soon as I sell the house, I'm out of here."

Something on the edge of the zucchini bed glinted in the sun. A Ziploc bag. Puzzled, he picked it up, then nearly dropped it. Inside was a gun. A note was tied to its handle, his name written in shaky ballpoint.

Neil,
You probably think I'm crazy for throwing this over your fence, but it's a lot safer with you than with Hank. He didn't have a license for this stupid thing, so either turn it in to the police or bury it. I already took the bullets out.
Becky

Under her signature, she had written, *Thank you.* Those two words leapt out at him—she had written them with such urgency that she had nearly pressed the pen through the paper. Thank you. What was she thanking him for—that sack of vegetables he had left on her doorstep? Then it sank in; Becky had left the guy. That fragile young woman with the matchstick arms had taken off.

* * *

On a mild September afternoon, Neil sat on the back porch and listened to the children next door squeal as they jumped into piles of raked leaves. A Hmong family had moved in after Hank left. The other day, a postcard from Becky arrived. She said she was waitressing in Madison and saving to go back to college. She got away, he kept thinking. She had to go and she went. But he had decided to stay. He had told Gina that he was too settled to pull up roots anymore. "I guess I'm going to grow old here, right in this neighborhood."

The garden rustled and whispered to him like an old friend. Looking at his birch tree, he thought of roots sinking into the earth, then watched its golden leaves reach into the intense blue of the autumn sky. The colors sang inside him as he began to play his flute.

THE GUY

BY PETE HAUTMAN

Linden Hills (Minneapolis)

J ane Day-Wellington said, "This thing is leaking."

"What thing?"

"This drain thingie." She pointed. "There's water under the sink."

Courtney Wellington fitted his Canterbury Park ball cap onto his head and shrugged. "So call the guy."

"What guy?"

"The drain guy."

Jane got down on her knees and looked carefully at the dripping pipe. "You can't fix it?"

"Do I look like the drain guy?" He did not look like the drain guy. He looked like a genetically dilute, down-on-his-luck aristocrat in a baseball cap.

Jane said, "It's just a little leak. If I call a plumber it'll cost us a hundred bucks."

"Old plumbing like that, it'll probably cost more."

"All the more reason to fix it ourselves . . . Where are you going?"

Courtney rolled his eyes and pointed at his lucky cap.

"You're going to play poker? Again? I was hoping you could help me with the yard work."

"Too hot. Besides, they're having a drawing for a bass boat in the card room. I've filled out about forty tickets for the thing, and you have to be present to win." He lifted his car keys from a set of hooks by the back door.

"What would *you* do with a bass boat?"

"Go fishing."

"Right. What about this leak?"

"I told you. Call the guy." And he was out the door.

"You fixin' this yourself, darlin'?" The man in the orange apron hitched up his jeans and waddled toward the back of the plumbing aisle.

Jane followed. "That's right. It's a U-shaped pipe." They reached a bin filled with PVC sink traps. "Like that."

The hardware guy held up one of the traps. "Where's it leakin'?"

"I think where it joins." She touched the open end of the plastic pipe. "Here."

The hardware guy—the name tag pinned to his apron read: *Doogie*—nodded seriously. "Well now, I would say that you have a partially clogged trap and a joint that's not quite sealed." He waited for a look of dread to appear on Jane's face, then smiled and said, "You should be able to fix it in a jiffy. Won't even need any tools."

Courtney Wellington returned to his Linden Hills bungalow from the card room at Canterbury Park shortly after 11. He had not won the bass boat. Just as well—where would he put the thing? He poured himself a scotch, then turned to the sink only to find a bucket over the faucet handle. Courtney frowned at the bucket, gave it a moment's thought, then removed it and turned on the water. He let it run for a few seconds to cool it, added a splash of water to his scotch, then looked down to see what was going on with his feet. Water was pouring from the cabinet beneath the sink. Courtney shut off the flow and marched directly to the bedroom where Jane was sitting up with a book, her reading glasses resting midway down her nose.

"What the hell happened to the sink?"

She looked up with a half-smile. "I'm fixing it."

"Fixing? My shoes are soaked."

"Didn't you see the bucket?"

"What am I supposed to think? There's a bucket over the sink. What's that supposed to mean?"

"I told you the drain was leaking."

"And I told you to call the guy."

Jane returned her attention to her book. Courtney slowly undressed, leaving his clothing in a pile on the floor. He donned his blue silk pajamas and got into bed with his wife and his glass of diluted scotch.

"Did you win your boat?"

"No."

"Did you win anything?"

"Yes. I won $37."

"That's why I'm fixing the sink myself."

Courtney frowned, struggling to make the connection. "Why?"

"Because we can't afford to call the plumber."

"You make good money."

"I bring home $370 a week. That's hardly enough for food and shelter."

"We have my trust fund."

Jane laughed.

"What's so funny?"

"The great Wellington trust fund. What is that? Another $200 a month?"

"$246."

"Yee-ha."

"Plus my poker winnings."

"If they're even real."

"What's that supposed to mean?"

Jane sighed. "Nothing." She did not actually doubt that Courtney won at cards. She had once gone to Canterbury to watch him play, just to make sure that was what he was actually doing. The image had stayed with her: Courtney in his lucky cap and sunglasses, wearing headphones attached to his iPod, sitting slumped at the hold'em table, $3 and $6 limit, folding hand after hand, waiting for the next "sucker" or "steamer" or "calling station"—he had a different name for every variety of loser—to join the game. Some days he won a couple hundred dollars, most days less than fifty. Sometimes he lost. As near as Jane could calculate—assuming that what he told her was true—Courtney was earning about $5 an hour playing poker. Less than she made at Cub Foods.

"Ya see, ya can't go metal to PVC without using an adapter," said Doogie. As if she should have known.

"I don't understand why you didn't tell me that last time I was here. This is my fourth trip back. First you sell me a pipe, then I find out I need a wrench, then I need another kind of wrench, and now this."

"Lady, I can't read your mind. How am I suppose to know you got metal pipes?"

Jane bit back her response. She said, "Do you have one of those . . . adapta things?"

"Adapter? Sure I do." He produced a white plastic ring from one of the wire bins. "Eighty-nine centavos, señorita. Only I think you ought to just go with a metal trap."

"But you already sold me the other one."

"Bring it back."

"But I don't want to come back."

"Then use the adapter."

Jane frowned at the device in the hardware man's hand. "And that's all I need? I put it on and my sink will no longer leak?"

"Lady, without lookin' at it myself, there's no way I can promise you anything."

"I don't want to have to come back here."

"You want my advice, lady? Call a plumber."

"You sound just like my husband."

"How so?"

"He's an incompetent chauvinist prick too."

"Whoa! Mee-yow!"

"I am most definitely not coming back here," Jane said as she turned away.

"Okay by me," Doogie muttered.

Courtney Wellington ate a slice of toast with apricot jam and watched his wife struggling beneath the sink. He said, "I told you to call the guy."

"If you say that one more time, I'm going to bury this wrench in your skull."

"You could call a guy for that too." Courtney sipped his coffee. "See, the way the world works is there's a guy for everything. I'm the poker guy. You're the grocery guy—only you're a gal. There's the drain guy, the cable guy, the lawn guy. That's your problem, Jane. You think you have to do everything yourself. Like you say, 'I'm gonna kill you.' What you should say is, 'I'm gonna have you killed.' You really want somebody dead, you call the guy."

"You got his number?"

"Matter of fact, I do. Meet all kinds at the casino."

Jane wriggled out from under the sink and sat up. "What is it?"

"What is what?"

"The number. The number of the guy I call to have somebody killed."

Courtney blinked. "Ha ha," he said.

"I'm serious. Do you really know such a person?"

He shrugged and looked away. "More or less."

"What is it? More or less?"

"I hate it when you get like this."

"I just wanted you to know that I know you're full of shit up to your ears, Court."

"Up yours, plumber lady."

Jane reinserted her upper body into the sink cabinet. "You let me know when you find that number."

"I find it, you better believe you're the last person I'd share it with."

"Probably a good idea," she said as she tightened the nut.

She was still struggling with the drain trap when Courtney left an hour later to play in a Sunday afternoon hold'em tournament with a $5,000 guaranteed prize pool. "Lotta dead money in this thing," he said, referring to all the weak players who would be entering. "See you around dinnertime."

"You better find yourself something to eat at Canterbury," Jane said.

Courtney got knocked out of the tournament on the "bubble"—one place short of the money. To make himself feel better he got into a juicy 6-12 hold'em game, took a couple of bad beats, and found himself down another $320. He tugged his lucky cap down low over his eyes, dialed up some vintage Pink Floyd on his iPod, and waited for a hand.

Four hours later he had come all the way back to even. He considered going home, but the thought of finding Jane still under the kitchen sink made him twitchy. Besides, had she not implied that there would be no dinner waiting for him?

He flagged down a waitress and ordered a cheeseburger, fries, and a beer.

Courtney pulled into his driveway at midnight feeling quite proud of his $130 profit. It was after midnight. Jane would be done with her little plumbing project and, he hoped, asleep in bed. He parked the car and quietly let himself into the house. All the lights were out. He made his way to the kitchen, thinking to have a little nightcap before bed. He turned on the light. The bucket was back over the kitchen faucet handle. He shook his head. There should be some kind of law against women wielding tools.

What was that sound?

He stopped, listening. Music. He tilted his head, searching for the source. Was it coming from outside the house? No . . . he turned in a slow circle, then focused his ears on the door to the basement stairs. He opened the door. It was definitely coming from the basement. Fleetwood Mac, Jane's favorite. He hated Fleetwood Mac. Why was Fleetwood Mac coming from the basement? Jane must have left the stereo in the rec room running.

Courtney flipped the light switch at the top of the stairs. Nothing. Another goddamn light bulb burned out. He started down the steps in the dark. On the third step his foot hit something slippery and the world turned sideways; he was falling, crashing down the steps in three incredibly painful jolts. He heard an ear-bending howl come from his own throat and landed hard on his hip in the dark at the bottom of the stairs.

Christ. Was he broken? Had he busted his hip? Or worse?

After several seconds he tried to move his right leg. It worked. It hurt, but it worked. He moved his left leg, then each of his arms. Everything hurt, but it all seemed to function. He untangled his body and got onto his hands and knees. He waited in that position until the spinning stopped, then carefully stood up and groped for the light switch at the bottom of the stairs, and turned it on.

What had happened? What had he slipped on? He saw something black puddled at the bottom of the steps. He picked it up. One of the slippery nylon things Jane wore under her dresses. A slip. He'd slipped on a *slip*.

Christ, he could have been killed!

Jane heard her husband's footsteps coming back up the basement stairs. She closed her eyes tight and took a deep, shuddering breath, her first since she'd heard Courtney's shout and the crashing of his body tumbling down the steps.

He had survived the fall, and he was walking.

"Goddamnit, Jane!" she heard him shout from the kitchen. She heard him stomping through the house toward the bedroom, the faint, steady beat of Mick Fleetwood on drums in the background. She turned on the light and sat up in bed. He came in gripping her lacy black slip in his fist.

"What the *hell* is *this*?" He shook the undergarment in her face. "I could've been *killed!*"

Jane shook her head. "I'm sorry, honey. I don't know what you're talking about."

"This slip! I fell all the way down the goddamn stairs . . ." He went on for some time, describing his fall in graphic detail. Jane stared up at him, waiting for him to wind down.

"It must have fallen from the laundry basket," she said as his rant faltered.

That set him off again. "I coulda been *killed*," he said for the third or fourth time.

"I'm sorry," said Jane. "I was careless." After all, he was absolutely right. He was right about the sink drain, and he was right about the slip.

Next time, she thought. Next time she would call the guy.

THE BREWER'S SON

BY LARRY MILLETT

West 7th-Fort Road (St. Paul)

O n the morning of June 10, 1892, as the Republican National Convention droned toward its uninspired conclusion in Minneapolis, the news across the river in St. Paul proved to be far more riveting. A great mystery preoccupied the Saintly City, and it seemed to grow more confounding by the hour. As a result, when a special edition of the *St. Paul Dispatch* appeared on the streets at 10 a.m., copies were snapped up so quickly that the newsboys were sold out within a matter of minutes. The story that everyone wanted to read sprawled across the front page beneath a headline of the size normally reserved for the outbreak of war or the death of a major advertiser. *RANSOM VANISHES,* screamed the headline above the story, which began as follows:

> *A shocking development occurred early today in the kidnapping of Michael Kirchmeyer, who yesterday morning was abducted by parties unknown while on his way to work at the brewery operated for many years by his father, Johann, at the foot of Lee Avenue.*
>
> *The Dispatch has learned that the police late last night set a trap for the kidnappers, who had demanded a $10,000 ransom for the young man's safe return. At precisely midnight, Johann Kirchmeyer, following new*

instructions from the kidnappers, personally delivered the money to a wooded area in a ravine near the brewery. Once again obeying instructions, he then returned immediately to his palatial home on Stewart Avenue.

The police, meanwhile, closed in. Under the direct supervision of Chief of Detectives O'Connor, a contingent of his best men secreted themselves in the woods so as to have an unimpeded view of the locale where the ransom had been left. A full moon provided ample illumination for the policemen, who formed what Chief O'Connor described as a "perfect noose" in which the kidnappers would inevitably be caught, or so it was believed.

During the long vigil which followed, however, the police detected not the faintest sign that anyone was trying to steal away with the ransom. As the sun rose, O'Connor's confidence in his "noose" began to fall. Fearing that his men had somehow been spotted by the kidnappers, the chief called off the surveillance at 6 o'clock this morning.

It was only then, when O'Connor went to retrieve the money, that he made an astounding discovery. The ransom was gone! A frantic search ensued but as this story went to press, there was no word as to where the ransom had gone or how it had been taken from beneath the very noses of the police.

As no fewer than eight policemen had the area in view and yet not one reported seeing or hearing anything of a suspicious nature, there appears to be but one possible explanation for the disappearance of the ransom. The chief, however, refused to entertain the possibility that one of his own officers might have absconded with the money,

saying they are "to a man of the highest moral character
and would never resort to thievery of any kind."

In the meantime, young Kirchmeyer is still missing,
and fear grows by the hour that he will meet with some
terrible fate, as it is now obvious that the police of this city
are far better at losing things than finding them. Indeed,
it is to be wondered now whether there is anyone in St.
Paul who can prevent a most awful tragedy from playing
itself out before long.

What the author of this melancholy prediction didn't
know was that Shadwell Rafferty—saloonkeeper, bon vivant,
private detective, and a man with an uncanny understanding
of the human animal—was already on the case.

Although best remembered for the remarkable series of
investigations he undertook with Sherlock Holmes, beginning with the ice palace murders of 1896, Shadwell Rafferty
had even before then made a name for himself in St. Paul as
a private detective. Saloonkeeping was, of course, his chief
occupation, but by the early 1890s his legendary watering
hole at the Ryan Hotel had proved so successful that he
found himself able to devote more time to the "detectin'
game," as called it. It was therefore hardly surprising that he
found himself in the midst of the Kirchmeyer affair almost
from the very start.

The facts of the case were simple enough, or so it seemed
at first. On the morning of June 9, Kirchmeyer, aged twenty-
four, left his family's towering brick mansion on Stewart
Avenue in the city's West End to walk to his job as an
accountant at his father's brewery. Located in a complex of
stout limestone buildings along the Mississippi River just

three blocks from the mansion, the brewery was famed as the home of "Kirchmeyer's Cavern Lager" or "Kirchy's," as it was commonly called, and so named because it was aged in a system of caves dug into the sandstone cliffs nearby. Local malt connoisseurs, Rafferty among them, regarded the dark foamy libation as St. Paul's finest beer, no small achievement in city that took its drinking seriously.

Young Kirchmeyer's walk was normally accomplished in a matter of minutes, but on this morning he did not arrive at the brewery as scheduled. Although not considered by his parents to be a perfectly reliable young man, he was seldom late for work and, if so, his tardiness was never extreme. When he became a full hour late, his father telephoned home to see what had happened. It was only then, after a brief search of the household, that Augusta Kirchmeyer, Michael's mother, made a frightful discovery. Lodged beneath the screen door on the front porch was a note, written in the large block letters a child might use. It said:

WE HAVE YOUR SON. PRICE OF HIS SAFE RETURN IS $10,000. DO THIS NOW: WITHDRAW $10,000 IN SILVER CERTIFICATES (DENOMINATIONS OF $100) FROM YOUR BANK. PLACE CERTIFICATES IN SEALED BOX OR OTHER CONTAINER NO LARGER THAN TWELVE INCHES LONG, EIGHT INCHES WIDE, AND SIX INCHES HIGH. HAVE MONEY BY 6 O'CLOCK TONIGHT. AWAIT OUR NEXT COMMUNICATION. DO NOT DOUBT WE WILL KILL YOUR SON IF YOU FAIL TO FOLLOW THESE INSTRUCTIONS.

It was signed, in a malevolent flourish of ink, *THE BLACK HAND.*

The police were called at once, and Chief of Detectives John J. O'Connor personally took charge of the investigation. He ordered a thorough canvassing of the neighborhood, which included the busy shops of the Chicago, St. Paul, Minneapolis, and Omaha Railroad, where a thousand men worked. Someone, the chief believed, must have seen or heard something. But the canvass turned up only one piece of useful information. A boy playing in the yard of his home saw Kirchmeyer walking down Lee Avenue toward the brewery. He was alone and gave no sign of distress. Beyond this meager report, not a single clue emerged as to the young man's whereabouts or how he might have been spirited away. It was, O'Connor remarked, as though Kirchmeyer had been "snatched up by the devil himself in broad daylight."

Like most of St. Paul, Shadwell Rafferty learned of the kidnapping that afternoon when the *Dispatch* reported the story under a headline that read, *BLACK HAND GRIPS BREWER'S SON.* The reference to the Black Hand was well understood by readers of the newspaper, which in recent months had presented a series of sensational articles about a supposed "terrorist organization" of that name. It was said to be controlled by "a gang of foreign-born criminals" operating from the shanty town that sprawled along the Upper Levee flats beneath the new High Bridge. Various acts of extortion and even murder were attributed to the shadowy group, though details were regrettably sparse, and no criminal charges had ever been brought against any of the alleged gang members.

A newsboy had brought in the *Dispatch* as Rafferty and his longtime friend and chief bartender, George Washington

"Wash" Thomas, were enjoying a late lunch of roast beef and boiled potatoes at the saloon, which was blessedly quiet after the noon rush. Rafferty read the kidnapping saga aloud in his powerful basso, pausing now and then to chew over a particularly intriguing detail.

When Rafferty had finished, Thomas said, "Well, it's a strange one, Shad. Maybe you should call Mr. Kirchmeyer and see if you can help. Don't you two go back a ways?"

"We do, Wash, though it's been awhile since I've seen him. Fact is, I think the last time we talked was after that business a few years ago when Jimmy O'Shea was cartin' away his prized lager."

Thomas, who was not fond of confined spaces, remembered the case all too well. He and Rafferty had spent hours in the dank brewery caves setting a trap for the elusive O'Shea, whom the police seemed unable to track down. Kirchmeyer had been so pleased by the thief's capture that he sent a month's worth of lager to Rafferty's saloon as a token of gratitude.

"What about Kirchmeyer's son? Do you know him at all?" Thomas asked.

"Met him once or twice. 'Tis said he's a bit on the wild side. Of course, so were you and I at that age. I seem to remember hearin' that the lad went off to school out east for a while to study surveyin' or some such thing but didn't stay for long. There was woman trouble, I think."

"I know all about that kind of trouble," Thomas said, a mischievous grin spreading across his broad black face.

"Yes you do," Rafferty agreed. "You are a regular expert in that department, Wash. Now then, what do you think about this kidnappin' business? Do you believe it is the work of the Black Hand, assumin' there is such a thing?"

Thomas knew that Rafferty had been skeptical of the earlier news stories. Unlike the reporters who wrote for the *Dispatch*, Rafferty actually knew many residents of the Upper Levee. If a cutthroat gang had been operating there, Rafferty thought, he would have been aware of it.

"I'm guessing you're not convinced," Thomas said. "Any particular reason why?"

By way of response, Rafferty picked up the paper and again read aloud the portion of the story dealing with the ransom note. Then he said, "I'm thinkin', Wash, that for a bunch of ignorant immigrants, or so the *Dispatch* would have us believe, these Black Hand fellows seems to be regular masters of the King's English. 'Await our next communication,' they say. Do you know anybody down on the levee who talks like that?"

"Can't say that I do," Thomas agreed, adding: "The instructions about packaging the ransom are also queer, don't you think?"

Rafferty nodded. "Queer as can be."

The telephone behind the long mahogany bar rang and Thomas got up to answer it. The operator came on, followed by a weary-sounding man who said in a thick German accent: "This is Johann Kirchmeyer. I need very much to talk with Mr. Rafferty."

The Kirchmeyer mansion, its high-hatted brick tower soaring above a broad lawn interspersed with oaks, stood at the end of a circular driveway, which was crowded with carriages by the time Rafferty arrived. Two coppers were standing outside the front door, smoking cigars. Rafferty, once a member of the force himself, stopped to chat. After the usual jovial banter, he quickly learned that there had been no new developments in the investigation despite an intensive search for the kidnap victim.

"The old man's in there waiting for the next message," one of the cops told Rafferty. "Did he send for you, Shad?"

"He did."

"Well, the Bull won't be happy, I can tell you that."

"The chief of detectives is never happy when I'm around," Rafferty said. "Must be my irritatin' habit of makin' a fool of him."

Rafferty turned to go inside, pausing first to look at the front screen door where, according to the *Dispatch*, the ransom note had been left. There were two large windows to either side of the door, both offering a clear view of the open porch. Placing a note beneath the door would certainly have been a risky proposition for the kidnappers.

A servant met Rafferty in the vestibule and ushered him upstairs to a small study at the rear of the house. There Rafferty found Johann Kirchmeyer, seated in an armchair next to a window that offered sweeping views of the river valley. Kirchmeyer was a short, heavyset man, with a bristly gray beard and small dark eyes behind wire-rim spectacles. Despite the heat, he wore a brown wool suit and vest, and he'd made no accommodation to the weather by loosening his tie, which was knotted with mechanical precision.

"Ach, it is good of you to come, Mr. Rafferty," he said. "Come sit down and we will talk."

After Rafferty had taken a seat, Kirchmeyer said, "I want my son back, Mr. Rafferty, and you, I believe, are the man who can do that for me."

Rafferty was taken aback. "I appreciate your confidence, but the police—"

Kirchmeyer cut in with surprising fierceness. "No, no, I

will not place my trust in the police, Mr. Rafferty, not for a single minute! You know as well as I why that is so."

Because half the cops are crooked, Rafferty thought, and the other half are lazy. "Yes, I understand, but—"

Kirchmeyer interrupted again. "Mr. Rafferty, I wish to hear no more of the police. You see, sir, I can tell you who really kidnapped my son. This Black Hand business, bah, it is nonsense. Do you agree?"

Rafferty said he did.

Kirchmeyer smiled for the first time. "I knew you would. You see, there is something that must be kept confidential, something about Michael which I must tell you. I fear he has become involved with gamblers and owes them a great deal of money."

"Ah, I see. 'Tis a common thing with young men, unfortunately. And you haven't mentioned this to the police?"

"No. It would be scandal and the death of my dear Augusta, if she knew."

"And how is Mrs. Kirchmeyer?"

"Not well. Not well at all. This has been very hard on her."

"I'm sure. Now then, do you know which gambler young Michael might owe money to?"

"I am told it is a man named Banion who operates some sort of gambling establishment downtown. Do you know him?"

Rafferty knew everybody. "Certainly. John Banion is his name but he goes by Red. He has a place on Hill Street a few doors down from police headquarters. 'Tis a cozy arrangement for all concerned, since the bribe money doesn't have to travel far. By the way, how did you find out about your son's involvement with Banion?"

"One of our housemaids told me. Michael had apparently shared a confidence with her."

Rafferty, who wondered what else the lad might have shared with the maid, said, "So you think Banion snatched your boy and wants the $10,000 to pay off what Michael owes him."

"Yes. I can only assume this Banion is a ruthless character and would not hesitate to kill my son. Yet I know the police cannot be trusted, and that is why I beg of you to help me. I have already obtained the ransom money and will gladly pay it for my son's return. But I am worried for this simple reason: What is to keep these kidnappers from murdering Michael once they have the money?"

"Nothing, if they're so inclined," Rafferty agreed. "And you have received no further word from the kidnappers, is that right?"

"Nothing. All I can do is wait and hope that you might be able to find my son."

Rafferty stood up. "That is a tall order, Mr. Kirchmeyer, a tall order. But I will do what I can. In the meantime, let me know as soon as you hear again from the kidnappers."

"I will, and I cannot thank you enough, Mr. Rafferty."

"Don't thank me yet," Rafferty said, patting Kirchmeyer on the shoulder before leaving.

O'Connor was striding up the front steps as Rafferty walked out on the porch. A dark scowl spread over the chief's splotched, unpleasant face and he stopped, blocking Rafferty's path. The two men might have been twins. Both were well over six feet, barrel-chested, large-bellied, surprisingly light on their feet, and invariably well-armed. Neither was a man to be trifled with under any circumstances.

"I'll have no tricks from you," O'Connor said without

preamble, as he fixed his poisonous green eyes on Rafferty. "You'll not be interfering in this business. Is that understood?"

"And good afternoon to you," Rafferty replied, staring back at the chief. "I'm here at Mr. Kirchmeyer's invitation, John. Apparently the police of this city do not have his full confidence. Imagine that."

The provocation was deliberate—Rafferty considered O'Connor to be nothing more than a thug with a badge—but also risky. O'Connor had beaten down many a man who crossed him and struck fear in countless others. Rafferty, however, was not among them.

"By God, I could arrest you right now," O'Connor said, moving toward Rafferty.

Rafferty stood his ground until the two men were eyeball to eyeball. "You could try," Rafferty replied, "though I'd not give good odds on your chances. Now, if there are no further pleasantries to be exchanged, I think I'll take a little walk."

"You do that," O'Connor said, glaring at Rafferty as he swung around him. "And don't come back."

Rafferty strolled over to 7th Street, where he found a drugstore at the corner of Randolph Avenue. There was a telephone inside and after favoring the store's proprietor with a silver dollar, Rafferty placed a call to Thomas at the saloon.

"Listen, Wash," he said when he heard Thomas's familiar voice, "I've got a job for you. I want you to track down Red Banion for me. Tell him he's a suspect in this Kirchmeyer business. Ask him how much the lad owes him and see what he says. And remind Red that he owes me a favor."

Thomas laughed. "Several favors, Shad. He'd probably be fertilizing the soil in Calvary today if you hadn't gotten him out of that mess with the Chicago boys."

The "mess" involved certain transactions with a Chicago gaming syndicate led by the notorious "Iron Pipe" McGinnis, so named after the weapon he favored for breaking the kneecaps, or in some cases the skull, of any gambler who failed to pay his debts.

Thomas said, "So you think Red snatched the kid to get his dad to cough up a debt?"

"Could be," Rafferty said. "Let me know what you find out. I'll call back later."

Rafferty left the drugstore after buying a couple of the cheap cigars he liked to smoke and headed back down Osceola Street toward the Kirchmeyer mansion. But he didn't go all the way there. Instead, he turned east on Lee Avenue, following the route Michael Kirchmeyer would have taken on his way to the brewery.

At Drake Street the "Omaha" shops, as everyone called them, came into view. The shops consisted of a series of low brick structures, including a roundhouse. Men in overalls were working on cars or moving locomotives in and out of the roundhouse on the north end of the property. Across Drake from the shops was a foundry, its wide doors open to dissipate the heat. A group of men inside were pouring molten iron into a sand mold. Other men were working in a small yard outside the foundry, loading finished goods onto drays. Teamsters with their wagons clattered along Drake, carrying supplies to the rail shops. Rafferty was struck by the amount of activity and the openness of the area. With potential eyes everywhere, it would hardly have been a good place to kidnap someone in broad daylight.

Farther down Lee, however, toward the river, the landscape abruptly changed. The street entered a long steep ravine, well-wooded, and followed it down to the river, where the brewery stood at the base of a low cliff. This rather secluded portion of the street, Rafferty concluded, would have been an ideal spot for the kidnappers to snatch young Kirchmeyer without being seen.

But where had they taken him and how had they spirited him away? At first Rafferty thought it likely the young man had been forced into a carriage or wagon, probably after being bound and gagged. But this theory had a problem. The street was very steep—Rafferty guessed the grade at twelve percent or better—and also quite muddy after heavy rain a few days earlier. Getting any kind of wheeled vehicle up and down the street under such conditions would have been very difficult.

As he was pondering this problem, Rafferty noticed something peculiar. A yellow ribbon—neatly tied with a square knot—dangled from a bush to his left where a goat trail led off into the woods. Curious, Rafferty turned up the muddy trail, instantly regretting that he had put on his best new loafers before going to the Kirchmeyer house. Rafferty followed the trail for perhaps a hundred yards, looking for any evidence that Michael Kirchmeyer and his kidnappers might have passed by. Before long, Rafferty saw a shanty, built of scavenged lumber and lodged up against one side of the ravine.

He scrambled over to take a look, fighting off a cloud of gnats that seemed to have been eagerly awaiting his arrival. The shanty looked as though it had been built by the hoboes who often camped near the railroad tracks. Inside, Rafferty found a fire pit, next to which was a crude plank bench supported by beer barrels. The dirt floor was littered with bottles of cheap whiskey, cans, and other signs of recent habitation. Rafferty sat down on the bench and used a stick to poke at the ashes in the pit, hoping he might find a clue. Almost immediately, he felt a peculiar sensation—at once cold and damp—around his feet. And in that instant, a most curious idea began to form in his mind.

By early evening, Rafferty was back at the Kirchmeyer mansion, waiting with everyone else for another message from the kidnappers. At around 6 o'clock, Rafferty called Thomas to see if he'd managed to talk to Red Banion. Thomas had, and the upshot of the conversation came as no surprise to Rafferty. The gambler, Thomas reported, was very insistent in stating that he'd had no involvement in Kirchmeyer's kidnapping and that the young man had never owed him anything close to $10,000.

"You know Red," Thomas said. "He's a very cautious fellow. You won't get much credit from him unless he's thoroughly convinced you're good for it. And when it came to young Kirchmeyer, Red wasn't convinced. He said $250 was the biggest debt the boy ever had and that he always paid up on time."

"How much did he gamble away in all?"

"About five thousand at most," Red said. "Anything happening on your end, Shad?"

"No, I'm just sittin' around like everybody else. But I have a feelin', Wash, that it won't be quiet around here too much longer."

Rafferty's prediction proved accurate. At 10 p.m. a boy arrived at the mansion's front door bearing an envelope that he said was to be personally delivered to Johann Kirchmeyer. O'Connor, who had returned to the house not long before after spending several fruitless hours trying to pry information out of the local hoodlum community, intercepted the boy at once. A quick grilling revealed that the boy had been given the envelope by a man of vague description who'd stopped him at Seven Corners and offered him a five-dollar gold piece to deliver it, no questions asked.

O'Connor took the sealed envelope, which seemed to have something heavy inside, and brought it upstairs to Kirchmeyer. The chief was peeved to discover Rafferty in the room, but kept his unhappiness to himself, since Kirchmeyer obviously had placed his faith in the saloonkeeper.

"This has just come, sir," O'Connor said. "I would think it is from the kidnappers."

"At last," Kirchmeyer said when O'Connor handed him the envelope. The brewer's hands were shaking as he opened it. Inside were a note and a gold pocket watch.

Kirchmeyer turned over the watch to inspect the engraving on the back. "It is Michael's," he announced. "I gave it to him on his twenty-first birthday."

With Rafferty and O'Connor looking over his shoulder, Kirchmeyer unfolded the note, which read:

MR. KIRCHMEYER: THE WATCH WILL TELL YOU THAT WE ARE NOT LYING. WE HAVE YOUR SON. IF YOU VALUE HIS LIFE, DO THIS: LEAVE YOUR HOUSE AT MIDNIGHT WITH THE RANSOM PACKAGED AS PER OUR EAR- LIER INSTRUCTIONS. ALLOW NO POLICE OR ANYONE ELSE TO FOLLOW YOU OR YOU WILL REGRET IT. BRING ALONG A LANTERN. WALK TO LEE AVENUE AND FOLLOW IT UNTIL YOU REACH A POINT APPROXIMATELY 200 YARDS TO THE WEST OF YOUR BREWERY.

THERE, ON YOUR LEFT, YOU WILL SEE A PATH MARKED BY A YELLOW RIBBON. FOLLOW THIS PATH FOR APPROXIMATELY 100 YARDS. YOU WILL SEE A SHACK TO YOUR LEFT. GO INSIDE AND PLACE THE MONEY BENEATH A BENCH SUPPORTED BY TWO BARRELS. THEN LEAVE AT ONCE AND RETURN HOME. IF THE RANSOM PROVES SATISFACTORY, YOU WILL RECEIVE INSTRUCTIONS ABOUT WHERE TO FIND YOUR SON. HE WILL NOT BE HARMED IF YOU COMPLY.

Once again, it was signed, *THE BLACK HAND.*

Kirchmeyer stood up and said, "I must do as they say."

"Of course," O'Connor agreed. "But don't worry. We have time. I will post my men all around the area. These criminals will not get away with their evil deed."

These words alarmed Kirchmeyer. "No, no. You have seen what the note says. No police. I cannot risk it. Do you agree, Mr. Rafferty?"

"I do. We can take no chances with young Michael's life."

"I do not think it would be wise to give up the money so easily," O'Connor said, shooting a nasty glance at Rafferty before turning to Kirchmeyer. "You have only their word that they will not harm your boy. I assure you that my men will be very discreet—"

"No," Kirchmeyer said sharply. "You are to instruct your men to stay well away. Is that clear?"

"It is," O'Connor replied, though Rafferty greatly doubted that the chief had any intention of living up to his promise.

After O'Connor left, Rafferty reread the note and told Kirchmeyer, "As it so happens, I was in that shack earlier today."

"In it? But why?"

Rafferty explained how he had run across the shanty. Then he added, "Now, I don't want you to worry. Just drop off the money as you were instructed to. I'm confident everything will be all right and you will soon see your son."

When Rafferty came downstairs, O'Connor was waiting for him.

"Kirchmeyer is a fool and so are you," he said. "That boy will be dead if we allow the kidnappers to get away with the ransom."

Rafferty was uncharacteristically silent for a few moments before he responded in a calm voice, "Well, John, I'm sure you'll do what you must. When Mr. Kirchmeyer returns from droppin' off the ransom, tell him I'll see him again in the mornin'."

"Tell him yourself," O'Connor said, and went off to round up his men. It was going to be, he knew, a long night.

The following morning was to bring two great surprises. The first concerned the seemingly unaccountable disappearance of the ransom, a development that left Johann Kirchmeyer in a fury while O'Connor struggled to explain why he had violated the brewer's express orders. Worst of all, Michael Kirchmeyer remained missing, and as the *Dispatch* stated, there was great fear for his well-being.

Not long after the newspaper's story appeared, however, came a second development far more startling than the first. Just before noon, as Kirchmeyer paced the floor in his study, a servant rushed in.

"It is Mr. Rafferty," he said excitedly, "and Michael is with him!"

The reunion that followed between young Kirchmeyer and his family was the sort of heartfelt occasion that members of the press, who had trailed Rafferty into the house like dogs on the scent of prime sirloin, were more than pleased to report upon. Johann Kirchmeyer fairly bounded down the stairs and wrapped his arms around Michael, a lanky young man who was a good half-foot taller and fifty pounds lighter than his father. Augusta Kirchmeyer, who had been confined to bed since the kidnapping, also made her way downstairs. At the sight of her son, she cried out, "Oh, Michael, my dear Michael, you are back," and then promptly fell to the floor in a faint. Father and son went to her aid as reporters crowded around, furiously scribbling in their small notebooks.

Amid all of this commotion, Rafferty slipped away down a hallway to the kitchen, then climbed up the back stairs to the study where he had talked with Johann Kirchmeyer the day before. Rafferty took a seat by the window and gazed out across the green expanse of the river valley. He was not looking forward to the task that lay ahead of him.

When Johann Kirchmeyer entered the study half an hour later, his face was a study in puzzlement. "Mr. Rafferty, why are you not downstairs? The reporters are asking for you. They want to know how you achieved this miracle. But Michael told me you were here and wished to see me alone."

Rafferty nodded as Kirchmeyer sat down in his favorite armchair. "Yes, there are some things you need to know, and the sooner the better. There is no way of sugarcoatin' what I am about to tell you. I only ask that you hear me out, and then you can decide what is to be done."

"Very well. I owe you that, at the least, for saving my son."

"Ah, I fear I didn't save the lad," Rafferty said slowly. "'Twould be more accurate to say that I captured him."

"What do you mean?"

"I mean this, Mr. Kirchmeyer: Your son was not kidnapped and he is the criminal responsible for this whole sorry business."

Kirchmeyer began to protest but Rafferty held up his hand. "Please, let me continue. Your son, I regret to tell you, staged his own abduction for the purpose of extortin' money from you. For the past twenty-four hours, he's been hidin' out in an abandoned portion of your brewery caves. It was he who placed that ransom note on your front porch. He also wrote the second note and had it delivered here with the help of a confederate, whose name I have if you wish to know it.

"Now, as for why Michael acted as he did, I fear you will find his motive most troublin'. You were right in thinkin' that he had run up debts in the gamblin' den operated by Mr. Banion. But as it so happens, I know Red Banion well and I was able to confirm that your son had in fact been payin' off what he owed, since Mr. Banion, being a cautious sort of fellow, would not extend Michael any great amount of credit. Trouble is, Michael had to get the money somewhere, and he got it at the brewery by stealin' money and cookin' the books, which he was in a position to do as your accountant.

"Unfortunately for him, he learned not long ago that his hand was about to be detected square in the middle of the cookie jar. As I understand it, you told him you were plannin' an audit at the end of the fiscal year this month because of some irregularities you'd run across. That's when Michael hit upon his desperate scheme. He'd pay back the money he owed, and maybe get a few thousand in spendin' money as well, by extortin' it from you. 'Twas certainly a brazen piece of work, I will say that for it."

Kirchmeyer put his hand to his forehead and said, "No, I cannot believe Michael would ever be capable of such a thing."

"Then you'd best take a look at this," Rafferty replied, retrieving a folded sheet of paper from the inside pocket of his gaudy seersucker suit. "'Tis Michael's confession, which I had him write out. I'm sure you will recognize that it is in his hand."

Kirchmeyer took the paper and read it slowly. The more he read, the more blood seemed to drain from his face. By the time he was finished, he had the desperate, stricken look of a man who had just buried his child. "Michael," he muttered, shaking his head. "Ach, my Michael, what have you done?"

Rafferty said, "I suppose you'll be wonderin' about the ransom. I have it. Michael was carryin' it when I apprehended him outside the old cave entrance west of the brewery. I guessed that's where he'd be sneakin' out."

"But how did he get his hands on it with all of those policemen watching?"

Rafferty smiled. "Ah, that was the true genius of his scheme. Michael had worked in the caves for a time and knew them well. I also recall that he had some experience as a surveyor, is that right?"

"Yes, he studied surveying, but what does that have to do with the caves?"

"Well, for Michael, it proved to be a handy skill. Because of his trainin' as a surveyor, he was able to figure out that one of the old caves passes very close to the edge of the ravine on Lee Avenue. And that gave him a stroke of inspiration. He figured out that by diggin' a short side tunnel no more than twenty feet long, he could punch a hole right into the floor of that shack. The sandstone down there is like hard sugar, as you well know, and a couple of men with a pick can cut through it easily. It probably took Michael and his confederate only a few nights to do the work. As they neared the ravine, they made the tunnel no bigger than a rabbit hole in hopes it wouldn't be discovered. That's why Michael was so insistent that the ransom money be put in a package of a certain size. He needed to be sure it would fit through the hole."

"How did you find out about this tunnel?" Kirchmeyer asked.

"'Twas a bit of luck. You see, Michael used rocks and dirt to temporarily plug the hole, but he didn't do quite a good enough job of it. When I came upon the shanty yesterday, I sat down on the bench while I was pokin' through the fire pit. Lo and behold, I felt a cool, damp breeze—cave air—at my feet. And that's when I had an idea that maybe, just maybe, somebody had come upon a foolproof way of gettin' their hands on the ransom."

"So you found the rabbit hole?"

"Well, I didn't open it, if that's what you mean. I didn't want to scare away anybody who might be hidin' out down there. But when the second ransom note arrived statin' where the money was to be left, I knew I was right about a tunnel comin' from the caves. The coppers never did figure it, since Michael did a better job of sealin' the rabbit hole the second time around, after he'd got the money."

Kirchmeyer said, "One thing is not clear to me. Did you suspect Michael from the very start?"

"No, I didn't know for sure until I caught him skulkin' out of the caves with the ransom money. He wasn't happy to see me and I had to do some persuadin' to keep him from tryin' to run off. After that, it didn't take long to wring the truth out of him. I can tell you he is mortified, though I'm inclined to think that the chief source of his unhappiness is that he got caught."

Rafferty looked into Kirchmeyer's tired, sad eyes and continued, "There is but one more thing for you to consider, sir, and it concerns the fate of your son. By all rights, he should be charged with his crime, not to mention the agony he put you and your wife through. Yet the fact is, you are the victim here and you must decide whether to prosecute the matter in the courts. What I'm sayin' is that I will not hand Michael's confession over to the police unless you ask me to."

"And if I decide to tear up the confession, what will the police be told?"

"Leave that to me," Rafferty said with a smile. "I have a fine Irish talent for embroidery. Besides, I believe I can convince Chief O'Connor to go along with whatever tale I have to offer, so long as he receives credit for findin' your son and retrievin' the ransom. He will be a regular hero by the time I'm through."

"You would do that to spare our family the shame of Michael's crime?"

"I would, but on one condition. The lad cannot be let off scot-free. You must see to it that he faces serious consequences for what he has done."

Kirchmeyer nodded. "I understand, Mr. Rafferty, and I assure you there will be consequences. To be betrayed in such a cold and calculating manner by my own flesh and blood is a terrible thing. I don't know that I will ever be able to forgive Michael."

"It will be hard," Rafferty acknowledged, "but perhaps one day, if Michael can prove himself worthy of forgiveness, you will be able to give it."

"Yes, perhaps one day," Kirchmeyer said as he stood up to

shake Rafferty's hand. Then he went downstairs to talk with his son.

Rafferty was as good as his word. When he talked to the reporters downstairs, he spun a lively yarn about how two unknown men—believed to be transients living in the shack—had snatched away Michael. The story was patently absurd, but Rafferty buttressed it with a glowing account of how Chief O'Connor and his men had allowed the ransom to be taken so that the kidnappers would think they had gotten away with their crime. Then, he said, he and the police had freed Michael and recovered the ransom yet the kidnappers had somehow escaped. The press was skeptical but Rafferty stuck to his story, and as there was no way to disprove it, the newspapers had no choice but to ratify it as the official version of events.

Johann Kirchmeyer was also true to his word. He banished his son from his home and business and wrote him out of his will. Soon thereafter, Michael left St. Paul for points unknown.

Five years later, in 1897, Johann Kirchmeyer died. His wife followed him to the grave a month later. With no heirs to take over the brewery, it soon foundered and was purchased at a rock-bottom price by an up-and-coming businessman named Jacob Schmidt, who eventually consolidated it into his large new brewery on West 7th Street. The old Kirchmeyer caves were then boarded up, and not long after that the brewery itself was demolished.

Michael Kirchmeyer never returned to St. Paul, not even for his parents' funerals. He was not heard of again until May of 1898, when a brief story appeared in the St. *Paul Pioneer Press*:

It has been learned that Michael Kirchmeyer, aged 30, formerly of St. Paul and the son of the late Johann Kirchmeyer, a well-known brewer in this city for many years, has died in the Klondike. Kirchmeyer was among seventy-three stampeders in search of gold who were buried by the great avalanche at Chilkoot Pass on April 3. His body in all likelihood will never be recovered, according to authorities on the scene.

Kirchmeyer will perhaps be best remembered in St. Paul as the victim of a kidnapping in 1892 in which his father was forced to pay a ransom of $10,000. Kirchmeyer was later found unharmed and the ransom was also recovered. No one has ever been arrested for the crime, believed to have been the work of railroad transients.

Thomas, who read the newspapers religiously, reported the news to Rafferty that morning as they prepared to open the saloon.

"Well, Wash, I guess it is the end then of the Kirchmeyer saga," Rafferty said. "Let us mark the occasion with due ceremony."

Beneath the bar, Rafferty—for reasons he could not readily explain—had saved a quart bottle of "Kirchy's" beer from the last batch made before the brewery shut down. He uncapped the bottle and poured out two glasses of the dark lager.

"A toast," he said, raising his glass, "to the brewer of a noble beer and to his wife and his son, all gone now. May the Kirchmeyers rest in peace, though I'm thinking that where Michael is goin' might be a tad hotter than the Yukon."

"Amen to that," Thomas said. "Amen to that."

LOOPHOLE

BY QUINTON SKINNER

Downtown (Minneapolis)

I should have known there was going to be trouble from the moment I discovered serious irregularities in Sam Vincent's books, but in my line of work "trouble" usually means nothing more than a procedural slap on the wrist or a threatening letter from the I.R.S. I've known of accountants who have gotten into difficulty for committing actual crimes, such as embezzlement. But for those of us who follow the letter of the law, the profession provides long, quiet, solitary hours. And that's precisely how I like it.

My ex-wife accused me of being "immune to passion." She may have had a point, but when she subsequently digressed about her fervid need for "a real man," it came to mind that she might have been missing the point about me. Maybe she always had. I possessed my share of passions, but they were quiet in nature: precision, detail, and the satisfaction of rows of numbers lined up and silently ringing with the celestial harmony of perfectly executed mathematics. And, besides, what exactly were these passions Barbara extolled from such heights of hauteur? Losing one's temper over nothing? Abandoning control in the name of "love" or "romance"? How about making constant, capricious, carping demands on one's spouse—now that was truly Barbara's passion.

It's not exactly that I prefer solitude but I can adjust to it easily. I arise, pour coffee out of my pre-programmed maker, eat a single low-carb breakfast bar (chocolate or zesty mango), then don the suit and tie I selected the previous night. I drive to my office in the Foshay Tower—not the trendiest Minneapolis address, but something about its humbleness in the face of its upstart high-rise rivals, like a quiet reserved type in the rough and tumble of a high school boy's locker room, has always appealed to me. I like to think that its old-fashioned charm gives clients a sense of permanence, decorum, and tact that keeps them returning to me (and referring their friends).

Sam Vincent was one such referral—he came to me by way of Lucas Huston, an executive who lived on Lake of the Isles and who had retained me as his primary accountant for the last seventeen years. Lucas isn't exactly a friend. He's never invited me to his house, for instance, for one of the glittering holiday fundraisers that I see written up in the *Star-Tribune* with clockwork regularity. But he often lingers in my office for a cup of coffee and sometimes a cigar, if I offer him one and its quality meets with his approval. It was during one such visit that Lucas informed me that I might be getting a call from an unusual prospective client.

"His name's Vincent," Lucas told me, squinting through a cloud of purplish smoke that he exhaled across my desk in my direction. "He's a building contractor. His company did some work on my house last summer, and he pestered me to find out who my accountant was until he got your name out of me."

I nodded in my usual friendly manner, wondering why Lucas might have been reluctant to recommend me to someone.

"See, this is the thing," Lucas went on. "The guy's

strange. Kind of a rough type. Makes a good living, I'm sure, but I didn't know if you wanted to be associated with someone like that. Feel free to turn him down. It wouldn't bother me at all."

I fretted all that night about whether or not Lucas was telling the truth, and whether my turning down his contractor would indeed be something to which he wouldn't take offense. In the process I rendered Sam Vincent, in my mind, into a slavering, drooling werewolf of a man, baying and clawing at my door with bone-sharpened claws.

Vincent showed up at my office the next day without calling ahead to make an appointment. He was no werewolf, but neither was he without certain fear-inspiring qualities. He was wearing a golf shirt, and its armbands strained against his considerable biceps. Under what I took to be a golf visor, his tanned face had frown lines where other people were wrinkled from smiling. His hair was so black that I figured he must have had it dyed. I wondered where vain rich men went to do such things—were there salons where intimidating building contractors were secretly buffed and pampered, their sun-damaged dermis lovingly tended to by smiling, silent young women?

"So can you do it?" he asked me.

"Beg pardon?" I said.

He shot me a look that implied people seldom dared drift off during his expositions. Somehow we had made it back to my office, where he was sitting in my chair, at my desk, and I was standing by my Twins 1987 World Series commemorative plaque.

"Nice plaque," he said, in a fashion that made it impossible to discern whether he was joking or not.

"I'm sorry, what were you saying?"

Vincent had some tax problems, nothing major, but he didn't care for his accountant and wanted someone to look over his tax returns from the last few years to see if he'd gotten a good break. He spoke of his accountant with the same disapproving regret one might reserve for a mouse that one had stepped on in one's apartment, a rodent that had run from under the sofa to an unfortunate end.

I examined Vincent's tax returns and saw that his accountant had indeed made a hash of them. There were all sorts of deductions missed and loopholes left unexploited. I got in touch with the I.R.S. on Sam's behalf, and within days he went from being a debtor to the government, to a man with a clean slate. Vincent was ecstatic, and the next day a case of single-malt scotch arrived at my office.

Two days later Vincent was back, partaking of the scotch that he had so generously bought for me and outlining the details of our grand future together. He had made a lot of money and invested wisely, he informed me, and henceforth I would manage his wealth and, in the process of seeing to it that he paid as little tax as possible, I would be the beneficiary of his well-known generosity and largesse. And if I ever needed a new room put on the side of my house, it was mine for the cost of the materials.

It is true that, for some time, I had entertained notions of a hardwood den with antique leaded-glass windows. I had plenty of space since Barbara left me, though I hadn't entirely given up on the idea that I might one day find another woman with whom I was compatible and who might one day share the home with me. There was, for instance, a secretary at my dentist's office who always brightened when I came to endure the latest installment of my painful and protracted gum work. She was quite a bit younger than me, but seemed to view me as likeable in a paternal sort of way.

I told Vincent I would do it. I wasn't wanting for work—my practice was doing very well—but I had to admit that dealing with Vincent brought a certain amount of excitement to my predictably stable professional life. He enjoyed telling me about his adventures, tales replete with withering impersonations of the "morons" and "assholes" he dealt with in the building trade. He told me about his girlfriends, and his wife, and his two sons who were evidently in a heated competition to see who could display the most appallingly antisocial qualities at the earliest age.

The honeymoon was short, but it was also enjoyable. Vincent sent me cigars, with which I impressed Lucas and other clients. His financial affairs were a tangle of handwritten receipts and slapdash spending, but I had seen worse. He liked to drop by, sometimes with motley offerings such as an Italian sub he'd picked up on the way from a building site. One time he brought me a brand new DVD player, still in the box. That seemed a little suspicious, but Vincent merely shrugged and smiled at me. We developed into a little comedy duo, with him exaggerating his roughness and his heedless rush through life, and me pretending to be a bit more scandalized than I really was. I knew Vincent viewed me as a fearful, drab creature constrained by convention and routine, but I didn't mind. It occurred to me more than once that Barbara would have thought he was quite grand, and that I would have gained in her estimation by his seeking out a sort of friendly relationship with me.

Then the trouble started. I initiated some routine cross-checking between his various accounts, and the numbers I produced were wildly divergent from the ones we had been supplying to the government. In addition, large sums of money were vanishing from Vincent's business funds into his personal accounts. A good deal of his income was disappearing without being reported.

Now, Vincent wasn't the first tax cheat in the history of the world, nor was he the originator of stealing from his own business. Yet both were crimes, and by their discovery I was implicated. I had never been a party to this sort of thing, nor did I plan to. I agonized for a couple of days, dodging Vincent's calls, until I hit upon what seemed the right course of action. I would not report him to the authorities, but I would no longer be his accountant. I called him at home to give him the news but immediately lost my nerve. Instead I asked him to meet me after working hours the next day at a bar downtown.

"What's the matter?" Vincent asked. "You don't sound right."

"I'm fine," I told him. "Just . . . a headache."

"Well, get some rest, kid," he said. "It's a good thing we're getting together tomorrow. I have something I want to talk to you about, and I'd prefer we didn't do it at your office."

I had suggested meeting at the Irish pub around the corner from WCCO because it was familiar to me. It was the kind of place where businesspeople had lunch, or stopped by for a drink before resuming their masquerade as loving family men. As soon as I stepped in, I instantly regretted the choice. People knew me there, or at least they used to. I hadn't gotten out much since I no longer had my wife to avoid, but the thought occurred to me that someone might see me with Vincent and associate me with some future crime he might commit.

But I was getting ahead of myself, wasn't I? I mean, he was a financial crook, but I had no reason to believe he was anything more nefarious. Money, after all, was just an aggregate of abstract sums to be played with and manipulated on computer screens and ledger sheets. It couldn't hurt, or kill.

He was different from the moment he sat down. He was wearing a suit, for one thing, a nice one, and he leveled me with a stare that immediately indicated his day had been far more arduous and treacherous than mine. He ordered two vodka tonics—one for each of us, it turned out—and sat a black leather briefcase on the table between us.

"Hard day?" I asked when the drinks came.

Instead of replying, Vincent lit up a cigarette. He blew out a big cloud of smoke and stared at me through it.

"You wanted to talk," he said.

"Yes." I paused. "Look, I'm sorry. I really am. It's just that you have to understand . . . I've come across certain discrepancies, certain things in your finances that make me very . . ."

"Uncomfortable?" he suggested sympathetically.

"Yes!" I said with relief. "Look, I have no intention of causing you any trouble. I've enjoyed working with you—"

He slid his chair closer to mine. "I hate to see you worried like this," he told me. "You're too serious."

"Well, that may be, but—"

"You don't want to be my accountant anymore."

And I experienced a tremendous, almost painful sense of regret. Sam, who understood me so well, had intuited the reason for our meeting. It was almost enough to make me take it all back, to go on as though nothing had happened.

"Okay," he said with a little smile. "That's fine. I don't want you to be uncomfortable."

"I'm really glad. I—"

"Forget it," he said, raising a hand to silence me. "Look, I want to tell you something. Come over here."

I obliged, moving my drink closer to his. I didn't even mind the cigarette smoke in my face.

"Look over there," he said. "Be discreet. But get a good look."

I glanced over to a table in the corner, where a man a few years younger than me was engrossed in conversation with a younger woman. They were both smiling, seemingly at ease in a fashion that admittedly filled me with a poison sting of jealousy. I looked back at Vincent, and took a long slug of my drink, then another.

"You think they're married?" he asked.

"I don't know," I told him.

"Believe me, they're not." Vincent smiled. "Not to each other, at least. You know what they're doing?"

I polished off my drink. Vincent seemed to approve. "What are they doing?" I asked.

"They're walking the line," he said. "A drink after work, they get home a little late. 'Honey, I got a call just as I was about to leave. Sorry about that.' Dinner, put the kids to bed, watch some TV, everything is fine. They walked the line, and they got away with it."

I was having a little trouble following what Vincent was saying. Another round of drinks had miraculously appeared. Though I usually stop at one, my mouth was dry, and soon I was nearly done with my second.

". . . matter of degrees," Vincent was saying. I felt hot, and a little nauseous. I undid my top button and loosened my tie.

"Go back," I said, surprised by how much my voice was slurring.

"All I'm saying is that we all have our little transgressions," Vincent added, nodding with self-satisfaction. "Big ones, little ones. Who cares? All that matters is getting away with it."

"But what about—" I started, in a voice not quite my own.

"You all right?" he asked me.

"I'm fine." But, in fact, that wasn't true. When I moved my head, it felt as though the contents of a swimming pool were sloshing around inside. I blinked, and saw that the lights of the bar had begun to undulate, fragment, and generally indulge in an orgy of visual insubordination.

"You don't look fine," Vincent said. "Maybe we better get out of here."

He helped me to my feet. I hadn't realized that I needed to be helped, but there it was. I teetered, wiped the sweat from my forehead, and nearly fell over. Through the fish-eye vantage of double vision I could detect that I was beginning to make a scene.

"No worries," Vincent said to out waitress, who had arrived with the bill and a look of concern that shifted to impatience when I nearly fell into her. "My friend here seems to have come down with something. I'm going to get him home."

We were in a car, Vincent's car. He was laughing and talking about one of his girlfriends. Rain seemed to be coming down on us, streaking and pooling on the window by my face, but I couldn't be sure. The town passed by, completely unfamiliar to me. I could have been in Kansas City; I could have been in Rome. I could barely see.

"You enjoying that little pill I slipped you?" Vincent asked me when we were stopped at a red light. "Boy, you made quite an impression back there. Don't think they'll be serving you drinks anytime soon."

For some reason this struck him as inordinately funny, and his laughter echoed in my ears as we drove on. I had the impression that we were someplace in the warehouse district when we stopped on a deserted side street. Sam came around, opened my car door, and helped me to my feet on the (wet?) pavement.

"You slipped me something at the bar," I managed to grunt.

"Smart boy," he said, one arm around me, half-carrying me to the doorway of a building.

"Don't want to," I slurred.

"Come on now," Sam insisted. "Be a good boy."

There were some stairs, fluorescent lights. No people. I could have done with some people.

I found myself on a sofa in a spare little office, with the lights of downtown sparkling like Christmas trees through the horizontal gaps in the blinds. I slouched back, my clothes soaked through with sweat, while Vincent was doing something at a near-empty desk.

The phone. He was talking on the phone. He pushed a pretentious pen set to one side as he opened the briefcase, still engaged in conversation, nodding, not smiling.

I entertained myself for a moment or two by trying to remember when last I had felt so out of control. I hadn't been much of a drinker in college, or anytime after. Maybe during one of the lengthy arguments Barbara and I had before our split, those eternal jousting matches that I always lost simply because Barbara would declare me the loser. I sat up a little straighter, my adrenaline burst of irritation serving to focus my senses at least a little.

Vincent hung up the phone. "Hey, look," he said.

He tilted the briefcase so I could see it. It was full of cash, neatly bundled.

"Forty grand," he said, giving me a lizard smile. "Big payout on that shopping complex I was telling you about. I wonder how much of it the I.R.S. is going to take when I declare it."

He froze, staring at me, waiting for my reaction. Then he burst out laughing.

"Problem is, I need to find a way to launder it squeaky clean. You know anything about that?"

I shook my head.

"I didn't think so." Vincent ran his fingers over the cash. "Too bad. I really liked working with you. I didn't think you were going to get cold feet on me."

I stood up and, with some measure of surprise, realized that I wasn't going to fall flat on my face. Vincent looked surprised too.

"Hey, pretty good," he said. He unbuttoned his suit and shoved his hands in his pockets. "I gave you enough to whack out a gorilla."

"Let me see," I said, or sort of said.

"See what?" Vincent asked.

"Money."

Vincent smiled. "Sure, kid, come on over."

I took a couple of unsteady steps. "Need help," I mumbled.

"Aw, Christ," Vincent exhaled. "Sure, why not? You know, there's someone coming over who I want you to meet."

"Someone?"

"Yeah, sure. Someone who's going to clear all this up for us."

Vincent helped me across the thin carpeting toward the

desk. My legs were heavy, and I heard him grunt with effort and finally place my hands on the edge of the desk.

"Like what you see?" he asked.

I stared at the money. It was in hundreds.

"All for you?" I rasped.

Vincent laughed again. "Know anyone else who needs some?"

I took a pen from the set next to the briefcase, turned, and, using all the strength I could muster, plunged it deep into the big artery rising from the right side of Vincent's neck. It was, frankly, amazing how deep it went.

His eyes opened with shock, a moment of rage, then something that I took to be a quick nod of respect, before Vincent fell to the floor and began the process of bleeding to death.

I wasn't particularly steady on my feet, but by holding the railing I was able to methodically get myself down to the lobby. I passed a man at the door who nodded when I held it open for him.

Outside I tucked the briefcase under my arm and made my way for the bright lights of downtown. Because, after all, business actually hadn't been going very well for me, and it was undeniable that it was time for a change. My friend Sam Vincent had just made one possible.

HI, I'M GOD

BY STEVE THAYER

Duluth (Up North)

The Tempest

All day long a Canadian cold front had been sweeping south
along the lake, bringing with it the first real storm of the win-
ter season. By the time the sun went down the temperature
was dropping at a rate of one degree a minute. Snow flurries
raced by sideways. Droplets of lake water shot by like bullets.
Waves thirty feet high crashed ashore, driven by winds up to
fifty miles per hour. These ungodly crests hit the Duluth Ship
Canal with a force so potent, so ferocious, that the earth
shook beneath the concrete.

The three high school boys standing at the foot of the
canal that hellish night had no way of knowing the
November gale was about to become another enchanting
piece of North Shore lore, a haunting story that would be
embellished and embossed and then served over beers at
waterfront bars for years to come. The boys themselves had
polished off a six-pack on their way down to the ship canal.
Sensing the storm, they had come to the lake to play the
game. But now, facing waves as tall as buildings, they were a
lot less enthusiastic than when they had started down the
steep hill.

"Have you ever seen them like this?"

"Never. My dad said in the old days they got this big, but
I never believed him."

"That is one angry lake."

"You guys talk like it's some kind of avenging spirit."

"It is."

"Bullshit . . . it's just friggin' water."

It was Pudge Abercrombie who muttered the bold remark. Pudge topped out at 5'7" in a pair of football spikes, and his weight often rolled past 170 pounds. He was a dark-haired, curly-haired, relatively handsome kid with something of a bulldog visage, which at an early age had earned him the nickname Pudge. And though he may have appeared short and pudgy, he was a good athlete. One of those bowling-ball type of runners. Built low to the ground. Hard to tackle, with good speed. Whether on a football field or a hockey rink, his stubby little legs had carried him fast and far. On the stormy night at the end of football season, those angry little legs of his had led him and his pals Jack Start and Tommy Robek down to the waterfront.

Along the canal where the giant ore ships came in, there was a long, wide walkway that speared its way into Lake Superior. The walkway was about the length of a football field. It ended at a lighthouse. On sunny summer days, crowds of people would line this walkway to watch the ocean-going vessels sail beneath the famous Aerial Lift Bridge and into Duluth Harbor. But at nighttime, the ship canal was a no-man's land. Shabby and neglected. Poor lighting. Once in a while, the Harbor Patrol would cruise Canal Park looking for prostitutes and drunken sailors, but for the most part the area was forgotten about until the sun came up.

The game the boys had come to play was as stupid as it was daring, and more than once in Duluth's long history the dares had proven deadly. The object of the game was simple: Sprint out the long walkway after a retreating wave, leap up the wide steps, tag the lighthouse, and then race back to shore before the next monster wave could wash over you. The concrete was wet, so the footing was treacherous. Debris washed over the walk. The strong northerly wind was right in your face. Worst of all, year round Lake Superior had only one temperature. Freezing. Paralysis could occur in seconds. Hypothermia took only minutes. If you timed it right, and you could run really fast, you could get back to the safety of the lift bridge without ever getting wet. But if your luck ran out—

These storms with the killer waves were at their deadliest in the early weeks of November. "My dad said, never challenge the lake."

Pudge Abercrombie smiled at his lifelong friend, the revolving beam from the lighthouse sweeping over his snow-soaked face. "But that's what makes the game so much fun, Jack. There is the real chance we could be killed."

Jack Start shook his head. "How many beers did you have?"

"Just two."

"Was she worth two?"

"You tell me."

Standing and shivering alongside Pudge Abercrombie and Jack Start that fateful night was Tommy Robek. Where Pudge and Jack had been the halfback and the quarterback, respectively, Tommy Robek didn't play sports. He was just the skinny kid from the neighborhood. The three boys had run together all their lives.

A malicious grin broke over Pudge's round red face. "Let's all go together. I mean, same time. One big wave."

Jack Start glanced out at a lake gone crazy. Glanced over at his friend. He shrugged his wide, athletic shoulders and smiled. Then he looked into the storm and quoted a line from one of their favorite movies, *Little Big Man*. "It is a good day to die."

They waited for a real live one, gambling that the wave that followed it, the wave that would be chasing them back to shore, would be the smaller of the two. They didn't have to wait long. A big black monster came crashing over the lighthouse like an invading army. Tons of freezing water splashed over the canal walls and raced up the walkway with a speed and rage the boys had never before seen. The angry lake water reached all the way to the tips of their toes. Washed over their ankles. Then suddenly the wave began its fast retreat. The two other boys echoed their quarterback's sentiments. "It is a good day to die." And the three boys were off and running.

They ran after the wave as fast as their young legs would carry them. Out onto the canal they ran. Out into the great lake. They hurled over the storm-strewn debris and struggled to keep their balance on the slippery concrete. They were screaming. They were laughing. They were so filled with adrenalin, youth, and beer, that all of the reasoning in the world could not have stopped them from challenging the lake. They were just seventeen, they were incredibly healthy, and their whole adult lives lay before them. And so what if they got a little wet.

Pudge Abercrombie reached the lighthouse steps first. Jack Start was right on his tail. The skinny kid brought up the rear. Pudge and Jack slapped the lighthouse wall, turned, and leapt back down the steps. That's when Jack Start slipped and fell. Pudge put on the brakes, barely keeping his balance. He turned and helped his friend to his feet. Now Tommy Robek tagged the lighthouse, jumped down the steps, and crashed into them. All three of them went rolling through the icy slosh. Their laughter was almost hysterical. They were having a real time of it because they knew it was going to be close. So now they were up and running. Running through the wind-driven sleet and snow. The Aerial Lift Bridge bathed in silver-blue spotlights looked like a giant goalpost, and they were about three-quarters home when the enraged lake caught up with them. It slapped them down onto the concrete and then buried them in freezing water.

The boys disappeared in an instant. All that could be seen was a ghostly wall of water washing down the canal. The giant ray of light from the lighthouse revealed nothing. Then, almost miraculously, all three boys toppled out of the storm, now separated by yards. They lay flat on their faces as the tail of the wave swept over them. When they lifted their heads, looks of pure fright graced their faces. The monster wave had stopped in mid-stream and now it began its determined return to the sea. The quarterback curled into a ball and steadied himself for the onslaught. Tommy Robek dove for a lamppost. He hugged it with all of his might. Pudge Abercrombie raced for another lamppost across the way, but he didn't make it. He went toppling down the walkway with the outbound water, somersaulting toward the lighthouse. When the wave was in full retreat, Jack and Tommy staggered down the walkway after him and retrieved their buddy Pudge just before he could be swept into the night. Now the three boys locked arms, the famous flying wedge, and they stumbled along the walkway as fast as their heavily sodden legs would carry them, trying to beat the next oncoming wave. At last, with only seconds to spare, they collapsed on their backs before the lift bridge. They were shivering. Coughing and swearing. Savage lake water swept under their heels.

After catching their collective breath, it was Jack Start who spoke first. "Well, that was the stupidest fucking thing I've ever done." He spit lake water from his lungs.

Pudge Abercrombie lay on his back staring up at a heaven teeming with rage. He was laughing, but it was a cold and bitter laugh. "Goddamn, that was the best." He fished a soggy pack of Marlboros from his jacket pocket and stuck a wet one between his lips. "In our entire lives we'll never again see waves like this."

So now, beneath the silvery-blue lights of the lift bridge, in the swampy black water left by Lake Superior, lay the three boys. They stared out at the long canal. They were wet and freezing. Beaten and exhausted. They had a buzz on from the beers. But they had challenged the great lake, and they had won.

It was the pugnacious Pudge Abercrombie whose voice finally cut through the icy storm. "I want to do it again."

Jack Start turned to him. The wind was in his face. "You're crazy."

"No, seriously. I want to go again. I feel unbeatable tonight."

"I wish I had felt unbeatable last night."

"I'm not thinking about that," Pudge yelled.

Jack Start had to scream to be heard over the storm. "Yes, you are. That's all you're thinking about . . . a football game, and a girl. There's more to life, Pudge."

Pudge Abercrombie got to his feet and began walking down the ship canal with the look of a man on a mission. A man obsessed. He turned to his friend, the limp cigarette dangling from his lips, the hellish lake framing his visage. "She wanted you to ask her out. She wanted to go to the dance with you. But you wouldn't ask her . . . because you're my best friend." The words *best friend* were dripping with sarcasm.

Jack sat up. "Who told you that?"

Pudge looked at Tommy Robek. Then Jack looked over at Tommy Robek. All the skinny kid could do was shrug his skinny shoulders.

"You're in love with her, aren't you, Jack?"

"We're all in love with her, Pudge. But you're the only one that's crazy in love with her. You scare her with your craziness."

"So ask her out, you dumb shit. Do you think a girl like that comes along more than once in a lifetime?" Pudge yelled the question into the storm. "Go ahead, ask her out . . . I'll get out of your way." He turned and started down the canal.

Jack Start climbed to his feet. "You're being stupid, Pudge. Come back here. It's not worth it . . . she's not worth it."

Tommy Robek worked his way to his feet. Wiped the sleet from his face. "You guys are just pissed because you lost a football game. Hell, it's not your fault. Coach Young was fuckin' drunk."

Pudge Abercrombie kept on walking, as if the lake were drawing him in. He threw his unlit cigarette to the side. "It is a good day to die!" they heard him shout.

Another monster wave broke over the lighthouse. It raced with a fury up the canal, drenching heart-broken Pudge up to his knees. It was only because Pudge was built so low to the ground that he was able to keep his balance. Then the wave began its violent return to the lake. And Pudge Abercrombie was off and running, chasing the black water. Sprinting toward the light.

The Wave

Pudge Abercrombie chased the retreating whitecaps down the ship canal, running faster than his stubby little legs had ever before carried him. The air temperature continued its assault on the freezing mark. The wind was howling mad. The big lake was black like ink. Crippling waves lashed at the mammoth rocks. But Pudge to the lighthouse was like a moth to the candle. He leapt up the wet concrete steps and tagged the monolith. Then he turned, jumped down the steps, and started for shore.

It is hard to say what was going through his mind that night, what made Pudge make that last run. Perhaps in high school the combination of losing the big game and then losing the girl is about as bad as it gets. Or just maybe Pudge Abercrombie was as crazy as everybody said he was. Either way, from the safety of shore, everything looked fine. Pudge was the fastest of them all. Though he was certainly being foolish, it appeared to his friends as if Pudge were going to once again beat the lake.

But then things began to happen. Strange things. Lights started going off and on all over town. Up and down the hills. The high winds and driving sleet were interrupting power. The Aerial Lift Bridge behind them seemed suddenly transformed into a giant strobe light. And that's when they saw it. Jack Start froze in horror. Tommy Robek, too, dropped his jaw, his eyes bulging from his head.

In every storm at sea there is one wave that dwarfs all others. The mother wave, if you will. The wave that sinks ships, and destroys homes along the shore. Suddenly and without warning, everything behind the sprinting Pudge went as black as black can get. From the sea to the sky, from the earth to the heavens, there was nothing behind the

Duluth teenager but the specter of utter blackness. It took a few seconds to register with the boys, but that blackness was a solid plain of water. It had shape and form. It seemed to possess life. And it was about to possess Pudge Abercrombie.

"Pudge, run!"

"Run, Pudge, run!"

He never looked over his shoulder, never broke stride, but the two boys could tell from the fear on his face that he was reading the terror in their eyes. Then Pudge Abercrombie, star halfback at Duluth High, was swallowed alive by Lake Superior.

The mother of all waves twisted young Pudge like a corkscrew. He was sent tumbling and spinning at the same time. Pudge washed up within ten yards of his friends, who were backpedaling for their lives. For a second, and it was only a second, it looked like he was safe, that he could stand and walk away. But then the wave from hell began its retreat, dragging Pudge Abercrombie with it. The sheer force of the raging water tore the lampposts out of the concrete. In fact, the whole scene seemed surreal, a desperate struggle for life played out in three-quarter speed. Pudge Abercrombie was being pulled into the lake by an unearthly force. It was clear that he was yelling, but his desperate cries for help could not be heard over the roar of the storm and the crashing of the waves. He went literally kicking and screaming. He fought the lake like a man afire, and it looked for an instant that he might be saved by the lighthouse. But it was not to be. The killer wave actually carried the boy up and over the light.

The last thing Jack Start ever saw of his friend Pudge Abercrombie was the boy's terrified face poking out the top of that wall of water. His mop of dark, curly hair was already frozen white. Icicles framed his jaw. His arms were stretched out to his side, like a bird in flight. Only Pudge was flying backwards, away from the lighthouse, away from life, back into the dark. Slowly disappearing into the raging abyss of black water.

Jack Start and Tommy Robek collapsed in shock, waiting for the next wave, hoping against hope that the big lake the Ojibwa called *Gitchee Gumee* would sweep their buddy Pudge back up the walkway and spit him out. But the next giant wave never came. On the contrary, there was a sudden cessation of the wind. Whitecaps washed over the lighthouse and the spray of icy water washed over the boys, but it was as if the great lake had gotten what it had come for, and now it was through.

As power was restored to the town, the two boys sat beneath the lift bridge staring into the blackness. They were freezing. Their wet clothes were stiff like boards. Their hair was frosty and hard. The revolving light of the lighthouse swept over their faces, revealing the tears that were spilling from their eyes. Superior, it is said, never gives up her dead when the gales of November blow early. Their friend, Pudge Abercrombie, was never seen again. Well, not on this earth, anyway.

25 Years Later

They were enjoying drinks at Grandma's Saloon the first time God showed his pudgy face. Grandma's was crowded that night, people streaming in from the Lakewalk. Every time the saloon door swung open, an end-of-summer breeze rushed in just in time to refresh the smoky joint. Jack Start and an old friend got lucky and found two empty stools directly beneath one of the television sets. Jack threw a copy of the *Duluth Newspaper* on the bar. He hung his walking cane on the rail and ordered two beers. The two men lit up cigarettes and caught the score of the Twins game.

Jack's drinking partner that warm summer night was Old Coach Young. As a much younger man, he had been the head football coach at Duluth High. The last football coach the school had. The kids had loved him, sober or drunk. But the old high school had been closed in the economic downturn of the 1970s. The big red-brick building halfway up the hill was still standing, but it stood empty. Lifeless. Nobody wanted it torn down, but nobody knew what to do with it. Nobody had known what to do with the football coach, either. With shrinking enrollments and closing schools, there were few teaching positions available on the Iron Range. For years the man simply drifted from shit job to shit job, until one day Coach Young became Old Coach Young. He was on disability now, and enough of his former players were still around town to loan him a dollar or two, or to buy him a beer. Besides, the coach knew everybody in town. On both sides of the law. For reporter Jack Start, new again in his old hometown, his high school football coach was a great source.

The television set flickering above them was tuned to KDUL-TV. Home of the Minnesota Twins. "Get this, Coach," said Jack Start, hoisting his first beer in twenty-four hours, "that cheerleader I interviewed, Miss Grand Tetons . . . she has an identical twin."

"Whoa! Do you mean to say there's four of those puppies?"

Jack Start spit laughter across the bar. Wiped his mouth. "I said identical."

The Twins were playing the Red Sox. The sound of the announcers could barely be heard above the buzz of the bar.

"I remember their mother was a real looker," the old

coach said in his deep, gravel voice. His gray-white hair was combed straight back, revealing the severe redness of his face. He carried the thick arms of an ex-athlete, and the overlapping belly of a lush. "A real looker," he repeated.

Jack Start nodded his head in agreement. "You know, I always wondered back then if you guys really looked . . . I mean, you teachers."

The coach laughed. "Kid, there was a lot more than looking going on back then."

"Really? Someday you and I are going to have to have a long, long talk, Coach."

It was a little past 9 p.m. They were waiting for the baseball game to end so that the local news could begin. It was the top of the sixth inning. The Twins were down one run to the Red Sox. Jack Start and his old coach ordered two more beers. And that's when it happened. It wasn't fast or flashy, it was just alien. Unexpected.

With a Red Sox batter at the plate, the TV signal went fuzzy. Then it faded away. Nothing but snow and static. When the picture cleared again, some guy was sitting at a desk talking into the camera. It looked like public-access cable, or like a cheap video taped in an old house. The strange man smiled, a truly engaging smile, and said, "Hi, I'm God." The man paused for effect. Then he held up a tacky little nameplate that read: I'M GOD. He added, "Don't worry about the game. There won't be any more scoring again until the pitching change in the eighth inning."

He was a fairly handsome man, in a slovenly sort of way. A heavyset guy who had a round, happy face, with thin brown hair on a receding hairline. There was something mischievous in his smile, but nothing malicious. A benign comedian. He was wearing a blue work shirt. The kind of guy who would fit right in at Grandma's Saloon. The messy desk he was seated behind looked as if it were located in a spare bedroom, or maybe a room in the basement. The background was cheap wood paneling, the kind installed to hide the holes in the wall. An old Hamm's Beer sign could be seen over his shoulder. In other words, it could have been in any one of a thousand homes in Duluth. In fact, the whole scene was no frills, no airs, North Shore Minnesota.

"This is the first of what will be seven appearances," the man who claimed to be God said into the camera. *"It is a new millennium."* Then he cracked up. *"Millennium . . . God, I love that word."* He caught his breath. *"So anyhow, the time has come to review where you are at as a people, and where you are going. And, quite frankly, if at the end of our little chats I don't like what I see, I'll probably flood the whole damn planet, starting with Duluth."* He began laughing. *"No, seriously, that was a joke."*

Jack Start and Old Coach Young were staring intently at the television screen, the image of God filtering through the haze of cigarette smoke. A hush fell over their corner of the bar as the bartender and the patrons surrounding them strained to hear the message, apparently being delivered from heaven.

God opened a desk drawer, pulled out a pack of Marlboro in the box, stuck a cigarette in his mouth, and lit up. He blew a long puff of smoke at the camera. He coughed, a nasty smoker's cough, and then cleared his throat. *"I think it's fair to say that you people eat too much, you drink too much, and you watch too much television. And you better cut it out."* He extinguished his mostly un-smoked cigarette in a dime store ashtray. *"Oh yeah, and on that religious thing . . . the Jews are the only ones that got it right."* He started laughing again, an infectious laugh if ever there was one. *"Again with the jokes."* He stuck up his hand and waved to the camera. *"Anyway, I'll be seeing you."*

The picture faded to snow and static. Then a Red Sox batter could be seen flying out to deep center field. The Twins had apparently retired the side. One, two, three.

Jack Start took a long swig and then dropped his empty beer mug on the bar. He wiped the froth from his lips. Stared up at the baseball game. "What just happened here?"

Old Coach Young shrugged his shoulders. "Some guy interrupted the Twins game and said he was God." He dwelled on the idea as he sipped his beer. "I'll bet it was one of those Volkswagen commercials."

"Where was the Volkswagen?"

"They never show it at first. It's a high-concept ad."

"Oh, please," begged Jack Start. "Did he look familiar to you?"

"Who?"

"The guy who played God."

"I think he might have been on a TV series. I know I've seen him before."

Jack Start was having a flashback. "He made me think of Pudge Abercrombie . . . I mean, you know, what Pudge might have looked like had he lived."

Old Coach Young smiled, a rueful smile. "Ole Pudge . . . I haven't thought about that kid in years."

"For years I couldn't *stop* thinking about him."

"That's right, you were on the ship canal that night, weren't you?"

Jack Start was suddenly drowning in his watery memories. A year earlier he had been diagnosed with multiple sclerosis. He had lost two wives to divorce, and two jobs to alcohol, but nothing haunted him more than watching his boyhood friend wash out to sea. "Yeah, I was on the canal."

"Who else was there?"

"Tommy Robek."

"The skinny kid. What ever happened to him?"

"He was killed in Vietnam."

The coach shook his head. "That fuckin' war." He sucked on his cigarette. "So you're the only one left alive?"

"Yup, I'm the only one left alive. I should have given the damn ball to Pudge."

"Say what?"

"Nothing."

The two men went back to their beer and their baseball, as did the rest of the bar. But a strange feeling had descended over the room. Something of a pall. There seemed to be more thinking going on than talking.

"Are you going to the reunion?" the coach finally asked.

"I didn't go to the ten. I didn't go to the twenty. Why the hell would I go to the twenty-five?"

"Because she's going to be there."

Jack Start felt his heart stop. After being fired from the only two newspapers in the Twin Cities, and then being diagnosed with MS, he'd had an overwhelming desire to return home. Somewhat of a calling. "How do you know?"

"She's divorced from the governor, for Christ's sake. It's all over town. She's driving up from St. Paul," the coach went on. "I think she has one son."

The veteran reporter exhaled into his beer. "Yeah, that's what I need in my life right now . . . a forty-three-year-old ex-cheerleader with the governor's kid."

"Maybe that *is* what you need."

"I don't think so, Coach. I've got plans."

The old coach rolled his bloodshot eyes. Snickered in his beer. He looked up at the television set, still a touch of the teacher in his voice. "Do you know how to make God laugh?" he asked. He answered his own question. "Tell him your plans."

Jack Start, too, looked up at the television set. He could see his reflection staring back. He raised his empty mug of beer in salute. "Here's to God and all his lovely plans."

The Red Sox made a pitching change in the eighth inning. Then the Twins scored two more runs to win the game. The next morning, in a box above the fold, the following article appeared on the front page of the *Duluth Newspaper*:

WAS GOD ON TV?

In a blatant violation of federal law, a man hijacked the KDUL television signal of the Minnesota Twins game last night and claimed he was God. The man, a white male, approximately forty to fifty years of age, with thin brown hair, took over the signal from 9:10 p.m. to 9:13. His height could not be determined, but he appeared to weigh over 200 pounds. He was wearing a blue jean shirt with a small red Levi's label visible on the right pocket. About halfway through his talk he lit up a Marlboro cigarette. What was most peculiar about the unauthorized television event was that the man made no attempt to disguise himself . . .

The Investigation
In the next three weeks God in a blue shirt interrupted two Twins game and the Viking's home opener. All on KDUL-TV. *"Hi, I'm God."* He held up his little nameplate: *I'M GOD. "Relax, the Vikings tie it up in the fourth quarter . . . but I won't*

tell you how it ends." Sports fans cried foul. Church groups cried blasphemy. In one of the broadcasts he asked, *"Where in God's name are you people getting these Presidents from?"* The FCC was not amused. FBI agents were dispatched from St. Paul. A media frenzy followed. The federal task force investigating the case set up operation on the top floor of a downtown office building, with a spectacular view of the lake.

In the reception area, Jack Start stared out the window at the harbor. The sky over the water was still a rich summer blue, but summer was over. The leaves had begun to change and more often than not the morning breeze was out of the north.

"Mr. Start, Inspector Whitehurst will see you now."

Jack Start took a seat in front of Inspector Whitehurst's desk. He placed his walking cane across his lap. Special Agents Black and Flannery stood behind him, guarding the door, but the two never spoke.

The inspector remained standing, shuffling files on his desk before finally breaking the tension. "Thank you for coming in, Mr. Start." He held up a pack of cigarettes. Marlboro in a box. "Smoke?"

"No thanks," said Jack. "I quit."

"Recently, I'm guessing. Maybe about the time God showed up on television?"

"So this is about God?"

"No, Mr. Start, he's all too human. And he's in a lot of trouble. So is anybody who is helping him. Hijacking a television signal is a serious crime. It hasn't been done successfully in over twenty years . . . and that was just a few seconds on a cable channel. This clown is hijacking signals from a network affiliate . . . and he seems to be doing it at will. Now, he'd have to have an uplink—"

Jack Start couldn't help but laugh.

Inspector Whitehurst glared down at him. The FBI man was a big man, and an older man, with thin, dark hair combed straight back. He may have been sent up from St. Paul, but the trace of a New York accent still punctuated his lawyerly speech. "Is something funny, Mr. Start?"

The Duluth reporter tried to wipe the smile from his face. "I'm sorry, it was just the thought of God needing an uplink."

The inspector picked up a file from his desk. Opened it and read, "*Lawrence Alden Abercrombie. Also known as Pudge Abercrombie. Do you know him?*"

"He's dead."

"Actually, his body was never found. He was classified as missing."

"And seven years later he was declared dead."

"Then why are you running around town telling people the part of God is being played by Pudge Abercrombie?"

Jack Start explained, carefully enunciating each and every word: "What I've said is, he looks like what Pudge might have looked like had Pudge lived."

The FBI inspector held up a sketch. A computerized sketch. "Our people in Washington put Abercrombie's high school yearbook picture on their computers and did an age-imaging analysis . . . what he would look like today. We know that Abercrombie is God."

"You believe what you want to believe, inspector. Pudge has been dead for years. I saw him die."

"That's right, you were his best friend, weren't you?"

"Yes."

"What would you say if I told you we traced Abercrombie to a house in Minneapolis, where he'd been living for the past twenty years? Not far from your old place."

"With all due respect, inspector, I'd say you're full of shit."

"Did you two cook this up while you were living down there in Minneapolis?"

"No."

"So it's a coincidence that Abercrombie shows up on television just weeks before his high school's twenty-five year reunion?"

"I don't know who that is on television, and neither do you."

"Did Abercrombie have a girlfriend in high school?"

"No."

"Did you?"

Jack Start thought about it. "No."

"Are you going to attend this reunion?"

"I hadn't planned on it, no."

"Why not?"

The old high school quarterback didn't answer the question. He stared out the window at Lake Superior. Seemed the great lake was the one constant in his life.

The inspector lifted a transcript from the file. "When God signed off last night, he went off the air singing a World War Two hit." Now the FBI man began singing, his fingers setting the tempo. "'I'll be seeing you in all the old familiar places . . . that this heart of mine embraces . . . all day through . . .' Did Abercrombie like that kind of music?"

Jack Start sat listening to the inspector warble, more amazed than amused. He scratched his head. "Actually, Pudge was more into the Beatles." Suddenly, he put his finger to his lips, as if something had just occurred to him. "There was one thing . . ."

"What?"

"Pudge liked the Partridge Family. I always thought that was spooky."

The FBI inspector was losing his patience. "Was there anything else . . . back in high school?"

Jack gave the question serious consideration. "Once, during our junior year, somebody commandeered the intercom system. Nobody was ever caught, but Pudge was the main suspect. It was pretty harmless stuff. He came on at 1 o'clock and dismissed school for the day. Before the vice-principal got back on the microphone, we were all heading down the hill into town."

Inspector Whitehurst dropped into his chair, seemingly exasperated. "We're going to find him . . . and we'd be surprised if you're not in cahoots with him."

"Well, that would surprise me."

"C'mon, Jack . . . a drunken, washed up newspaperman with a degenerative disease suddenly finds himself with the big scoop. An exclusive interview with God. You'd be back in the game, wouldn't you?"

Jack had to chuckle, more to himself than the FBI man. "You're not really from Minnesota, are you?"

The inspector smiled, an evil little smile. "Let's talk about that night on the canal . . . the night he disappeared. Do you think he was suicidal?"

Jack Start took a moment before answering. He was startled, as if some revelation had just come to him. For the first time in years a twinkle appeared in his eyes. "You know, maybe that's how he gets back and forth."

"Who?"

"God. He comes down here to live for a while, and then to get back, he stages some spectacular accident."

"So now you're saying you went to high school with God?"

Jack Start, one-time star quarterback for Duluth High, raised an eyebrow in delight. "Wow!" he exclaimed. "I never thought of it like that before. And we were in the same back-field."

The Reunion
Under the suspicion that God might be there, so many people signed up to attend the twenty-five-year reunion that it was moved from a private room at Grandma's Saloon to the ballroom at the Convention Center, overlooking Canal Park. By the time the reunion was in full swing, non-class members outnumbered the real class members by ten to one. FBI agents were planted at the entrance and the exits. Satellite trucks ringed the parking lot. Reporters were interviewing anybody they could find.

Old Coach Young was popular. "Pudge was a great ath-lete," he said into a battery of microphones. "But he lacked discipline. Do you know what I mean?"

"Are you saying God was lazy?"

"No, no. I'm saying the God I knew was something of a screw-off."

Television sets were scattered around the ballroom in case God made his seventh appearance over the airwaves. Only the night before, in his sixth appearance, God had entertained the Iron Range by popping a beer and choking on a pretzel.

"*Hi, I'm God,*" he said, coughing up the gooey mess and spitting it into a paper towel. He held up his nameplate: *I'M GOD.* "*I have some really bad news for you people. I've thought about it, and I've thought about it . . . and I'm moving to Wisconsin.*" His belly laughs filled the television screen. "*You know I'm joking you. If it's the end of the world . . . I'll let you* know." He held out his hands, as if baffled. *"And what is with all you people falling in love with the wrong person? Open your eyes, for God's sake."*

The reunion continued. A local band was playing Beatles songs. Badly. More and more drinks were poured. The room grew increasingly louder. And hotter.

"Get you a beer, Jack?"

"No thanks, I'll stick with the ginger ale."

"Ginger ale. What's wrong with him, Coach?"

Old Coach Young raised his hands in surrender. "I can't figure it out. He quit smoking, he's not drinking. I swear the devil has gotten ahold of him."

There was another round of laughter as Jack Start made his way through the crowd. He was actually enjoying himself. In fact, it was almost overwhelming. He set his ginger ale down on a table and walked to the end of the ballroom, where the bay windows over the lake were twenty feet high. Glass from the floor to the ceiling. The old high school quarterback stood there alone looking down at Canal Park. Beyond that was the utter blackness of Lake Superior.

"That's quite a view. I miss it."

He turned when she said that. Turned too fast and almost lost his balance. She met his eyes with a smile, and twenty-five years melted away in an instant.

"Hello, Jack," she added.

He smiled, a genuine smile he hadn't felt in years. "Hello, Mary." She was taller than he remembered. Her hair was longer and a bit lighter. And those eyes, the eyes that had crushed little boys' hearts, were still as bright as any star that hung over the North Shore. In short, she was even more strikingly beautiful than he'd tried to forget.

She gave him a hug, and he embraced her in an awkward

manner, not knowing what to do with his cane. When he'd steadied himself, he said, "You're supposed to be dumpy and all wrinkled up."

"They told me you weren't coming."

"I wasn't, but then . . ."

"Then what?"

"I don't know. Might have been something I saw on television."

She glanced at his cane. "Can you walk?"

"Oh, yeah. The cane is mostly for insurance. It's my left leg," he explained, a touch too excited. "Sometimes it just goes to sleep, and then I fall down. It's kind of embarrassing to be falling down at my age."

"I meant . . . would you like to go for a walk?"

The sea breeze in his face felt good. The woman beside him felt heaven sent. Jack Start stared at the long walkway leading out to the lighthouse. Where Canal Park had once been the purlieu of prostitutes and sailors, a multimillion-dollar renaissance had brought restaurants, shops, and hotels, not to mention a million tourists every summer. But on this night the park was quiet. In fact, the great lake itself was as calm as he'd ever seen it. The waves were small, and they lapped against the shore in perfect harmony. It was early October now. There remained only two weeks of decent weather. Then the cold would set in. And the storms would follow.

Jack Start found himself doing something he thought he would never ever do. Never in a lifetime. "I've walked past it," he said. "I've stared down at it. But I haven't set foot on this walkway in twenty-five years."

"How does it feel?"

"With you, it feels good."

"Should we walk out to the lighthouse?"

It was a remarkably clear night. Every now and then the revolving beam of light sailed over their heads. Jack and Mary stopped halfway down the walkway. The shadow of a man could be discerned standing at the top of the stairs, at the foot of the lighthouse. They wanted to be alone. So they stood where they were and stared at the galaxy of lights that ran up and down the steep hills. Illuminated hills that rolled up and away from the lake. And at the foot of those hills, throwing an eerie, translucent glow, were the klieg lights from the television crews that surrounded the Convention Center.

With his back to the lake, Jack Start shook his head in amazement. "What a circus," he said. "You know, excuse the pun, but he really hasn't said a goddamn thing."

"It's those three little words that are driving people crazy."

Jack had to laugh. *"Hi, I'm God."*

She laughed too, but it was a laugh tinged with regret. "Do you think he's out there somewhere?"

"Who, Pudge?"

"No . . . God?"

The cynical reporter turned back to the lake. "Me and him have had our differences over the years. I can't really answer that one."

She joined him at the wall, staring out at the endless water. "Well then, how about Pudge?"

"You know, Mary, I've thought about it, and I've thought about it, and it certainly sounds like something Pudge would do."

"Do you remember when he took over the intercom system?"

"Remember? Hell, I told the FBI about it."

"But, Jack, would he really hide out for twenty-five years?"

Jack Start shook his head in wonder. "Had to be one hell of a broken heart."

She thought about that. "He really did love me, didn't he?"

"Oh yeah. He was crazy in love with you."

It is said that a friend is someone you can stand in silence with and not be embarrassed by the silence. The two high school friends stood shoulder-to-shoulder facing the great lake—gazing far out into the past, where the water meets the stars. The only sound was the wind whistling over the shore, and the waves washing over the rocks. Time drifted by. At last she took a deep breath and sighed. "Well, I suppose."

He looked over at her and smiled. "Yeah, I suppose."

She slipped her arm through his and they walked away from the lighthouse, back up the hill toward their reunion.

God never showed his face again. Never made a seventh appearance. The FCC stiffened the fines for anybody interfering with the airwaves. And Congress passed a bill approving longer prison sentences for any person caught hijacking a television signal. But nobody was ever arrested. The case remains open.

EMINENT DOMAIN

BY JUDITH GUEST

Edina (Minneapolis)

Eminent Domain: In law, the right of a government to take or authorize the taking of private property for public use, just compensation being given to the owner.

—Webster's New World Dictionary

T hey were to meet at Beaujo's on France. Kendra wore dark glasses and a black silk scarf tied over her red hair, even though she was certain no one would recognize her; she seldom frequented these chic, upscale wine bars sprouting up like wild mushrooms in her neighborhood. One of them even bore the name Wild Mushroom.

She sat at the L-shaped bar, trying not to fidget or look like she was on the prowl. Even though she was. It's just an experiment. Research. Investigating the possibilities.

She glanced around the room: no curtains on the windows and no rugs on the floor made it a bit noisy, but for her this was perfect. They wouldn't be overheard; that was essential. And the lighting was dim, so that no one could say for sure that it was the famous Kendra Schilling they saw that night, dressed all in black, black high heels hooked over the rung of the bar stool.

No, not dim; that wasn't precise. She prided herself on the accuracy of her descriptions. She was a writer, after all. Soft, murky lighting. Yes, that was better. Making everyone look a little more chic, a little less desperate. Were they desperate? She wasn't sure. She only knew that she was. She tapped one perfectly manicured nail against the rim of her wine glass containing Trentadue Petite Syrah . . . inky, big, and powerful with intense blackberry syrup and ripe plums, leather-like aroma. She had ordered it purely for the fancy lingo.

Glancing at her watch she took in the cast of characters, wondering if she might have overlooked her fellow assignee. Was that the right word? Perhaps accomplice would be more accurate. For surely that's what they were: accomplices. Partners in crime. For a moment she thought of quitting while she was still ahead. She'd wrestled with her conscience all day, balancing need against self-respect. No, she'd come this far; she wouldn't wimp out now.

I'm tall, he had told her over the telephone. *Blond hair and brown eyes. I'll be wearing a brown leather jacket with a red carnation in the buttonhole.* Nobody in the bar fit that description. But she knew he'd come. It was still early; the salesclerks from Chico's and Anthropologie had already quaffed their beers and left; the après-movie set had yet to arrive.

At the end of the bar sat a pale girl wearing a paisley dress two sizes too small for her. She was hunched over a plate of fried calamari. Hunching and munching. Could be a useful phrase in the short story she was working on. In fact, she might just lift the whole scene, excising the rather plain-looking old man sipping a glass of oily clear liquid (Absinthe? No, that was illegal, wasn't it?) and reading the *Edina Sun.*

"This seat taken?" a voice asked at her elbow.

Tall. Blond. And yes, the red carnation in the buttonhole. "It is now," she said, taking the hand extended toward her.

"I'm Hiram."

"You're younger than I expected."

"Did you specify an age?" His smile was friendly, curious. "Because you could have. Not that it makes any difference. We all do pretty much the same thing."

"Do you?" She looked him up and down thoroughly. "How many of you are there?"

"Lots." He slid onto the bar stool. "More every day." The bartender glanced down the length of the bar, and Hiram raised one finger. "Wine cooler, please."

Uh oh. What kind of yahoo was this? She half-expected the bartender to laugh in his face, but he brought out a bottle of Bartles & Jaymes and set it in front of Hiram.

"I'm not much of a drinker," Hiram apologized, and glanced at her nearly empty glass. "Another for you?"

She shook her head. He was a handsome young man, not that this was any requirement. In fact, it couldn't matter less to her what he looked like. That thought made her shiver slightly.

"Something wrong?"

"I'm just not sure exactly what I'm doing here," she said.

"Not nervous, are you?" He looked her straight in the eye. "Don't be. We're just talking. Nothing's written in stone."

But she felt herself blush to the roots of her hair. Was she going to be able to go through with this, after all?

"I wouldn't trust you if you weren't feeling just a tad apprehensive," Hiram said encouragingly.

And you're just a tad too glib, she thought. Suddenly it seemed important to knock him down a peg. "A better question," she said, "would be whether or not I can trust you."

He smiled, not in the least offended. "We do have a reputation to maintain. If a client doesn't feel at ease, it'll be a no-go from the get-go—"

"Stop sounding like Chili Palmer. I already feel like I'm in an Elmore Leonard novel."

"Just trying to loosen you up a bit. Gain your confidence. Think a minute—how did you hear about us?"

She hesitated. "From a friend."

"Exactly. I'm betting it was one of our satisfied customers." He took out a small green notebook, gave her a grin. "We don't have any unsatisfied ones."

"Who are they?" she asked. "Your customers. In general, I mean."

"In general?" He shrugged. "Ordinary people. Angry housewives. A shadow baby or two. Sometimes it's just . . . what a woman must do."

"So it's mostly women."

"Oh, no. A lot of men hire us too. Let's just say your needs are not unique."

"That's how you look at it then? You're supplying a need?"

"Absolutely," he said. "I assume you've read our brochure?"

She nodded.

"And was there anything that particularly caught your eye?"

"Would it make a difference?" she asked. "In terms of cost?"

"Most definitely. It's a bit like ordering pizza—the more toppings, i.e., the more exotica, the more expense." He clicked the point of his Cross pen—a cheerful gesture designed to put her at her ease. But it didn't. She'd been lying to herself, she suddenly realized. Pretending to explore her options. She had no options. She was in this for keeps. She gave a long sigh.

"If anyone were to find out—"

"No one will," he assured her. "Anonymity is our motto. And it works both ways. For instance, I'm just the one who signs you up. I won't be providing the services."

She laughed in spite of herself. "Too bad. I was just beginning to like you, Hiram."

Again he grinned. "That's my job. Do you have any questions? Any preferences?"

"Yes." She almost whispered it. "I want to know what happens to . . . the leftovers."

"The remains? Not to worry. We take care of all that. It goes to a place where the sea remembers. A rainy lake. And there's no telling. After all—the body is water, you know . . ." He paused and gave her a quizzical look. "Would you mind if I asked you a question? For our private files? How much did they take you for?"

"Twenty thousand," she said gloomily.

He whistled. "The price keeps going up."

"At first they said it would be $688. But when they found out I wasn't just another crook like them—that I was the real Kendra Schilling trying to buy back my own domain name— they jacked the price up."

"Highway robbery," Hiram said.

Kendra took the last swallow of her Syrah. "You know, I never thought it would come to this. When my lawyer said there was nothing I could do—"

"Nothing legal, that is." Hiram smiled. "People don't usually find out about this scam until they decide to get a website. And suddenly you discover that someone has bought your name, and for a tidy little piece of your income they'll be only too happy to sell it back to you."

"The worst part is how darned chipper they are about it," Kendra said. *"Hey, congratulations, you lucky thing, now you own your own name again!"*

"Kind of sticks in your craw, doesn't it?"

"Like having a bee in my bonnet."

"They're jackals," he said. "Hanging's too good for them."

"They prey upon a person's ignorance and lack of computer savvy."

"You're savvy-less," Hiram said. "But not helpless. Not anymore. Not when you've got us. We're Assassins Anonymous. The score-settlers." He leaned back on his stool. "So have you picked out a weapon? We have some premium choices—the 9mm Glock, the Mercedes-Benz, the magic whip . . ."

She waved them away. "Nothing that smacks of luxury."

"Right. Sets the wrong tone. Something cruder. Baseball bat. Clothesline. Hair dryer in the tub—"

She covered her ears.

"Or you can simply leave it to us. Some prefer the hands-on approach. Others only want to be informed after the fact. Are there any modes of elimination that especially interest you?"

"Yes," she said carefully, "I like cruel and unusual."

He entered this in his green notebook. "Multiple woundings? Dismemberment? Recitation of suitable Bible verses . . . ?"

"You mean like in *Pulp Fiction?*" she asked. "That was effective, wasn't it? Samuel L. Jackson played that to the hilt. Yes, I think a Bible verse might be appropriate. Do I need to come up with it myself?"

"Not at all," Hiram said. "We have a number of them in stock. *You are of your father, the devil* . . . John, Chapter viii,

Verse 44. Or, *It biteth like a serpent and stingeth like an adder* . . . Proverbs, Chapter xxiii, Verse 32. Another favorite is *Sweet is revenge—especially to women*. Lord Byron. From *Don Juan*."

"Could I get back to you on this?" Kendra asked. "I think I may want to compose something."

"Very good." He made a note.

"Now, about payment—" Kendra said.

His turn to wave. "Someone else handles all that. You'll be contacted on completion of the contract. We're flexible. If you like, you can spread the payments over a number of months."

"I was more concerned about how to get the money to you," Kendra said. "I don't want to write a check."

"Nor would we want to cash one," he agreed. "No—unmarked bills in a number 10 envelope works best for us. After the damage is controlled."

"And the score is settled. I guess you're the Venus flytrap of the cyber world these days."

He nodded. "The cat's pajamas."

"The tiger rising."

"The strangler fig."

Kendra laughed. "You're a trickling tributary of truisms tonight, Hiram."

"A churning channel of chestnuts," he said cheerfully. And before she could top him, he got up from the stool, dropping a twenty onto the bar. "A pleasure doing business with you, Kendra." And with that he was gone. Kendra, too, rose from her stool. She felt like a million bucks. Life was good. People would get their just desserts. She picked up the red carnation—proof of purchase—and tucked it into her purse. Come to think of it, there were several messy situations in her life that could stand some cleaning up. Hiram, she thought. Hire'em she would. Hang the cost; it would be worth every penny.

BLASTED

BY MARY LOGUE

Kenwood (Minneapolis)

W hen were you the most scared in your whole life?"

Claire Watkins looked over at her gangly teen-aged daughter Meg, who was somehow managing to slouch while still wearing her seat belt. Nice to have her darling self-involved daughter ask her a question.

Claire was driving them up to the big city. The Mississippi River flowed in the opposite direction as they passed along it going to the Twin Cities. Specifically they were headed to Minneapolis to go shoe shopping, a big treat for both of them. School was starting soon.

"The most scared?" Claire stalled. She didn't need to think about it. There was no contest. One moment in her long career in law enforcement stood out in her mind.

"Yeah, you know, heart-zapping, teeth-chattering fear. You know, the whole ball of wax?"

"The whole ball of wax? Jeez, you sound like Rich."

"Whatever, Mom, you know—petrified?"

Claire had never told Meg about this event in her life, had always thought that she would save it for when she was older. But Meg was going to be fifteen in a few months; maybe she was old enough to hear it.

"There was one time when I was pretty petrified."

"Tell me, tell me." Meg pulled herself up straighter.

"Are you sure?"

"Come on, tell me. We have an hour before we get to DSW," Meg said, referring to her favorite shoe store.

"Well, this was a long time ago. I was still new at the job, working in Minneapolis. Not quite a rookie, maybe I had been a cop for a few years. I answered a call. A domestic. It's the worst call a cop can get."

"Why?"

"Well, because people are usually killed by those that love them. Passion gets out of hand very fast."

"Go on."

"I remember it was very late at night. Technically, early morning. Three-thirty, as I recall."

"What was your shift?"

"I was working the midnight-to-8 shift. Brutal. I don't know how I could have done that. I certainly couldn't do it anymore. Good thing we moved down to Fort St. Antoine."

Claire saw they were catching up to a northbound train near Diamond Bluff. She loved this drive up along the river. She had driven it so many times, it demanded nothing of her. She could watch the scenery and talk to her daughter.

When Meg nudged her, she continued her story: "The wife had called in, the dispatcher told me—she sounded drunk, he said. She claimed her husband was threatening to kill her."

"That sounds bad."

"Yeah, and I was on my own, which was unusual. My partner had gotten sick in the middle of the shift and I had dropped him off at home. I was heading back to the squad room to do some paperwork when I got the call. My mistake was I took it.

"The first surprise was the address the dispatcher gave

me. It was in Kenwood, an older, very nice neighborhood in Minneapolis. I drove up to the house and wanted to move in. It was probably built in the '20s and had leaded windows, a tiled roof, even a turret. I remember walking up to the house and lusting after it."

"Then what?"

"Well, the lights were on in the house. I mean they were all on. When I rang the doorbell, a blond-haired woman came to the door. I guessed she was in her late thirties. She asked what I wanted."

"You mean she wasn't the one who called?"

"She hadn't remembered she'd called. She was sloshed. I think she had a drink in her hand as she was talking to me, but getting drunk in your own home wasn't any kind of offense. I asked her if I could come in and just see if everything was all right. At first, I didn't think she would let me, then her husband yelled from the other room and she stepped aside.

"As soon as I was in, I could see that a battle had been going on. Dishes broken on the kitchen floor. A mirror shattered over the fireplace. But this elegant older guy stood as I entered the living room and asked what seemed to be the problem."

"Was he drunk too?"

"Yes, but he held it very well. One of those drunks that pronounces their words even more carefully, trying not to appear drunk." Claire caught sight of a bird flying along the bluff. Looked like an eagle. She pointed it out to Meg.

"I told him I had received a call. And I wanted to check out the situation. He assured me that everything was fine. His wife had been a little difficult, he explained, but he had calmed her down. I was turning to leave when he said something to her. I didn't hear what it was, but she exploded. Said she wanted him out of there. Said she hated his guts. He stayed very calm. She turned to me and said, 'Make him leave.'

"The husband sat down on the couch and said, 'I'm not going.'

"The wife said he had been beating on her and showed me a badly bruised arm. I asked him if this was true. He didn't say anything. I suggested to him that maybe he should go to a hotel for the night, come back in the morning. He said he wasn't going anyplace. Then he pulled a gun out from between the couch cushions."

"A gun? Wow, is that when you were afraid?"

"No, not really. He wasn't pointing the gun at me, and it all seemed a little unreal. He was waving it at his wife and yelling that she wasn't going to tell him what to do. She was screaming, 'Why don't you go see that woman you've been seeing?'

"I told him to put his gun down. He wasn't really listening to me. He kept talking in this very controlled voice to his wife, and then he let loose a shot into the ceiling. The sound of it was incredibly loud. I realized that was what had happened to the mirror. He had shot it.

"He was so gone, ranting at his wife, he wasn't paying any attention to me. All his anger was focused on her. They were in this huge war, screaming at each other. I walked up behind him and chopped the arm that was holding the gun. It went flying. At the same time, I grabbed him in a chokehold."

"Way to go, Mom."

"Yeah, it worked. He collapsed, didn't put up a fight at all. I felt reasonably in control. The wife started crying. She was sitting on the couch. I dropped the husband to his knees and put cuffs on him. Then I helped him up to take him away. And that's when it got really bad. You see, the wife had grabbed his gun and was aiming it at me."

"Was this it—the time you were most afraid?"

"Not quite yet. Not the most. But I was afraid. She was only about three feet away from me, too close to miss."

"Why was she doing that?"

"She was crazy, hysterical, screaming, saying things like, 'Let him go. I love him. You can't take him away. I won't let you.'

"For what seemed like a long moment, I could think of nothing to do. I had both hands on the husband and my gun was in my holster."

"Mom, what did you do?"

"I knew I had to distract her. I pushed her husband hard and he fell to the ground. She shrieked, dropped the gun, and went to his side. She was asking his forgiveness when I snapped the cuffs on her, too."

Meg stared at her. "Then what happened? Was that it?"

"Not quite." Claire looked for a place to pull over. She needed to stop to tell the end of the story. She pulled onto a field road, cornstalks rustling in the slight wind. She looked over at her daughter, so happy and easy in her life. A beautiful, healthy girl. How she loved her.

"Then I heard a noise upstairs. I left the two of them sitting on the living room floor and bolted up the stairs to see what was up there. I found a baby sitting in her crib. I almost fainted when I saw her. I couldn't breathe, I couldn't move."

Claire reached over and pushed back her daughter's hair, then said, "She reminded me of you, my own baby home asleep. I've never felt such pure panic."

"I don't get it. Why?"

"Because there was a hole in her bed, a gunshot hole that had blasted through her mattress and into the ceiling of her room. All I could see was this smiling baby."

IF YOU HARM US

BY GARY BUSH

Summit-University (St. Paul)

I t was dusk as the train rounded the bend and I saw the skyline of St. Paul for the first time in five years. It looked different. I turned to the Pullman porter leaning next to me on the half-open car door. "What's that big building with the red neon '1' on the top?" I asked.

"Why, that's where the money's at. That's the First National Bank. Thirty-two stories high, they built it in '31. You'd think there was no Depression on, looking at that, would you?"

"I guess not," I replied. The train slowed as it approached Union Depot.

"You're Jake Kane," he said. "I recall you from the old days."

"Leonard Charles," I said, suddenly remembering. "We played baseball together at Mechanic Arts. Class of 1917."

He nodded. "I heard you got sent up. Nice to see you home."

I thanked him. As the train pulled to a stop, he swung down with a step stool in his hand and placed it next to the bottom step.

I followed him, carrying my valise with my meager belongings.

"Warm," Leonard said. "For November, that is."

But I was cold. I was wearing the same tropical suit the

marshals had nabbed me in when I walked off the boat from Havana in 1929. After spending the last four years in Leavenworth, I was glad to be home. I had unfinished business.

I took out my sack of Bull and started to roll a smoke. "Have one of mine, kid—it's your old brand, Sweet Caporals." I looked up to see Frank O'Hara.

"How ya doing, Frank," I said, taking the cigarette. "You look like you put on some weight. The police business must be good."

"It ain't bad," he replied, patting his stomach. "I see you lost weight. That suit is a little loose and probably too light for St. Paul."

"I guess so. So what brings you down here, Frank?" I asked, bending to light my cigarette from his cupped match.

"You, Jake," he said, shaking out the match. "We got a wire that they sprung you early."

"Good behavior. If you dicks got the word, the whole town probably knows by now."

He chuckled and nodded. Then his demeanor changed. "Jake, the rumor is that you're gunning for Tommy Macintyre. They say you have a score to settle with him. Talk is, when he disappeared for a year, he left you holding the bag."

"You shouldn't listen to rumors, Frank."

"Kid, I think the world of you and Tommy; I know how you guys kept Frank Jr. alive after he got gassed in France. I'll never forget it. They called you the Three Musketeers back at Mechanic Arts High."

I nodded. "Lot of water under the bridge since then. And by the way, how is Frankie? I got a letter from him in the can. He says he's a new papa and living in Arizona."

"Yeah, the climate out there is good for his lungs. He's in

the radio business, there's a big future in radio. Owns two stores in Tucson." Frank pulled out his wallet and showed me a Kodak of a baby. "That's the grandkid. Francis X. O'Hara III. Handsome kid, huh?"

"Looks like his mother, not one of you ugly micks," I laughed, remembering Frank Jr.'s pretty wife, Beth.

"You got that right, boyo." But he became serious again. "Listen, Jake, this town's changing. The kidnappings of William Hamm and Edward Bremer brought that on. The rules have been broken. Dutch Sawyer's on the run, they nabbed his old lady in Cleveland."

Harry "Dutch" Sawyer had been the number-one fixer in town. He, his predecessors, and the cops kept the O'Connor system going for more than thirty years. John O'Connor had been police chief at the turn of the century. With the city fathers' tacit approval, he created an arrangement where criminals could seek haven in St. Paul as long as they checked in with the police and kept their noses clean when in town. There were fewer bank robberies and for the most part "honest" citizens were left alone and safe. That didn't stop us homegrown boys from running our own rackets. Hell, Prohibition made us fortunes.

"Jake," Frank said, "since Repeal, things have changed. The papers are getting religion, going after corruption. The G-Men are all over the place. Hoover is going to shut this town down."

"Hoover's an asshole, Frank," I said, taking a drag off my smoke. I hadn't had a tailor-made cigarette since 1929. "Look how his agents shot up Little Bohemia over in Wisconsin going after Dillinger. They shot three innocent bystanders and killed one. They're the laughingstock of the whole country."

"Don't underestimate the Bureau, Jake. Dillinger's dead, Pretty Boy Floyd is dead, Machine Gun Kelly's in stir. Hoover's hot to recover his reputation. I tell you, he's coming after this town. I'm getting out myself. By New Year's Day I'll be retired and living down in Arizona."

"That's good, Frank. You been on the force, what, thirty-four years?"

"Yeah. I came in with the O'Connor system and I'm going out with its demise." He rubbed the back of his neck and I could see how tired he was. Then he looked up. "But I ain't done yet, and if you go after Tommy Macintyre I'll have to come after you."

"I wouldn't expect any less from you, Frank."

"I love you boys like my own sons. I don't want to see either of you die."

"It will work out, Frank."

"Jesus, I hope so. Come on—I'll buy you dinner."

We took the escalator up to the busy concourse, its high ceiling decorated with carvings of stagecoaches and trains. I noticed the women were wearing their dresses ankle length. The flapper look went out with the crash.

Our footsteps echoed on the stone tile floor of the great lobby as we walked toward the depot restaurant. I glanced at the big clock above the baggage claim; it was 6 o'clock on the dot.

We sat in a booth and a world-weary waitress took our order.

"Tell me," Frank asked. "How was it? Was they tough on ya?"

"It was okay, once I got off hard labor. First a job in the furniture shop and finally one in the library. I think I have you to thank for that."

Frank shrugged. "Kid, I still don't know why you didn't stay in Cuba until things cooled down."

"Maybe I don't like rum," I said, digging into my steak when it came.

Frank snorted. "If you was coming back to deal with Tommy, he had already disappeared. Lot of people thought he was dead," Frank told me between bites.

"Look, Frank," I said, pointing with my knife. "This is my country. I shed blood for it in France. I have the medals to prove it. That's why I came back. It was unfortunate that someone tipped off the marshals when I landed in Tampa, but that's all behind me."

"You know, kid, they wouldn't have been so hard on you if you hadn't killed that Prohibition agent."

I put down my knife and fork. "That son of a bitch was on the take. He was supposed to let us run the booze down from Canada. Instead, he opened fire on us, no warning, no nothing. It was the dark of night and I shot back. I ain't sorry he's dead. I hate double-crossers."

My lawyer had made the same argument. He went over my war record and the fact that we were ambushed. He was able to get my charge knocked down from murder to manslaughter. Of course, in court I showed remorse, but that bastard had it coming.

Frank put his hand on my arm. "You got a tough break, kid."

"Yeah," I said. "But it could have been worse. Now, since you're buying, how about some pie?"

Frank ordered the pie—it was apple and damn good. "Looks like you're going to fill out that suit of yours just fine," he said.

I just nodded, my mouth full of pie.

"You set up? Got a place to flop?"

I took a swallow of coffee and answered. "Yeah. I'll be staying with my Uncle Izzy. He has a room for me in back of the pawn shop."

"That's good." He picked up the check, flirted with the cashier, and turned to me.

"C'mon, kid. I'll give you a ride up to Izzy's. It's raining and that linen suit ain't gonna keep you dry."

He drove out of the garage and up 3rd Street. "It's all torn up," I said.

"Yeah, they're going to widen it, make a boulevard out of it. Named after that guy from St. Paul who outlawed war. Ain't that a laugh? You know—Frank Kellogg. Your uncle will have to move his shop over to East 7th with the rest of the pawns."

Frank pulled up in front of Izzy's shop and shook my hand. "Remember, Jake, don't go after Tommy."

"Thanks for the lift, Frank," I said, and I got out of the car and went into the pawn shop.

Isadore Goldberg stepped out from the cage when I entered. He looked older but still had the robust body of the wrestler he had been back in Russia. "*Nu*, Jakey, you lost weight." He came over and hugged me, his arms like iron bands.

"Hi, Uncle Izzy," I said, hugging him back. "You look good."

"*Ess hat mir oisegegangen die kayach.* My strength's left me, Jakey."

"You're still a *shtarker*," I said, rubbing my sore ribs.

He shrugged. "Doesn't matter. They're going to tear down the building soon and I'm going to California to live with your cousin Rebecca."

We talked into the wee hours of the morning getting caught up. Finally, I began to yawn. In the pen, you go to bed a lot earlier.

Izzy had a couple of rooms in the back of the shop, where a bed was made up for me. As soon as I hit the pillow, I fell asleep.

I took a good look at myself in the shaving mirror. My hair had turned gray at the temples and there were deep lines around my eyes. I stropped my razor, soaped my face, and scraped off two days' growth.

Izzy had laid out some clothes. Old but clean work pants and shirt, along with fresh underwear, socks, and sturdy brogans. I dressed and went into the shop. Izzy had a customer. I waited while the man pawned his watch. He was well-dressed, but he looked defeated.

When he left, my uncle turned to me. "That fellow used to be a bank clerk, but with the Depression he lost his job. You know, I'm getting out just in time. How many more watches, radios, jewelry can I take in?" He spread his arms, pointing around the shop. "Who's going to buy?"

I shrugged. "Listen, Uncle Izzy, I'm going up to see Pinsky the tailor. Then I'm going to walk around for a while. I'll see you later."

"Okay, Jakey." He went to his safe, opened it, and handed me a stack of twenties. "You need more? It's your money."

"Not now, but thanks for taking care of it for me."

He spread his hands in a broad gesture as if to say, *I'm your uncle, what did you expect?*

Before I left, he handed me a leather jacket and a fedora.

I walked up to Pinsky's on Wabasha and bought new duds—everything from suits to evening clothes. Men's fashions had changed. The jackets were fitted with wide shoulders; the trousers were straight with wide cuffs turned up. Shirts had attached collars. In the old days, I would have had clothes tailor-made, but Pinsky had some good off-the-rack items and promised he'd have them altered by late in the day.

I ate breakfast at the St. Francis Cafeteria, and then caught the matinee of The Thin Man at the Paramount. It had been known as the Capitol Theater when I went away, but whatever its name, it still retained its elaborate façade of terra-cotta molding and Spanish grillwork. Sound had just come in when I was last at a picture show. Now I was fascinated by the dialogue between William Powell and Myrna Loy. I had read the book in prison, but I still enjoyed the picture. Myrna Loy was the kind of gal any guy in his right mind would want.

I took a streetcar up to the old neighborhood just for old times. I climbed Mount Airy Street to look over the city. Like Rome, St. Paul sits on seven hills. The town had changed despite the Depression. Along with the First National Bank building, the new city hall–courthouse had been built. And the old Victorian buildings along the river bluffs were coming down. I remembered what Frank O'Hara had told me about change. St. Paul was going to eliminate the criminal element. But what hadn't changed was my unfinished business.

I walked down the hill to the wooden stairway that led me to Canada Street. I stood in front of my old house. My folks had died of the influenza when I was in France. I said a little prayer, then walked to the corner grocery at Grove and Canada.

The lady behind the counter recognized me and asked if I had been away. I smiled and nodded and bought a pack of

Sweet Caporals, a Coca-Cola, and a Hershey's bar. I walked over to the Franklin Grammar School where I first met Tom Macintyre and Frank O'Hara Jr. Not much had changed.

There was a Russian bath over on Mississippi Street near the rail yards. I paid my dime and steamed for an hour, trying to get four years of Leavenworth stink off me.

It was about 4 when I hailed a cab and had him take me to Pinsky's to pick up my clothes. By the time the cabbie dropped me at Izzy's shop, it had started to rain—not hard, but steady.

I put my parcels in my room. Back in the shop, Izzy was dickering with a man trying to hock a tuba. I stepped outside to stand in the entrance and watch the rain.

I had been locked up so long I wanted lots of fresh air, even if it meant a little rain. I took out a cigarette and had just struck a match when someone bumped into me with an umbrella and knocked the smoke from my hand. "Watch where the hell you're going, fella," I said, bending to pick up my snipe.

"I'm sorry," she replied. I stood up and looked into blue eyes so dark they were almost black. I checked out the rest of the package. She had a beautiful face, oval, with dimples and a sweet mouth. Blond hair peeked out from her wide-brim hat; its feather sadly drooped in the rain. Her fur coat hid her figure, but I was certain it was a swell one.

"Sure your eyes can handle it?" she asked, not smiling. She was struggling to fix her umbrella, which the wind had turned inside out.

"I'll take a chance I won't go blind," I answered, giving her the once-over again. "Can I give you a hand with your umbrella?"

"I have it," she said, closing it.

"You know," I said, "this neighborhood isn't exactly safe for a pretty girl like you, dressed to the nines."

"I can take care of myself." She glared, clutching her handbag.

"I'll bet you can, but don't worry, I'm not interested in your belongings. I never was a purse snatcher."

She looked into my face. "Wait a minute. You're Jake Kane, aren't you?" Her voice mellowed, "I've come to see you."

"I'm Kane. How do you know who I am? And how did you know I was here?"

"The whole town knows you're here. Someone with your reputation doesn't come into St. Paul unnoticed." She took a copy of the *Pioneer Press* from under her arm. There was my picture plastered on the front page. The headline read, *Former T-Man Killer Freed After Four Years*. The photo wasn't very flattering. It was the mug shot they took when I was arrested in Tampa.

I shrugged. "What do you want to see me about?"

"We can't talk here." She looked in the window where Izzy was still bargaining with the tuba player. She thought a second. "I have an apartment at the Commodore. Meet me in the bar in an hour, and try to look more presentable." I guess my work clothes bothered her.

She turned on her heels, put up her collar, and opened her umbrella, which immediately turned inside out again. I heard her curse under her breath.

I watched her walk to her car. I liked the walk and I liked the car—a brand new, fire-engine-red Duesenberg convertible sedan.

Whoever this blonde was, she had dough, living at the Commodore and driving a new Duesy.

242 // Twin Cities Noir

The tuba player came out, minus his horn, and I walked in.

I told Izzy about my encounter with the dame and described her to him. "Do you know her?"

"Where would an *alter kocker* like me meet such a hotsy-totsy woman like you give a picture of? Listen," his voice shifted. "You have to be careful. Whatever this *maydel* wants could mean *tsuris*. Big trouble."

I nodded and went in the back to change into something "more presentable."

"You look like a *mench*," Izzy said when I returned. "But you ain't dressed yet." He handed me a Luger. "It's loaded. I'm sure you remember how to use one."

"Thanks, Uncle."

I took off my jacket, slipped on the shoulder holster he gave me, checked the action on the Luger, nodded, and set it in the holster.

"You ain't going to catch a cab in this weather," Izzy said, pointing to the rain-snow mix. "I've got an Overland coupe out back. It's ten years old, but it runs." He tossed me the keys.

The Commodore was a chic apartment hotel up on Western and Holly in the exclusive Summit neighborhood. Over the years the hotel hosted famous and infamous clientele—Scott Fitzgerald and his wife Zelda, Al Capone, the Barker gang, and a gaggle of other celebrities.

I walked up the steps, through the courtyard, and into the lobby. The bar was to my left. It was a grand-looking place, decorated in the Moderne style. Glass mirrors and chrome sparkled throughout. A bartender in a white shirt and black bow tie stood behind the small but luxurious bar mixing a cocktail in a shaker. Off to the side a group of happy drunks were gathering around a small piano, giving out with a dirty version of the song, "If I Could Be with You One Hour Tonight."

The place was intimate enough for me to spot the blonde at a small glass table at the back of the room. She was dressed in a blue silk dinner number, ankle length, cut high in the front and low in the back. It did nothing to hide her lush figure. I had been right when I guessed it had to be swell under her fur wrap.

I said hello and started to sit, but she pointed to the singers and said, "It's too noisy here. Come up to my apartment in ten minutes—number 402." She stood and left.

I stopped at the bar and ordered a scotch, my first drink since I left Leavenworth. The singers had switched to "Let's Do It." It was kind of nice just watching people have fun.

I finished my drink and went up to her apartment. She opened the door at my first knock. I pushed past her, Luger in hand, in case this was a setup. I checked the place over. When I was satisfied we were alone, I turned to her. "Okay, baby, spill. Start with who you are and what this is all about."

She blinked her dark blue lamps and said, "My name is Claire Blake, Mr. Kane, and I need your help." And tears began to flow.

I handed her my handkerchief, led her to a settee, and sat beside her. "Tell me about it." What guy isn't a sucker for a beautiful dame with tears in her eyes?

She wiped the tears away and looked at me. "I heard you've come back to town to settle a score with Tom Macintyre."

I didn't answer her, so she continued. "Macintyre is a dangerous man. You could get killed."

"Why should you care what happens to me?" I asked.

"Because I know what Tommy Macintyre did to you. The whole town knows. What they don't know is what he did to me."

Through sobs she revealed her story.

Just a small-town girl, she had come to the big city to be a singer. Not much different than others with the same dream. She ended up working for Macintyre as a hostess in his club. When Tommy found out she could sing, he gave her a break.

"But there were strings," she said. "I don't love him; I don't want to be known as Tommy's bim. But . . ."

"But what? Are you telling me that Macintyre wouldn't let you sing unless you slept with him?"

"Yes, he made it clear that it was part of the deal." She lowered her eyes as if she were ashamed.

I raised a skeptical eyebrow.

"It's true—I swear."

"If you say so."

"You don't believe me." More tears. "Look, Mr. Kane. I may not be a virgin, and I might be ambitious, but Tommy Macintyre owns me. I am so afraid of him. I've an offer for a radio contract in New York, but he won't let me go. He told me he'd kill me if I ever left him."

"What's that got to do with me?"

"Everyone knows you're gunning for him. But he's dangerous. I can distract him and maybe you can take care of him. It's to both of our advantage."

"What if he kills me first?"

"I have a friend to back the play." The tears were gone and she was all business. "He wouldn't dare go up against Tommy alone, but with you . . ."

"Who's your friend?"

"You can meet him tonight. Come out to Tommy's club, The Rose of Tralee, around 8. If you need money, I can pay you." She took a roll out of her purse as big as a grapefruit.

"If this isn't enough . . ."

"I don't need to be paid for what I'm going to do," I said, pushing the roll back at her. "Looks like Tommy's been generous," I added.

"Material things. A girl needs more," she breathed softly.

"How much more, baby?"

She smiled. Next thing I knew she was in my lap, her arms around my neck, and her tongue down my throat.

I picked her up and carried her to the bedroom. She whispered, *"Fuck me,"* a phrase that you didn't hear from nice girls, but I hadn't been with a nice girl since Mary Agnes Murphy back in 1917 before I joined the army. I must have made some impression on Mary Agnes, because when I was in France, she became a nun.

I had known bad girls from Paris to Havana. And Claire was definitely a bad girl. She made love like an alley cat—the scratches on my back would hurt for days. It was a great ride, especially since I'd been without for four years.

We went at it a couple more times and when it was over, I said, "You were swell, baby. I like the way you move."

"No complaints from me either, big boy." Claire planted a honey-cooler on my lips and went into the bathroom.

She came out wearing a silk kimono, sat at her dressing table, and proceeded to fix her hair and makeup. I dressed and she walked me to the door.

"You'll be out to the club by 8?"

"Yes." I leaned in to kiss her.

She turned her head. "Jake, my makeup."

"Sure," I said, and left.

Back at Izzy's, I cleaned up and changed into my new tux, transferred the Luger to that outfit, and grabbed my hat and coat.

Izzy had gone home, which was good. The less he knew, the less he would worry.

It was cold in the Overland as I drove out Fort Road. The heap had no heater and I had to keep the windows down so the windshield wouldn't fog over.

The Rose of Tralee stood on a bluff overlooking the Mississippi. It was a nice-looking place, nightclub in front, illegal casino upstairs.

The valet sniffed when I handed him the key to the Overland. I gave him a fin and he put a phony smile on his face.

I checked my hat and coat with a cutie wearing a sexy little green satin number. I ran my fingers through my hair, turned, and came face-to-face with my ex-partner. No, not Tommy Macintyre, but Maurice "Mummy" Lamott. Tall, with hooded eyes and hollow cheeks. Always a menacing figure. We had parted ways early in the '20s.

"Hello, Jake," he said, holding out his hand.

I shook it, fighting off the urge to count my fingers.

Mummy was a hard mug and more than a little dangerous. We went back as far as Franklin Grammar School. His gang had jumped me on the playground and beat the shit out of the "sheeny bastard." I was saved by Frank Jr. and Tommy Macintyre.

I caught up with Mummy a few days later and kicked his ass. We had sort of a truce after that—never buddies, but we got along in high school. When Frank Jr., Tommy, and I came back from France in 1919, Mummy was setting up a bootleg-ging operation. He needed tough guys who knew their way around a gun. Tommy and I didn't see anything better com-ing our way, so we joined his gang. Frank Jr. declined. He had seen enough of war and his health was frail.

But Mummy was too free and easy with his rod; you never knew when he would start throwing lead. His antics brought down the big *machers* who ran the rackets in town. Tommy and I were able to square ourselves, but Mummy had to leave St. Paul. He went to work for the Chicago Outfit where his special talents got him in good with Capone. He'd drift in and out of town after that, on errands for the Outfit. Now here he was togged to the bricks, in a fine set of white tie and tails.

"You the doorman?" I asked.

"Always the kidder, aren't ya, Jake? Na. Ain't you heard? I'm Tommy's partner now."

"Yeah?"

"Yeah, since last month. He needed someone to run the casino. Now, Jake, I know you're here to settle a score, but you gotta be careful. Tommy's no pushover."

"Shouldn't you be worried about your partner?" I asked, lighting a cigarette.

"Look, Jake, we been pals since we were kids. I don't want to see you get hurt. And to tell you the truth, Tommy ain't the best partner a fella ever had."

"So you're telling me you'll back my play?"

"If I have to." He pulled back his tail coat and I saw his gun.

Before we could continue, Tommy came walking through the crowd, glad-handing patrons left and right. Then he spot-ted me.

"Hello, Jake," he said, but didn't offer his hand. "You here to see me?"

"We have some business to finish," I replied, looking into his broad black Irish face.

"I suppose we do. But it will have to wait. I have a club to run and the show's going to start. C'mon—you can sit at my table and I'll buy you dinner. I have a torch singer here with a voice like an angel and a face and figure like a Greek goddess."

Tommy turned to Mummy. "Mummy, before the show starts, check the casino receipts."

"What about him?" Mummy asked, pointing at me.

"There won't be any trouble, will there, Jake?"

"Our business waited this long. For a free meal and show, it can wait a little longer."

Mummy nodded and I followed Tommy to his table. Tommy ordered steak dinners for each of us. This wasn't the place for conversation, too many people watching. Small talk. He told me I looked thin, I told him he had put on weight.

Then the lights dimmed and the orchestra struck up "How Deep Is the Ocean." A spotlight came on and there stood Claire, clad in a long red evening gown. I could see every curve of her body; the gown had no buttons. She must have shimmied into it. Claire leaned into the microphone and began to sing in a dark, throaty voice.

The crowd that had come for dinner and a show certainly got their money's worth. Every guy in the place thought she was singing to him, especially when she let go with "The Man I Love."

When she finished, the applause shook the place and Tommy was beaming. Had the big goon actually fallen for her?

"Want to meet her?" Tommy asked.

"We have to talk."

"Yeah, we do." He stood up and walked toward his office; I followed. Claire and Mummy sat at a table next to the office. She gave me a barely perceptible nod; Mummy gave a tight-lipped smile.

"Mummy," Tommy said, "stay close, I might need you." Mummy nodded and winked.

Tommy's office was paneled in dark mahogany; the wood was dense and made the room practically soundproof, which suited my purposes just fine.

Tommy walked to a small bar in the corner and took down two glasses. He lifted a bottle. "Single malt, twenty years old."

"Why not?" I said, and he poured.

He handed me the glass and said, "To old times."

"Some need to be forgotten," I said, and sat down in a big leather armchair.

"But not all of them?" Tommy asked.

"Not all of them."

"Well, if it's going to be business, maybe I should call Mummy in."

"You know something? You can still be a dumb schmuck when it comes to women."

"What the hell does that mean?" Tommy said, putting his drink down.

"Claire. She came to see me today, told you were holding her back, wouldn't let her go to New York for a radio contract."

"What?"

"Later I went to the Commodore. She told me you threatened to kill her if she ever tried to leave. After that we screwed like minks."

Tommy looked angry. Double-crossed by a dame.

"Why don't you call Claire in here," I suggested, taking out the Luger and setting it in my lap. "Mummy too."

"That's how it's going to play, huh?" Tommy asked.

I nodded and he opened the door and beckoned them in.

They entered and sat down side by side on a small sofa facing me.

Tommy glared at Claire. "So you want to go to New York, huh?"

"What are you talking about, Tommy?" Her voice was so sweet; you'd swear bees were nesting in her mouth.

"Jake told me that you said I'd kill you if you ever left me. That's how you see our relationship?"

"No, Tommy." She began to cry. "Kane came to my apartment, forced his way in, and raped me. He told me it was to get even with you."

I started laughing. "You tell a great story, baby. But I like the one you told this afternoon better."

"What story?" Tommy asked.

"That the only way out of the relationship was for you to be dead. And since she figured I was going to kill you anyhow, I'd do her a favor."

"That's a lie, Tommy," Claire said.

"Oh, there's more. She was afraid I might have lost my edge in stir, so she told me she had arranged backup for me, and guess who that is?" I said, pointing to Mummy.

Mummy started to his feet.

"Sit down, Mummy, I'm not through." I showed him my Luger. "Here's how I figure it," I said to Tommy. "Claire wants to be more than just a chanteuse. She wants power. By seducing you she could get it. But you kept it strictly business. So Mummy was her fallback. He was for it. Why not? He'd get a swell dame and your operation. But he didn't want to go up against you alone. When he heard I was getting out, he assumed I would kill you and then he and Beautiful would take care of me."

"That's a great story, Jake," Mummy said. "But it's bullshit. I'd have no reason to kill you."

"Really? Remember that Prohibition cop I killed? He was supposed to be on the take, but someone got to him and paid him more than Tommy and I did. When I was in the pen, I found out who the double-crosser was. It was you, Mummy. You let your mouth run free with one of Capone's hitters. You remember Santino? When he was sent to Leavenworth, I saved him from a shiv. He told me what you had done. You wanted that booze, you greedy bastard, it was worth a hundred grand. I also know it was you that tipped the law that I was coming back from Cuba. You hoped they'd kill me."

"How do you know Santino wasn't lying?" Mummy asked belligerently. "How do you know it wasn't Macintyre that set you up?"

"Because when we were jumped, it was Tommy that took the bullet meant for me and saved my life. He got patched up by an abortion doc in Minneapolis. Then we both lit out for Cuba, so Tommy could recover. I came back to find the rat that double-crossed us."

Mummy went for his .38. I raised the Luger and put a 9mm Parabellum slug right through his heart. His pistol fell from his hand.

Claire screamed, "You son of a bitch!" She dug a little automatic out of her purse and aimed it in my direction. Tommy grabbed up Mummy's .38 and shot her in the head. Her gun went off as she fell and the bullet put a hole in Mummy's shoulder.

* * *

In December, I was behind the wheel of the Duesenberg, driving Tommy to see a surgeon at the Mayo Clinic in Rochester. We shot the breeze about the events.

"Didn't go as planned," Tommy said.

"It went better," I said. Originally, Tommy brought Mummy back from Chicago by offering him a partnership in the casino. We were just waiting for me to be sprung, so I could be in on the kill. We made everyone think I was gunning for Tommy, to throw the rat off base. Mummy should have known, if you harm us, you pay.

"Claire was the joker in the deck," Tommy said. "But it worked to our advantage."

We told Frank O'Hara that Mummy had wanted to take over Tommy's operation and tried to kill him. Claire attempted to stop him. But Mummy shot her with his .38. As Claire fell, she shot him in the shoulder. Before he could get off another shot, I killed him.

Frank went through the motions, but he bought our story because he wanted to.

"You know Claire had talent and would have gone far," Tommy said. "But I wonder, was she a good lay?"

"Not as good as that Follies dancer in Paris," I said.

"Yeah," he chuckled. "Now she was a good lay! After this operation I'm going to have to make up for lost time."

You see, I knew Claire was lying when she said Tommy had made her his mistress. When Tommy took that bullet for me, it clipped a nerve and rendered him impotent.

CHILI DOG

BY CHRIS EVERHEART
Downtown (St. Paul)

A quick chili dog for lunch and I gotta get moving. There's never enough time in this racket. I start driving across town at 8 a.m. collecting the receipts, drive all the way out west to Lake Minnetonka to get them looked at, pick up a bundle of cash there, and drive back to the east side of St. Paul, stopping along the way at each establishment to distribute the money. I tell you, it's a meat grinder. But this is the best part of my day—a quick stop at the Gopher Bar and Café on 7th Street in downtown St. Paul for a beer and a Coney Island—a chili dog piled so high with toppings that you have to eat it with a knife and a fork. This is what accounts for a lunch break—twenty minutes with an axe hanging over my head. Then back on the road again, driving clear out to Hudson to pick up yesterday's receipts and drop off yesterday's cash. Hudson is always a day behind because they're way out there. Benno could front them the money, but he doesn't trust anyone—not even me. I hate to think what would happen if he knew I stopped here every day, leaving his payroll in the car, even for only a few minutes.

But what the hell am I supposed to do, eat lunch in the car? I ain't no pig! I hate eating in the car, spilling food all over my custom upholstery. And trying to keep a big Continental on the road and eating a chili dog at the same time is more frustration than I can stand. Hell, if I wanted to work under those conditions I would have taken a job at my uncle's foam factory over in Northeast and spent my life working on the dock, breathing truck exhaust and wrenching my back every other day. I chose a life on the streets because it had more pizzazz, more excitement, and, for Christ's sake, more money. Now I end up working for Crazy Benno, still humping an impossible schedule and making minimum organized crime wage. It ain't fair. So, yeah, I guess my little chili dog break is a "fuck you" to the new gangster order.

I rush out the front door of chili dog heaven, digging a piece of sweet onion out of my teeth, and head toward the parking lot. I hate to leave the car sitting very long. You can't be too careful when you're carrying $70,000 in cash. Granted, it's in a strong box in the trunk and only me and Benno know the combination, but I still get nervous every time I stop—kind of like driving without car insurance: You know nothing is going to happen, but you're worried anyway.

As I round the corner of the building, headed for my car, someone slams into my shoulder, knocking me down as I say, "What the . . . ?"

Next thing I know, the guy is on top of me. "Where are they?" he says.

I quick reach for my gun but it ain't there, and I feel a sharp, sweet whack at the back of my head. I look up and there's this grubby tattooed guy with my gun in his hand.

"He said, where are they?" growls Tattoo, and whacks me again. I'm not sure what they're talking about, then I realize Dude #1 is digging in my pocket.

"Hey!" I say, as if it's gonna stop him. I take a swing at him but he's already on his feet, my keys sparkling in his hand. "Motherfucker," I yell, "get back here!" But he keeps on going, running toward my Lincoln, Tattoo following.

I immediately stand up, and my head spins. Fucker hit me harder than I thought. I stumble and grab the wall as the bums start my Lincoln and peel out of the space, spitting gravel everywhere. Goddamnit, I just had that thing painted and they're gonna scratch it all up. As they spin past me and I watch helplessly, I see Tattoo smile slyly behind the passenger window and wave my gun, taunting me. "SHIT!" I yell. What am I gonna do?

When from around the corner, I hear, "Davy? Are you all right?" I look over to see Curtis, one of the regulars at the Gopher. He's a small-time hood and a real likeable guy. He's always nice to visit with on my little lunch breaks. I guess I overlooked him in there today, but I'm happy to see him now.

"Curtis," I say, "thank God! You gotta help me! These two assholes just did a job on me and took my car."

"Let's go," Curtis says, and from behind him appears a heavyset guy I haven't seen before. He doesn't say anything but he moves with us in the direction of Curtis's car, so I figure he's with him.

I jump in the front seat, Heavy in the back, as Curtis starts the ignition. "I saw them go toward Jackson Street," he says. "They're probably heading up to the interstate. We can catch 'em." He leaves the gravel driveway and squeals the tires onto 7th.

"Oh man, am I glad you came along when you did, Curtis. I'm dead meat if I don't get that car back."

"How much is in there today?" Curtis asks, jerking the wheel to pull around a slow-moving milk truck.

"Over seventy thousand," I answer. "I gotta get that money or Benno will kill me."

"I wouldn't worry about Benno," Curtis says. "We'll take care of this."

We reach the interchange at 35E and Curtis automatically takes the northbound onramp.

"Are you sure they headed north?" I ask. "Maybe they kept going east up to 94."

"No," Curtis shakes his head, "they went this way. I saw them take this right."

Thank God he can see what's going on. My head is still ringing from the thumping Tattoo gave me. We scream up 35E and nearly reach the 694 interchange when we spot my Continental cruising north, just like Curtis said.

"There," I say. "Hang back a little. Let's follow them to where they're going. I'm gonna fuck these guys up when we get there." I reach for my gun and remember I don't have it anymore. "Shit, they got my gun."

"Don't worry about it," Curtis says reassuringly, "I got one with your name on it." Heavy doesn't say anything from the backseat, so I assume he's just enjoying the ride, but I hope he's ready to rumble when we get where we're going, because I'm not just gonna get that money back, I'm gonna take a surcharge out of their hides.

We follow these clowns—who don't seem to be in any big hurry—clear up past Forest Lake, where they finally pull off the interstate and head east to Lindström. Once through that dinky town, they go north on a narrow highway.

"They gotta know by now that we're following them," I say to Curtis, who is driving casually along now, unconcerned about tipping them off.

"Yeah," he says, "but they're not worried."

"You think they're planning to shoot it out?" I ask.

"Don't know," Curtis replies, as he turns off the narrow

highway onto an even narrower gravel road, "hard to say what people will do to get their hands on that much money."

That much money. I suddenly realize how odd it was that he asked me in the parking lot how much was in the car today—in all the months I've been stopping at the Gopher, I never mentioned what my day job is—and how I didn't see him inside the bar but he appeared as soon as those jerks took my car. Now here I sit in the passenger seat, with this guy driving who I really don't know that well, and Heavy in the seat behind me who I've never seen before, and I start to wonder. And my wonder turns to worry. I look at Curtis as he pulls the car off the gravel road into a tree-obscured lane with two wheel ruts, and I say, "No, no way."

Suddenly, from behind, Heavy clasps my shoulder with his meaty hand and presses the cold barrel of his pistol against the base of my skull. I get the message—don't move—and I don't. I just sit there and say the Lord's Prayer in my mind.

We come to a stop in a leaf-canopied clearing where a broken-down old cabin stands, roof covered with moss, and there next to my beautiful baby-blue Lincoln Continental stand Dude #1 and Tattoo. Son of a bitch, am I a schmuck! Tattoo steps up to the passenger side and opens the door, covering me with my own gun, and I hear the key alarm bong as Curtis and Heavy get out of the car. I stand up and shake my head.

"You ain't gonna get away with this," I say, as Heavy pushes me toward the back side of the cabin.

Curtis sneers at me. "You're such a blowhard, Davy. I've been sitting in that bar listening to your bullshit for so long I can't wait to hit the off button. But you're gonna talk right up to the end, aren't you?"

"You can make this personal if you want, Curtis. But I ain't gonna tell you the combination to the box. It'll take you a year to get it open, and when Benno finds out he's gonna skin you motherfuckers alive."

"I already have the combination," he says with a velvety satisfaction in his voice. "And what makes you think Benno doesn't already know what we're up to?"

"*Shit*," I whisper.

"That's right," Curtis says. "Benno didn't give you no lunch break." He steps away and tells Heavy, "Pop this jerk so I can get to work. I got deliveries to make."

It's all clear to me now. "Go ahead and take the fucking job, Curtis. I'm sick of it anyway. And by the way, the fringe benefits suck."

Heavy pushes the gun against the back of my head and squeezes the trigger. Ah, what the hell, it was worth it—that's one hell of a chili dog.

ABOUT THE CONTRIBUTORS:

GARY BUSH recently finished a novel featuring private detective Max Coppersmith. He is currently working on a second Coppersmith novel and researching a historical mystery. His short fiction has appeared in *Flesh and Blood* Volume 3, *Fedora 2*, *Small Crimes*, and *MXB Magazine*. Bush lives in Minneapolis with his wife Stacey.

K.J. ERICKSON writes the Marshall Bahr mystery series, set in the Twin Cities. The fourth title in the series, *Alone at Night*, won a 2005 Minnesota Book Award.

CHRIS EVERHEART, a Minnesota native, is a fiction and screen writer. He has worked in film and advertising in Minneapolis, where he lives with his wife and stepson.

JUDITH GUEST has lived since 1976 in Edina, Minnesota, where she has been gathering lots of material, which could take another thirty years to be disseminated. She is the author of five books, including *Killing Time in St. Cloud* and *The Tarnished Eye*. She has one husband, three sons, and three daughters-in-law, plus seven of the best grandchildren known to man (or woman).

PETE HAUTMAN has written novels for both adults and teens. His poker-themed crime novels *Drawing Dead* and *The Mortal Nuts* were selected as *New York Times Book Review* Notable Books. His latest novel, *Invisible*, is about model railroads, pyromania, friendship, and window-peeping. Hautman lives with novelist and poet Mary Logue in Golden Valley, Minnesota, and Stockholm, Wisconsin.

ELLEN HART, five-time winner of the Lambda Literary Award for Best Lesbian Mystery and two-time winner of the Minnesota Book Award for Best Crime Fiction, has written twenty-one mystery novels in two long-running series, all set in the Twin Cities. She teaches crime writing at the Loft Literary Center, the largest independent writing community in the nation, and lives in Minneapolis with her partner of twenty-eight years.

Kathleen L. Kruger

STEVEN HORWITZ has worked in publishing for twenty-five years. He lives with his wife and two dogs in St. Paul, Minnesota.

Julie Schaper

DAVID HOUSEWRIGHT is a former newspaper reporter and advertising copywriter, who was born, raised, educated, played hockey, discovered girls, and currently lives in St. Paul. He is the author of several Twin Cities–based novels, including *Dearly Departed, A Hard Ticket Home, Pretty Girl Gone, Dead Boyfriends, Penance*, which won an Edgar Award for Best First Novel, and *Practice to Deceive*, which earned the Minnesota Book Award.

Renee Valois

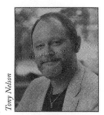

WILLIAM KENT KRUEGER writes the award-winning Cork O'Connor mystery series set in Minnesota's great Northwoods. With his wife and family, he lives in St. Paul, a wonderfully noir city that he dearly loves.

Tony Nelson

MARY LOGUE was born and bred in the Twin Cities. A poet and writer, she has strayed occasionally, but always manages to find her way back home. A new book of poetry, *Meticulous Attachment*, and a new Claire Watkins mystery, *Poison Heart*, were published in 2005. She lives with Pete Hautman on both sides of the Mississippi.

Tim Francisco

LARRY MILLETT is a Minneapolis native who spent much of his career as a writer, reporter, and editor for the *St. Paul Pioneer Press*. He is the author of four works of nonfiction, including *Lost Twin Cities* and *Twin Cities Then and Now*, as well as five mystery novels in which Sherlock Holmes and Dr. Watson travel to turn-of-the-century Minnesota to solve cases at the behest of railroad tycoon James J. Hill. He currently lives with his wife and two children in St. Paul.

Lorna Sullivan Rubenstein

BRUCE RUBENSTEIN is a crime writer who grew up in the Twin Cities and knows a great deal about the events, places, and people upon which his tale is based. He's written many crime stories, and recently published a book, *Greed, Rage and Love Gone Wrong* (University of Minnesota Press). His wife is his inspiration because of her constant demands for more money.

Tom Oaks

JULIE SCHAPER has been a Twin Cities resident for eleven years. She lives with her husband and two dogs in the Merriam Park neighborhood of St. Paul.

Dirk Vietzke

MARY SHARRATT grew up in the Twin Cities and currently lives in a dark satanic mill town in Lancashire, England. A Minnesota Book Award finalist and winner of the 2005 WILLA Literary Award for Contemporary Fiction, she is the author of the novels *Summit Avenue, The Real Minerva,* and *The Vanishing Point,* and coeditor of *Bitchlit,* a fiction anthology celebrating female antiheroes.

Sarah Walter

QUINTON SKINNER is the author of *14 Degrees Below Zero* and *Amnesia Nights*. He lives with his family in Minneapolis.

STEVE THAYER is a *New York Times* best-selling author. His novels include *Saint Mudd*, *The Weatherman*, and *The Wheat Field*. He lives in Edina, Minnesota.

BRAD ZELLAR has lived in the Twin Cities for more than twenty years. He is a writer and editor for the *Rake*, a monthly magazine, and has a lousy relationship with sleep.

Also available from the Akashic Books Noir Series

D.C. NOIR
edited by George Pelecanos
304 pages, a trade paperback original, $14.95

Brand new stories by: George Pelecanos, Laura Lippman, James Grady, Kenji Jasper, Jim Beane, Ruben Castaneda, Robert Wisdom, James Patton, Norman Kelley, Jennifer Howard, Jim Fusilli, Richard Currey, Lester Irby, Quintin Peterson, Robert Andrews, and David Slater.

GEORGE PELECANOS is a screenwriter, independent-film producer, award-winning journalist, and the author of the bestselling series of Derek Strange novels set in and around Washington, D.C., where he lives with his wife and children.

BROOKLYN NOIR
edited by Tim McLoughlin
350 pages, a trade paperback original, $15.95
*Winner of SHAMUS AWARD, ANTHONY AWARD, ROBERT L. FISH MEMORIAL AWARD; Finalist for EDGAR AWARD, PUSHCART PRIZE

Twenty brand new crime stories from New York's punchiest borough. Contributors include: Pete Hamill, Arthur Nersesian, Maggie Estep, Nelson George, Neal Pollack, Sidney Offit, Ken Bruen, and others.

"*Brooklyn Noir* is such a stunningly perfect combination that you can't believe you haven't read an anthology like this before. But trust me—you haven't. Story after story is a revelation, filled with the requisite sense of place, but also the perfect twists that crime stories demand. The writing is flat-out superb, filled with lines that will sing in your head for a long time to come."
—Laura Lippman, winner of the Edgar, Agatha, and Shamus awards

DUBLIN NOIR: The Celtic Tiger vs. The Ugly American
edited by Ken Bruen
228 pages, trade paperback, $14.95

Brand new stories by: Ken Bruen, Eoin Colfer, Jason Starr, Laura Lippman, Olen Steinhauer, Peter Spiegelman, Kevin Wignall, Jim Fusilli, John Rickards, Patrick J. Lambe, Charlie Stella, Ray Banks, James O. Born, Sarah Weinman, Pat Mullan, Reed Farrel Coleman, Gary Phillips, Duane Swierczynski, and Craig McDonald.

MANHATTAN NOIR
edited by Lawrence Block
257 pages, a trade paperback original, $14.95

Brand new stories by: Jeffery Deaver, Lawrence Block, Charles Ardai, Carol Lea Benjamin, Thomas H. Cook, Jim Fusilli, Robert Knightly, John Lutz, Liz Martínez, Maan Meyers, Martin Meyers, S.J. Rozan, Justin Scott, C.J. Sullivan, and Xu Xi.

LAWRENCE BLOCK has won most of the major mystery awards, and has been called the quintessential New York writer, although he insists the city's far too big to have a quintessential writer. His series characters—Matthew Scudder, Bernie Rhodenbarr, Evan Tanner, Chip Harrison, and Keller—all live in Manhattan; like their creator, they wouldn't really be happy anywhere else.

SAN FRANCISCO NOIR
edited by Peter Maravelis
292 pages, a trade paperback original, $14.95

Brand new stories by: Domenic Stansberry, Barry Gifford, Eddie Muller, Robert Mailer Anderson, Michelle Tea, Peter Plate, Kate Braverman, David Corbett, Alejandro Murguía, Sin Soracco, Alvin Lu, Jon Longhi, Will Christopher Baer, Jim Nesbit, and David Henry Sterry.

BALTIMORE NOIR
edited by Laura Lippman
298 pages, a trade paperback original, $14.95

Brand new stories by: David Simon, Laura Lippman, Tim Cockey, Rob Hiaasen, Robert Ward, Sujata Massey, Jack Bludis, Rafael Alvarez, Marcia Talley, Joseph Wallace, Lisa Respers France, Charlie Stella, Sarah Weinman, Dan Fesperman, Jim Fusilli, and Ben Neihart.